I0741493

Polish to *Perfection*

Rachel W. Jones

This novel is a work of fiction. Names, characters, places, and incidents are either the products of the author's imagination or are used fictitiously. Any resemblance to actual persons living or dead, business establishments, events or locales is entirely coincidental.

Polish To Perfection

COPYRIGHT © 2018 by Rachel W. Jones

Thank you for purchasing this book.

All rights are reserved.

No portion of this book may be used or reproduced in any manner whatsoever without written permission from the author except in the case of a brief quotation embodied in critical articles or reviews.

This book may not be redistributed to others for commercial or non-commercial purposes.

Please do not participate in piracy of copyrighted material.

Cover Art by Lee Hyat Designs

Published by Rachel W. Jones

ISBN: 978-1-7329392-0-2

Dedication

To all the talented musicians I have known throughout my musical journey. There are more beautiful sounds in the world because of your talent and effort.

Chapter One

The aircraft's wheels touched down on the asphalt runway, and the anxiety churning in the pit of Ella's stomach began to grow.

San Francisco.

Home.

The place she could no longer avoid. But after two years, shouldn't an intelligent thirty-one-year-old woman have worked through her grief?

Her parents' untimely deaths had taken its toll.

Perhaps the unexpected event bringing her here was a sign to suck it up and move on. Wasn't she trying to do that by leaving the touring track to find a new career direction?

Ella followed the other passengers through the jet-way. As she entered the baggage claim area, an uncomfortable heat as warm as another layer of clothing crept over her body. Lightheadedness followed. She stepped out of the flow of people and leaned against the wall until the sensation passed. The dizziness was yet another reason to break from touring. Along with the weight loss and fatigue, the signs she should see a doctor were piling up.

Rest and a less hectic schedule is what I need. Then everything will be okay.

She surveyed the crowd. No uncle. A frown settled on her face as she continued her search.

A man, sharply dressed in dark trousers, a crisp blue oxford shirt, and a Ralph Lauren tie, stalled her gazing. She had a thing about neckties. At an early age, Ella had learned from her mother how to manage a four-in-hand knot, along with other essential pointers for buying ties for her father. Narrow, not skinny and the tip should hit at the belt line. He got it right — this guy knew how to dress. A little preppy for a chauffeur who could certainly pass for a male model, but she wouldn't judge. She focused on the sign he held.

That's me.

She walked toward him. "Hi, I'm Ella. Nice of my uncle to send a car service. I could have taken a taxi."

A half smile slid across the stranger's face so quickly Ella wasn't sure she had seen it. A sparkle of mischief in his green eyes held her attention for an exaggerated moment.

"Nice to meet you, Ms. Craig. May I take your bag?"

She took a step back. "No thanks, I'll carry it." After almost losing her precious music bag at the airport in Madrid last year, she kept it close when she traveled. "What's your name?"

"You can call me J."

"Okay, Jay. Let's grab my suitcases and get out of here."

They approached the rotating carousel.

"What color is your luggage?"

"I bought red this last time, makes it easier to spot between all the black and navy suitcases."

"Smart idea."

"It works." Ella studied the stranger. Light brown hair tapered short on the sides and back, but longer on top. A clean-cut business look. The tanned skin of his Olympic physique attested to time spent outdoors, and it made her wonder what he did to keep in shape. His smooth baritone voice completed the package.

She shifted her gaze from the driver to the carousel. The luggage dropped onto the conveyor belt and traveled along the circular path. As she watched, a spinning sensation grabbed Ella's attention.

Not again, not now.

Ella swayed, but there was no wall for support. When her legs turned to jelly, her only option was to grab the nearest arm. Mr. Olympic Physique's arm. Her knees buckled, but he kept her from hitting the floor.

"Hey, let's have a seat." He led her to a bench.

She sat with her head bowed, but very aware of the man beside her. Pulling in a full breath, she looked up. "Thank you. I'm fine now," she lied.

"Are you sure?"

"I've not felt this way before today."

"You look a little pale to me."

"It might seem that way to someone with a prime California tan. I skipped breakfast this morning, probably not a good idea."

She closed her eyes, hoping when she stood, she would be able to walk without wobbling. As she rose, the stranger did too.

A flash of red on the baggage carousel caught her eye. "There's my luggage."

"I'll get it." He lifted the suitcases with ease and turned. "Are you sure you're okay?"

She raised her hand; her fingers splayed as if to hold him in his place. "I'm all right."

They stepped outside. "Have a seat over there while I bring the car around."

He's not buying it. But hopefully the family won't notice.

While Ella waited, she took her phone off airplane mode and saw the text message:

Emergency surgery — not sure how long I'll be. Dinner at your aunt's townhouse tonight at 7 PM. See you there.

She should expect nothing less from her uncle, Chief Surgeon of Bayview Medical Center. Prioritization, a necessary element of his job had made meeting his niece at the airport drop lower on his list.

Jay opened the door to the back seat. She slid in, grateful for the time to regroup.

"I got this key at the hospital from Dr. McMillan." He passed it to her before closing the door.

A minute later, her eyes met his in the rearview mirror. Concern replaced the mischievous look she had noticed earlier.

"Where are we going?" he asked.

Ella recited her uncle's address. Settling back into the seat, she resumed her mental struggle of cutting her agent loose, a woman who ran 24/7, giving all to her career. The fact Ella had remained on the touring track since her parents' deaths, taking no time off, had pleased Rita.

In the beginning, touring had held an enormous appeal, but the last year had been more of a chore than a delight, a signal that it was time to re-evaluate her life and find something to bring her out of her funk. Her mother's words surfaced from the recesses of her brain.

All work and no play is never a good thing, sweet girl.

Rita was a tough cookie. Had she been on the path to becoming a Rita by agreeing to one piano concert after another? Her body's protest, aligned with her manager and friend, Pamela's advice was the only reason Ella had decided on her present course of action. Otherwise, she'd have kept running at top speed — just as her agent wanted.

At this morning's meeting, Pamela encouraged her once again to step away from touring. Rest and refocus. Ella felt bad that she had dropped her decision on Rita so unexpectedly. It was a well-known fact that her career had been lucrative for the agent, and she'd take a hit financially because of Ella's action. Pamela had assured her that Rita's love of money would find her moving on to a new client quickly.

The stop here for a concert with the San Francisco Philharmonic Orchestra was a personal favor for Pamela. She'd do anything for her manager but wished the concert had been with another orchestra in another city.

I'll be here less than two weeks. I can do this.

Jay's voice pulled her from her thoughts. "I'll take your bags up the stairs."

Ella stepped out, relieved that her feet felt solid on the driveway. She placed the strap of her music bag over her shoulder. When they reached the door, she held a twenty out to the handsome driver.

He waved her offer away. "My fee included gratuity."

"Thank you," she said, as he retreated down the stairs.

Taking control of her life had to be a priority. Then perhaps she could rediscover the joy of performing. The joy that had been missing for far too long.

JACKSON WEAVED THROUGH the early afternoon traffic, attempting to make it back to the hospital without delay. At the end of his shift, he'd begin five days of downtime. The vacation hours were mounting, and his boss insisted that Jackson utilize a portion of them. Which translated into a lot of free time without much to fill it. He had resumed surfing a few weeks ago after a four-year absence from the waves. At least there was that. Tonight he had a dinner invitation from the two people who had made his life bearable for the last year and a half. An invitation to dinner to meet their niece. Then Bill had made things interesting, asking Jackson to meet the woman at the airport and take her to Bill's house where she would be staying.

Why had he jumped on Ella's incorrect assumption that he was a chauffeur and run with it? The contact with the pleasant woman had pulled the jokester side of him to the surface. A part of his personality that had disappeared two years and eight months ago when the light in his life had been snuffed out. The spontaneous act at the airport had surprised him as much as the spark that had ignited when he met Bill's niece. There had been no sparks since losing Beth. He'd exchanged spontaneity for a rigid, predictable lifestyle. Taking care of his patients consumed most of the hours. It was not unusual for him to start his day waking patients for morning rounds before the sun peeked around the edges of their window shades. Or to be the last doctor to leave at the end of a full day.

His time away from Bayview continued in a regimented fashion. A few hours at the gym, home with take-out or an occasional microwave meal, an hour or so of TV or reading, and then to bed. It sounded like the life of a seventy-year-old rather than someone at the prime age of thirty-five.

The physician side of him revisited the episode of Ella nearly fainting in the airport terminal. Should he mention it to his boss? No, it wasn't his place to do that. It was Ella's choice to share with her aunt and uncle. He would take the position of the proverbial fly on the wall on that one.

Nearing the hospital, Jackson made a mental list: stop by medical records, round on his patients, then home to shower and change before heading to Maxine's for dinner. As he pulled into the hospital parking lot, the thought of seeing Ella again made him smile. Something he didn't do very often.

ELLA GROANED AS SHE ROLLED onto her side and blinked to focus on the alarm clock. When was the last time she'd spent three hours sleeping in the afternoon? Her rigid schedule never included soothing naps. The best her timetable allowed was dozing on various methods of transportation while traveling from one location to the next.

After a good stretch, she looked around the room. Her aunt's touch was everywhere, even though Maxine no longer lived in the house since the divorce. With the break-up three years in the past, how could it be Ella expected her to pop into the room for a casual chat?

Through emails and phone calls, her cousin Claire had leaned heavily on her for support during that time, and she had come through for her. But Ella hadn't asked the same of Claire when her parents died. The denial came easier if her emotions about their deaths stayed rolled up tight, keeping the details of her last visit home in a remote place.

So she toured, long and hard. But all the traveling around the world couldn't erase the scene embedded into her memory. It would sneak up when she was alone, taking her by surprise. Two caskets. The mahogany one, covered with white roses, mums and snapdragons accented with greenery sitting beside a coffin of cherry wood. Pink and white roses and white football mums draped over the lid. The glossiness of the wood and the flowers always vivid. How she wished she could wipe away the scene in the cathedral! Perhaps then she could move on to the next phase of her life, whatever that was to be.

She blew out a breath as her eyes took in the space of her temporary home. The walls were a delicate gray. Full-length drapes with alternating dark gray and white stripes hung at the side of the windows bordering white sheers that covered the panes of glass. A charcoal linen chair sat by the window with a small pink pillow resting on it. There were other splashes of pink arranged throughout the room. Ella smiled and warmth spread through her chest, helping her appreciate the fact she had family that loved her and wished for her happiness. She planned to revel in their love during this short visit and hoped it would overshadow her loss.

Ella ran her hand across the smooth wood of the ebony dresser and decided to empty the contents of her suitcases into its drawers. She showered and dressed in record time, then debated between Uber and a local taxi service. Her mind drifted to Jay the chauffeur. Too bad he didn't have an Uber business on the side. Having the hunky guy drive her to her destination wasn't a bad way to start the evening.

Stop your daydreaming. Things like that only happen in movies.

She dialed the number of the San Francisco Taxi Service, and within an hour, Ella stepped into her aunt's townhouse. Her eyes paused at the reflection in the mirror above the foyer table. The dress she chose tonight would have hung loosely on her frame if she hadn't added the belt. Even knowing she would be facing a head-to-toe inspection from her aunt, it would just have to do. Her appetite had been off for a few months, and most everything in her wardrobe looked shapeless on her body.

"Ms. Maxine come right out." An older, petite Asian woman dressed in a server's black outfit relayed the message. A clean, white apron covered her dress, and she wore her dark hair pulled back in a bun.

"Thank you," Ella murmured. Her eyes swept over the pictures of her cousins on the table. They had grown up together in San Francisco and had been very close. Touring over the past eight years had put distance between them. It would be good to see Claire and Jeremy again.

The muffled sound of a woman's voice became more distinct as her aunt's steps advanced toward the foyer. A darting gaze to the door made her wonder if she could bolt, to stop the encounter before it had a chance to start. Her aunt was quite the expert at extracting information that one preferred to keep tucked away.

And then she stood eye to eye with the woman in question, dismissing her thought of escape. Ella marveled at how her aunt, a woman in her fifties, had managed to keep her curvaceous figure. Short, curly brown hair without a speck of gray in sight. Flawless makeup that revealed tiny wrinkles at the edges of her eyes when she smiled. Tears sprang to the surface when Ella saw the familiar face. She had been wrong to stay away so long.

"Ella, it's so good to have you home." Maxine hugged her and added a kiss on the cheek. "Where's your uncle?"

"He's still at the hospital, so I took a taxi."

"That man! I don't know what to do about him."

"You're divorced. Uncle Bill's not your problem anymore."

The sound of the doorbell interrupted them before Maxine could get worked up any further. She twisted the doorknob. "He's going to get an earful — Oh, Jackson. Come in."

"Thanks for the invitation, Maxine." He stepped across the threshold and gave her a quick hug. His full attention fell on Ella.

She did a double take.

What's the chauffeur doing here?

His watchful gaze caused a shiver to scurry down her spine.

Maxine continued talking, oblivious to the couple's visual exchange. "Jackson, this is my niece, Ella." She turned to Ella. "This handsome man is Jackson Hart, a surgeon at Bayview. Let's have a seat."

She ushered them ahead. They both obeyed and sat as though they were school-aged children.

"Jackson, do you know if my ex-husband will be joining us?"

"Soon. He had a last minute consultation."

"I'm not surprised. Would you like a drink?"

"Thanks. I'll take a Scotch, neat."

"Ella?"

"Thank you, nothing right now."

Crossing her arms, Ella glared at Jackson. "I don't understand. Why did you pretend to be a driver sent by my uncle?"

"The opportunity presented itself when you made an incorrect assumption."

"What are you talking about?" Maxine asked.

Ella pointed an accusing finger. "He called himself Jay and said he had picked up Uncle Bill's house key from him."

Bill stepped into the sitting room. "Hi, everybody. Sorry, I'm late. Did I miss anything?"

Ella turned at the sound of his voice. "Uncle Bill." The excitement swirling around her shifted from irritation at Jackson to delight at seeing her mother's brother. Despite having less hair on his head, he looked the same, a solidly built man in his late fifties whose gray eyes filled with delight at seeing his niece. She stood and rushed toward him.

"Ella, baby, how are you?"

Sinking into the comfort of his embrace lessened the ache she had carried but denied for two long years. She was glad to be home. The simple gesture of being held in his arms accented how empty her life had been in regards to family. How long had it been since she'd had someone to cling to physically? Her chest heaved with a new peacefulness. "I'm so glad to be here."

He pushed her back at arm's length, studying her with sharp eyes. His penetrating gaze caused her to peer at the floor as uneasiness rose in her chest. If he had noticed the paleness or the thinness of her face, he did not comment.

"It's about time you came home. You haven't been here since the funeral."

She shrugged. "It's been impossible. Rita kept acquiring performance opportunities that were too good to pass on."

"You look like you could use some rest." His voice gave away his concern.

He knows something's off. Please, Uncle, give me some space.

The beginning of her visit home was starting off rocky. Attempting to take control, she coerced a bright smile on her face and planted a hand on her hip. "Uncle, is that your way of saying I don't look my usual fabulous self?"

Before he could reply, Maxine moved to her ex-husband's side and placed a hand on his arm. "Hello, William. It's not the norm, but I'm glad you're here. We're just getting started with drinks. The usual?"

"I'll go with that."

While Bill and Maxine conversed, Ella took in Jackson's casual but neat appearance, focusing on how the material of his Polo shirt stretched across his well-defined pecs. Her heart jigged an erratic beat as her body played traitor with its reaction to the visual stimulus of Dr. Jackson Hart.

Unprepared to reveal her medical issues to her family the first night home, her eyes became wide with apprehension. Would this good-looking MD keep her near fainting episode to himself? How he proceeded would reveal a piece of his character.

But she couldn't leave it to chance. She wanted to approach her medical symptoms on her terms, at the time that was right for her. In an attempt to redirect the conversion, Ella said, "You haven't answered my question, Jackson. Why did you lead me to believe you were a driver instead of my uncle's colleague?"

"What?" Bill asked.

Jackson sat his glass on a coaster. "I figured the easiest way for us to find each other was the old 'write her name on a card' trick. You approached me and assumed I worked for a car service. Something inside of me said 'go with it,' and I did."

"Fine. Let's put this behind us and move on." Along with the suppressed appetite, her olfactory senses had dimmed as well. Ella relied on her memory and said, "Dinner smells great, Aunt Maxine. I've missed your cooking."

Maxine approached Ella with a glass of wine. "Let's sit."

Maxine joined her on the sofa and touched Ella's cheek. "Honey, you look so tired and pale. I believe you've lost weight."

Minimal answers. Short and sweet.

Ella shrugged. "Jet lag can be tough."

"I hope you're planning to rest during your break. Maybe you should have a physical. William, what do you think?"

Bill took a drink. "Here, we go."

His statement brought a smile to Jackson's lips.

"I think Ella is old enough to know what she needs." He punctuated his statement with a wink at Ella.

"What plans do you have while you're home?" Maxine asked.

She had forgotten how exhausting her aunt could be. But her concern came from her heart, and that was what mattered. Ella dug in, launching answers she hoped would satisfy her aunt's curiosity without revealing a whole lot.

"I don't have big plans, just the concert with the SFP Orchestra. When I'm not practicing, I plan to read and catch up on the movies I've missed. This past year has been busy with little downtime. As for my paleness, I think time in the sun instead of all the time I've been spending in hotel rooms and on airplanes will take care of that."

She ignored the comment about the physical exam and turned to Jackson, using him as a scapegoat to take the focus off her. "So, how long have you been at Bayview?"

"Roughly two years."

"He was hired to fill your father's position," Bill said.

The knot in her stomach tightened. She took a sip of wine. "I see. Good luck, my father was a phenomenal surgeon."

It wasn't fair to him that her words came off as a challenge, but this was her father they were discussing. The man she had always thought walked on water. This newcomer had some big shoes to fill.

"People speak well of him," Jackson replied. "I hope to one day be as good a surgeon as Dr. Craig."

Maxine checked her watch and stood. "Dinner should be ready. Let's move this party into the dining room."

The table glowed with candlelight, emphasizing the beauty of Maxine's good china. Tonight she had prepared bourbon chicken, sweet potatoes with pecans and steamed asparagus with a cream sauce. Maxine's reputation as an excellent cook was well known, so it was no surprise the food looked and smelled delicious. Even so, it did nothing to revive Ella's long-lost appetite. Not wanting to give her aunt a reason to direct the conversation back to her health status, she pushed herself to eat, but without much success.

Though Maxine's incessant chatter during the meal initiated a dull throb at Ella's temples, she took pity on Jackson, who was the current target of her aunt's interrogation. Knowing questions about dating could be easily directed at her, she waited for the right moment to come to his rescue. As Maxine paused for breath, Ella interrupted.

"Did you grow up in California?"

"No, I'm from Atlanta. I was looking for a change when I read about the position at Bayview Medical Center. The job was offered to me when I applied for it."

"We're lucky to have you," Bill said. "You're an excellent surgeon."

Jackson smiled at his boss's praise, and the sexiest dimples Ella had ever seen appeared on his face. Her stomach quivered.

Maxine pointed a finger at Bill. "Don't even go there, William. No shop talk tonight."

Ella was pleased her aunt and uncle were still a part of each other's lives. They had split up a year before her parents' deaths. When she had come home for the funeral, she watched them comfort each other through that devastating time. A stranger would never have seen them as a divorced couple.

"Jackson, we'd rather hear about what you do away from the hospital," Maxine said.

Ella tried to ignore the look her aunt passed her way, but if she didn't react now, she'd face a lecture later. "Yes, what do you do on your days off?"

"Recently, I've been spending time on the beach. Surfing is my thing. But I'm not opposed to taking an occasional day trip to wine country."

Maxine looked at Ella. "Maybe you should join Jackson on the beach to get out in the sun."

The excitement in her aunt's voice was apparent. She glanced at Jackson. Though he remained quiet, the mischievous smile on his lips sent Ella reeling toward long-ago teenage emotions. Her cheeks heated.

Bill's pager beeped. He stood. "Jackson and Ella are old enough to decide if they want to spend time together. I need to answer this page."

Ella and Jackson returned to the sitting room as Bill finished his phone call. Maxine arrived from the kitchen with coffee and an invitation for dessert.

"Max, I'm sorry to cut the evening short, but I have to go back to the hospital."

"You know that's a big part of why we're divorced."

"We may be divorced, but I still love you."

Maxine's sigh of disappointment did nothing to deter his departure.

He leaned over and kissed her on the cheek. "Dinner was delicious as always. Jackson, would you mind dropping Ella at home? Just because I'm leaving doesn't mean the night has to end. I'm sure she and Maxine would like to visit for a while."

"I don't mind as long as it's okay with Ella," Jackson replied. He gazed at her, waiting for a response.

"Do you text while you drive?" she asked, her words sounding strained.

"I can't say I've never done it. As a general rule, I don't."

"If you agree to keep your phone in your pocket, I'd appreciate a ride home."

"No problem."

"Wonderful." Maxine's eyes sparkled. "Be right back."

Although known for her decadent creations, Maxine returned with a simple chocolate cake.

Ella watched as her aunt cut and plated three pieces. She worked to swallow past the lump in her throat. "You remembered chocolate is my favorite."

"I couldn't forget that. You always had chocolate cake at your birthday parties."

While the trio ate, Maxine managed to slip a few funny stories about Ella's childhood into the conversation. She also beamed with pride over Ella's talent and performance abilities. "If you ever have the chance to hear her in concert, you should."

Could she be any more obvious about my upcoming performance?

Ella spoke up. "Aunt Maxine, I'm sorry, but this jet lag is kicking my rear. I should probably go home."

"No worries. Go and get some sleep. I'll call you in a few days." Maxine wrapped her in a hug and gave her a squeeze. "I'm so glad you've finally come home, even if only for a short time."

Ella nodded and smiled. She wouldn't be able to contain her emotions if she spoke. Jackson had hugged Maxine before they walked out together.

Traffic was lighter than usual, and the drive from Pacific Heights to the Marina area where Bill lived was a short one. Ella had hoped they'd exchange polite chitchat about the weather or the types of music they liked. Instead, when the car slowed to a stop at the first traffic light, Jackson turned to her and said, "Why don't you want your family to know you're ill?"

"I don't know what you mean."

"Oh, come on. Your eyes said it all. You were freaking out that I might mention the incident at the airport."

"Thank you for not saying anything."

"You're welcome, but you didn't answer my question." The light turned green, and Jackson focused on the road.

"It's difficult to explain."

"Go ahead, give it a whirl."

"Please, you can't say anything. They'll hover over me and insist I see a doctor immediately. You heard Aunt Maxine already mention a physical exam."

"And that's a bad idea, why?"

"The concert, of course. I have committed to perform with the orchestra. My goal for the next ten days is to polish the Tchaikovsky concerto. I can't do that if they hover."

Jackson pulled the car into the driveway and cut the engine. Moments later, he opened Ella's door. She stepped out into the cool night air. As they walked toward the stairs, a feeling of comfort surrounded her. As she spent time with this man with sexy dimples, the fatigue she had professed to her aunt lightened.

"I sound like an ingrate." Ella took a seat on the third step while Jackson leaned against the stucco wall.

"I love my family, but things are different. I'm the orphaned niece slash cousin. It's like I'm a square peg trying to fit into a round hole." Ella looked around. "I love this house. Spent a lot of time here when I was growing up. My cousins are more like siblings."

"So, your family is tight. That's good. Bill told me about your parents and the car crash. I'm sorry you lost them."

She pushed her lips together in a slight grimace. A long exhalation spilled from her chest. "I feel their loss every day. Sometimes it's in the tiniest way, but it's always there. I used my music for comfort, but it also helped hide the awful reality they were gone."

"How'd it do that?"

"When I'm on stage, my focus is to provide the best musical experience as possible for my audience. There's no room to think about anything else. I was able to pretend Mom and Dad were still alive and well in San Francisco." It surprised her how the words began tumbling out, how easy to talk to this man about something so private.

Jackson joined her on the step.

"When I was on tour they used to meet me about every three months on location for a few days. After they died and the visits stopped, I was forced to admit they were gone, and that's when life got tough."

Staring at nothing, he finally said, "I lost my parents when I was eleven. It was an airplane crash, no survivors. Time makes the pain fade, but you had your parents a lot longer than I had mine. So, I'm sure it's tough for you, even now. You'll deal with it when you're ready."

Overcome with an immediate urge to take on his pain, Ella touched his arm. "Oh Jackson, you lost your parents when you were just a boy."

"Well, it looks like we've found some common ground."

"Does it bond us enough to keep you from talking?"

"Here's the deal. I won't say anything to Bill or Maxine if you come clean with me about your symptoms."

Ella remained quiet; her lips pulled into a tight line.

"If I think you can hold off seeing a physician until after the concert, I'll keep quiet."

It wasn't a yes, but he held all the cards. "Today was the first time I was dizzy. I'm always tired, have no appetite, and I've lost weight. The headaches are nothing new. I've had those for several years. I think things will be better now that I'm slowing down." She stood. "I need to get through this concert. Then I'll see a doctor. I promise."

"Your time frame is too vague."

"I'll see a doctor the day after the concert."

"Make the appointment tomorrow."

"I can do that."

Jackson stood. "I don't like it, but I'll stay quiet. Which means I'm keeping my eye on you." He followed her up the stairs.

Ella unlocked the door and made a hasty retreat inside. Turning around, she said, "Thanks for the ride home. See you."

"You can bet on it."

AFTER LEAVING ELLA, Jackson had been tempted to take a drive up the coastal highway, something he had done many times since moving to San Francisco. He would drive for miles before heading back to his rented condo facing the bay. The hum of the highway lulled him into quiet contemplation about his presence on the West Coast and where he thought his future should be. Driving to clear his head and formulate goals, Jackson never allowed thoughts of his past to intervene. Building a foundation for his future required he stay grounded in the present since wallowing in the past had kept him anchored to Beth's absence and his life in chaos.

The change in locale had been positive. Jackson's professional life was taking off. He was a skilled surgeon, making a name for himself at Bayview and the surrounding medical community. The two recent offers to move elsewhere to practice came to mind. Offers that were still on the table. His life was coming together, and a lot of that was due to Bill and Maxine. They had taken it upon themselves to pull him into their lives after the death of his wife, to help him heal and he was grateful. Still, he needed to separate his gratitude from the facts while making his decision to stay at Bayview or move on.

At thirty-five, it was time to put down some roots, not just medical but community ties as well. Why hadn't he acted on the other offers? He had no inclination to leave San Francisco, but he needed confirmation from the chief of surgery that Bayview believed he was the kind of doctor they wanted to offer a long-term commitment. A niggling of misgiving about leaving his grandparents in Atlanta pinched his heart. He should call them soon.

Jackson parked his car but couldn't bring himself to go inside. Though the evening was chilly, he walked toward the marina, the water calling to him. His thoughts shifted to Ella. At the airport, by instinct he had reacted to keep her from falling. But as he sat with her, he had felt a pull that this woman needed safeguarding. He'd felt it again tonight when panic had shown in her eyes causing her to shut down the discussion about their initial meeting, in particular the part about how she nearly fainted. Ella had involved him in keeping her secret. That wasn't true. He had allowed himself to become involved. And now, less than twenty-four hours after meeting her, he wanted to see her again. Something about

Ella had ignited a spark that he thought had died three years ago with his wife.

CHANGED INTO PAJAMAS and washing her face, Ella heard a knock. She slipped on a robe and tied it before opening the door.

"I wasn't sure you'd be awake," said Bill.

"I had a nap when I got in from the airport, so I'm not ready for bed. Come in. Have a seat." She pointed to the gray chair by the window then settled on the bed.

"Since Max has always taken care of our guests, I wanted to know if I missed anything."

"You did good." Ella's attempt to hold a grin at bay failed.

"What?"

"I just washed my face. There's enough linen in the bathroom for my entire stay."

"Well, I'm green about these things." His eyes remained on her face. "I didn't notice the dark circles under your eyes until now. You must have covered them with your makeup."

Silence.

"Is everything okay?"

Childhood memories flooded her, reminding her she could never keep anything of importance from her parents. A sense of déjà vu haunted her. "Ohhh, this is about Aunt Maxine's comments. You know she obsesses over things."

"Max is right to be concerned. I have eyes, too." He leaned forward. "So do you want to tell me what's going on with you?"

He had just given the opening Ella needed to concede about her symptoms. She didn't take it. "Nothing terrible, a nagging headache and some tension in my neck. Do you have any ibuprofen? I took my last tablets yesterday."

"Let me check." He disappeared down the hall and returned momentarily with a small, white bottle. After removing the childproof lid, he shook out two tablets.

"I need four. This headache is a mean one."

"Do you *usually* take four at a time? Eight hundred milligrams is a lot."

"These stress headaches don't go away with two."

He gave her two more tablets. She breathed an inaudible sigh of relief.

"I don't like the idea of you taking this much medication. We should try some other meds. Are these migraines you're having?"

"Can we talk about this tomorrow? It's been a long day."

"Sure, get some rest."

Bill started to the door and turned around. "I should probably mention I had your piano moved from your house to my library. I didn't think you'd want to practice there. I hope that's okay."

Her pulse raced at the thought of her childhood home. All the memories it held. How would she ever step inside that house again? She attempted a smile. "Perfect. It doesn't make sense for me to stay here and have to go there to practice."

"Good. I'll see you in the morning."

"Goodnight, Uncle."

How could she have thought he wouldn't look at her through physician's eyes?

"I'll just have to stand up and remind him I'm an adult. I make my own decisions."

But the little girl inside wished her mother and dad were here to hold her close and tell her everything would be all right.

Chapter Two

The next morning Ella found her uncle sitting in the living room drinking his coffee and reading a magazine. Upon closer inspection, she saw it was a medical journal.

"Good morning, Uncle."

"Morning, baby. Want some coffee?"

"Maybe later." She took the seat adjacent to the sofa.

Bill laid his journal aside. "How'd you sleep?"

"Like a dream."

Except for the stomach pains that woke me two hours ago.

Ella suddenly realized she hadn't mentioned the pains when reciting her list of symptoms to Jackson the night before. Confessing to this the next time he came around might make him reconsider his agreement. And it had been an honest omission.

Looking around the room, she said, "You've done some remodeling since the last time I was home. I like it." She summed up her appraisal with an approving nod. There were multiple windows on the wall behind her. The morning sunlight spilled into the room. Hardwood floors gleamed under her feet, and the area rug in front of the sofa boasted vertical lines of muted colors. Red, green, and brown blurred together, lending a masculine feel to the space.

"Max picked out everything."

"She has a gift for décor, and she loves taking care of her family."

"How could I not let her, especially now that she's a bona fide interior designer? I would never have trusted anyone else with changing so much when I updated the house. You know she opened a shop in Pacific Heights about fifteen months ago."

"I think Claire mentioned in an email that Aunt Maxine was considering it. Good for her."

"With an empty nest followed by the divorce, I guess she had a lot of time on her hands."

Ella stood and walked toward the fireplace. What was wrong with the world? People who loved each other giving in after a long marriage, and people so in love with each other dying too early. She turned around, her nostrils flaring and hands planted on her hips. "If you love each other, I don't understand why you got divorced in the first place."

"Saying it's complicated would be the easy answer. The simple truth is Max was tired of having a part-time husband. I don't blame her for the divorce, for wanting more than I was giving. So I gave her what she needed — because I love her."

Ella reached up to touch the necklace resting on her chest. The last birthday present her parents had given her. Tears threatened. What hope did she have for herself if love wasn't enough to hold people together?

"Things weren't supposed to change when I left for New York." Defeat closed in, the tears becoming a reality.

Bill crossed the room and wrapped her in a hug. Patting her back, he said, "I know, but change is inevitable, and most of the time it brings good things."

"Not always." The tears became a steady flow as she began sobbing.

Bill held her tight and whispered, "It's okay." Wrapping an arm around her shoulder, he led her back to the sofa and sat beside her.

With thoughts of her parents now planted firmly in her mind, heaviness settled on her chest. Making a temporary home with her mother's brother instead of going home to the house on Filbert Street brought the absence of her parents crashing down around her.

Bill grabbed the box of tissue from the side table and pushed it toward her. She wiped away her tears. "I miss them so much."

"I know, but looking forward is what you need to do. Even if you're only looking as far ahead as the next twenty-four hours. What are your plans for today?"

"Practice and then more practice."

"Maybe you'll play for me tonight?" He checked his watch. "Hey, I've got to get going." He stood, slid the journal into his briefcase, and picked up his cup.

"Don't bother with that. I'll take it to the kitchen."

"Thanks," said Bill as he headed to the foyer. He stopped and turned. "If it's too difficult practicing on your baby grand, if it stirs up too many memories, we can get a rental in here to use for practice."

Ella attempted a smile. "Good to know."

After hearing the front door close, she took the coffee cup to the kitchen, rinsed it out, and placed it in the dishwasher. Having no appetite for breakfast, she moved on to the library and stood in the doorway, taking it all in.

It was an impressive room with dark mahogany paneling. On the left, the entire wall was floor-to-ceiling bookcases; a small library filled with medical, historical, biographical, and fictional books. Uncle Bill's desk now rested in front of the bookshelves. On an adjacent wall, the fireplace that had housed crackling fires on nippy days while she and Claire had spent afternoons reading jarred her memory. Her eyes continued the visual tour around the room, stopping when she saw her baby grand piano. It was like seeing an old friend.

Ella sat at the piano, her hands resting in her lap, not yet ready to touch the ivory keys. She closed her eyes and visualized the room where it had resided in her parents' house for the last fifteen years. It had been her seventeenth birthday gift given in celebration of being accepted to the Eastman School of Music to study piano performance.

Memories broke free, flooding her mind. Ella struggled to hold the tears in check. She'd already cried a day's worth of saline fluid this morning. How was she ever to feel relief from this weight on her heart?

She needed to take a step forward toward her future, to complete her grieving, and reach acceptance. Right now, she was a prisoner in the past and spent her present days spinning in a circle with no particular plans for her future other than touring.

Gently, she placed her fingers on the familiar keys and in a reserved manner began playing Debussy's *Claire de Lune*. The calming music drew her thoughts to quiet visions of the sun shining through trees to a forest clearing and then to a still lake at sunset. Transported for a time, she didn't have to think about her life and the changes she should attempt.

The urge to play continued, so she moved on to Rachmaninoff's *Opus 3 No. 2 in C Sharp Minor*. It had a haunting sound that built up to loud crescendos of chords then returned to echo the quiet sounds at the beginning of the piece. She reached the end. Ella remained seated.

Her emotions were mixed. Joy at the beautiful sounds she pulled from her beloved instrument.

Sorrow that her mother and father would never again hear her play. Any chance of a practice session ended with that last thought.

She stood and walked around the room, stopping in front of the bookcases. The sight of the books brought memories from her past rushing over her like rapids on a river. As far back as she could remember, each day had ended with one or both of her parents sitting at her bedside reading to her. The ritual was a remarkable time for them, and the memory was almost too much to bear as she stood staring at the books.

Ella suspected her uncle expected to talk about the house on Filbert Street, maybe even go to the house. How would she ever manage to see her mother and father's possessions if looking at her uncle's book collection brought such intense and distressing memories to her mind?

Ella left the library and returned to her room. Sitting on the bed, she opened her laptop to make some notes about new pieces to conquer and add to her repertoire. Suddenly Ella felt drained, and the niggling about her health resumed. She wasn't sure how to approach her uncle, but that wasn't an issue for today. She'd figure it out after the concert.

JACKSON STEPPED OUT of the shower and dried off, using his last clean towel. An afternoon of laundry duty loomed in his future. Maybe he should look into getting a housekeeper to come in once or twice a month. He wasn't the best at cleaning, but he did like things neat and tidy, a credit to his grandmother's influence. She always kept her house clean and comfortable for her family. Thinking about his grandparents brought a smile to his face. They had been an acceptable replacement for his mom and dad. Loving him, providing for him, and encouraging his ambition toward medicine. He couldn't complain, because life with them had been first-rate. Then he'd met Beth, and life had become outstanding.

He rubbed his wet hair vigorously with the towel as if he were trying to send his thoughts of Beth back to where he kept them locked away. Three years was a long time. Thoughts and visions of his wife came to the forefront of his mind with less frequency, a testament to the fact he indeed was moving on with his life.

Relocating to the West Coast two years ago had been the right decision. A decision credited to his grandparents' gentle but persistent encouragement that a complete change was needed to jump-start his life again. He recalled his grandfather saying that merely existing was not living, and that as much as it might hurt he needed to get on with the business of living. He had a long life ahead of him, and he shouldn't remain a widower. After submitting applications to several hospitals, he found himself packed and ready to move to San Francisco. He had thrown himself into his work at Bayview Medical Center.

Ready to tackle the day, Jackson picked up a small bag as he headed out the door to his car. He'd begin his time off by running some errands. A dismal thought pinched his mind. Almost two years in town and he had no one to hang with. How would he, since all he did was work? The remainder of his time he spent in near solitude. That needed to change. After a year, with Bill and Maxine's encouragement, he had relaxed enough to begin socializing. Most of his acquaintances were couples, but that was okay. He found he had missed the non-medical interaction with people, but dating held no appeal to him. And then he'd met Ella.

Now standing at Bill's front door, Jackson angled the borrowed golf clubs against the porch before pushing his warm, sweaty hands into his pockets. From the moment they had met, he felt a pull toward Ella and her hazel eyes. Maybe it was time to come out of his self-imposed shell. Time to feel and live again.

His heart thrummed in his chest as he rang the doorbell. He twisted the ring from his alma mater around his finger as he waited for a response.

The door swung open, jerking his attention to the beauty in a red dress and beige sandals, her dark brown hair pulled back into one long braid.

"Jackson, hello." Her forehead puckered into a small frown before it skirted away. Peering around him, she surveyed the street.

"Did I miss something?" he asked.

"You're not exactly who I was expecting, but it's nice to see you."

He was caught off guard by her statement. It had taken him most of the night to talk himself into coming here today, and she was expecting someone else at her doorstep. "I can come back later."

"There's no need to leave. My trunk from New York arrived at the airport this morning. I'm expecting a courier. I hope he won't take all day. I need to practice. Please, come in."

Jackson stepped inside pulling the golf bag behind him. "Why do you have to hold up your rehearsal until you get your trunk?"

"I guess I don't have to, but I tend to tune everything out when I'm in practice mode. I'm afraid I might not hear the doorbell, and I need my trunk." She noticed the golf clubs. "Looking for Uncle Bill?"

"I know Bill's at the hospital. I have the day off and was running some errands. Returning the golf clubs was on my list, and I figured since you were here…"

"You mean my uncle lent you his golf clubs? That's hard to believe. He's very protective when it comes to his golf game."

"Well, this is his old set. I was trying them out to see how I feel about the sport." He shrugged. "It's okay, but I prefer surfing."

"Let's put them in the front closet." Ella reached for the bag.

"Let me," said Jackson. As their hands touched, an electric jolt zipped through him. They looked at each other for an exaggerated moment. As Ella backed away to allow him access to the closet, Jackson wondered if she had felt it too.

There was a quiet pause before Ella asked, "So what else is on your list for today?"

He followed her into the living room, and they sat on the sofa. "Giving you this." He held out a handled bag that advertised Get More At Way Lo.

"For me?"

Jackson nodded.

She took the bag and peeked inside. Pulling several DVDs out of the bag, the corners of her mouth turned up into a smile. Her full, red lips caused a dip in his belly. They were the kind of lips made for kissing.

"Some of last year's blockbusters. Thank you, I can't wait to watch them."

"I'd be willing to watch some of them with you. I'm a great commentator."

"Good to know."

"As long as I'm here, I do have a question for you."

"Okay."

He cleared his throat. "I've accumulated a lot of vacation hours at work, and my boss, a.k.a. your uncle, suggested I should take a few days off here and there. He pointed out everybody should have some downtime—"

The doorbell interrupted his words.

"I hope that's the courier." Ella stood, and he saw her sway unexpectedly. She touched the arm of the sofa for stability and closed her eyes.

Jackson moved quickly, reaching for her shoulders to steady her. He pushed her gently onto the couch, his eyes fastened on her colorless face. "Are you alright?"

"I guess I stood up too fast."

The doorbell rang again.

"You stay here." Jackson opened the door to a courier and had him wait in the foyer while he hurried back to Ella. He sat beside her, his MD senses on high alert. "Feeling better?" he asked.

She squeezed her hands into fists, then relaxed them. "I'm okay."

"Good. Now, where do you want your trunk?"

"Upstairs would be great." She started to stand, and he put a hand on her arm.

"I'll take care of it. Up the stairs...?"

"To the left, at the end of the hall," she finished.

He returned a few minutes later with the courier, tipped him as he showed him out, and then returned to the living room. Making a quick assessment of Ella, he was glad to see the familiar paleness had returned to her face. "One trunk settled in your room," he said.

"Thanks. I appreciate your help."

"You're welcome. Now, where were we?"

"You have lots of vacation time."

Diverting my attention from the incident — smoothly done.

Jackson decided to give her a pass from a medical interrogation. "That's right," he replied. "So, my boss, who never takes time off himself, tells me I should consider some downtime."

I did take that long weekend in Atlanta last year.

"I'm taking a drive to Napa Valley on Saturday, and I wondered if you'd like to go. Last night you mentioned how busy the last year has been. I usually find a drive to the wine country relaxing."

Ella sat quietly for a moment before answering. "I have plans tomorrow with Claire. But there's nothing on my calendar for the weekend, except for practice of course. Can I think about it and get back to you?"

The disappointment he felt at her words surprised him. He rubbed the back of his neck. Their short talk the night before had convinced him he wanted to know all about her. He hadn't considered the possibility she might not feel the same way.

While his initial thought when they met had been that she needed safeguarding, his conclusion today shifted to she might not allow it. As the proffered invitation dangled between them, Jackson stood to leave. "Sure. Bill has my number."

She pulled her cell phone from her pocket. "I want to be as little a bother to my uncle as possible." She held her phone out to him. "Please, just add your number."

When he finished, he handed her phone back, and for the second time during their visit was caught off guard when a current rippled across his fingers as they made contact. They moved to the foyer. Jackson stepped outside and turned around. As he watched her leaning against the opened door, he took the time to store the image in his mind before he said, "Just call or text me."

It was quick, but Jackson's trained eyes caught her anxious intake of breath. "I'll call you. I don't text."

Chapter Three

Already awake, Ella reached over and silenced the alarm clock. She had been awakened twice during the night with the familiar gnawing pain in her stomach. The idea of remaining in bed kept her from moving until she recalled her agenda for the day.

She sat up and murmured "Claire." Meeting her cousin for shopping and lunch were toward the top of her list, but the piano practice had to come first.

As she stood under the showerhead, the hot water massaged away the tension taking up residence in her neck and shoulders. Her life needed some significant alterations. Decision time. It had to happen. But her heart had a mind of its own. Over the past two years, her once engaging personality had shut down. She'd built a wall around herself, cementing in the grief of her parents' deaths. This self-imposed prison had affected her health. And for the past few months her performance abilities. Not to the degree that her audience noticed, but the slips clanged in her head.

Ella applied her makeup with care, covering the circles under her eyes and adding blush to her pale cheeks. If she didn't pass muster with her uncle, she had no hope of convincing her cousin that her life was all good and on track. She made it downstairs just in time to say goodbye.

"No time for coffee?" she asked.

"Early meeting this morning. I'll get my coffee at the hospital, and I'll see you tonight." He kissed her on top of her head before closing the front door behind him.

Ella wandered into the kitchen and nibbled at a banana before going to her piano. Warming up on scales and arpeggios then a few Hannon exercises, her mind fell into practice mode as well as her fingers. Finished with her warm-up routine, she pulled the pages of the Tchaikovsky piece from her music bag and placed them on the music stand of the piano.

She began playing the concerto from memory, the pages in front of her intended only as a reference, if needed. It didn't take long for Ella to realize her fingers and mind were out of sync, but she persevered. Halfway into the first movement and three unbelievable mistakes later, Ella banged her fingers on the keys, and a conglomeration of sound assaulted her ears. Where was the control she'd exhibited over the piece when she'd recently performed it and during all the time she had spent at the keyboard practicing? The concentration she needed wasn't present this morning. Her head was full of Rita and Claire. And then thoughts of Jackson popped up.

Chalking her fumbles up to the anticipation of spending time with her cousin, Ella decided practicing later in the day was a good plan. And she wouldn't have to admit to defeat over her lack of concentration. She stood and moved away from the piano. A wisp of excitement about seeing her cousin took hold. Another distraction to keep thoughts of lawyers, documents and the house on Filbert Street pressed back in her mind.

She agreed to meet her cousin at Union Square in front of Saks on Post Street. Excitement skipped through her again, squeezing her heart as she drove her rental car into the parking lot. It had been several years since her last shopping trip with Claire, and the memory of good times warmed her heart. As quickly as the feeling came, it vanished. Maybe they had been apart so long their sisterly connection would be gone. The thought stabbed at her as she left the car and walked toward the uncertain reunion.

She had to think hard about the last time she had taken personal time on tour. For shopping or doing the touristy thing in any of the remarkable places she had been. Finally, she remembered. She had visited the Haus der Musik in Vienna a few months before her parents' deaths and since that time had tightly cushioned herself into the world that included only her music, her agent, and her assistant, Dory. Her days had consisted of practicing, performing and traveling until recently she was not even doing that well.

Waiting at Saks, Ella pulled her sweater close as cool air swirled around her. Turning to her left, she saw Claire and all thoughts about touring and her parents fell away as they hugged each other. Clinging to the woman who had been a huge part of her past, tears formed in her eyes. The enormity of how much she needed her and the rest of her family hit Ella with unexpected force.

Claire pulled away from their embrace, her hands sliding down Ella's arms to catch her hands. "Ella, you're finally home. So why the tears?"

"I've missed you." She dabbed at the corner of her eyes.

Touching the ends of Ella's brown hair, Claire said, "Your hair is so long now, it's beautiful."

Ella laughed. "I told Rita I'm going to throw in some blue streaks. She almost had a heart attack. It's so easy to punk her."

Claire took Ella's arm and moved toward the store's door. "Wait!" said Ella. "Don't take another step until I see it."

"I don't know what you're talking about." Claire's face became all smiles as she held out her left hand. The solitaire diamond sparkled in the sunlight.

"It's beautiful." She pulled her cousin into another hug. "I'm so happy for you, and I can't wait to meet Ed."

"Yeah, I need to bring you up to speed on the wedding preparations. I'm excited your tour schedule allowed for you to be my maid of honor. But you bummed me out saying you'd be coming home the day before the wedding and leaving right away. Now you'll be here for everything. And we're starting your vacation off right with shopping. What are we shopping for today?"

"The truth is, I haven't been shopping for quite a while. I need everything."

"Music to my ears," said Claire.

Ella spent the morning trying on outfits, shoes, and jewelry. In the fitting room at Talbots, Claire sat on a leather seat and critiqued the options. Being with Claire was comfortable, making it easy to assume her old life as if distance and death had never been a factor in her present state of being.

"Have you met Jackson?" asked Claire.

"Yes, I have."

"Isn't he hot? I could sell anything with that face and body. And he's a nice guy, too. I don't think he's dating anyone."

Ella pulled a soft black knit top over her head and said, "When did you leave advertising for sleuthing? And why do you care? You're engaged." She stepped into a straight denim skirt with the black top and got a 'thumbs up' from Claire.

"Mom and Dad know him pretty well, and I've been around him enough to know he's not seeing anyone. He's probably just not ready."

"What do you mean?" asked Ella.

"He's a widower, but I don't know the details. I'm sure my parents probably know the whole story."

"Oh," said Ella. She should cut him some slack.

"Hey, you and Jackson should go out."

Ella could feel heat explode on her face.

"Are you blushing?" asked Claire.

As teenagers, the girls had held nothing back from one another. Guilt stabbed at Ella. Her actions had caused the geographical and physical distance between them. Maybe spending some time in San Francisco would pull them together again.

"Jackson asked me to go for a drive to Napa on Saturday."

Claire helped gather up the discards. "Well, maybe he is ready to date again. I'll need all the details afterward, cousin."

"I didn't give him an answer, just said I'd think about it."

Claire cocked an eyebrow upward. "Why in the world won't you go with him?"

Ella looked away. "I don't know — I haven't dated since Patrick."

"Patrick was three years ago."

The quietness grew as the unspoken words, 'and then your parents died' rested between them.

"You have to go with Jackson. He's trying to re-enter the social scene, so you can't disappoint him. And you can't leave him hanging the whole day. When we get outside, you have to call him and tell him you'll go."

"You know, missy, you're getting more like your mother every day."

Claire raised her chin. "I like my mother."

Ella laughed. "Okay, I want to hear you say that five times on your wedding day when Aunt Maxine is everywhere you don't want her to be."

Claire's laughter mingled with Ella's. "I know you're right. Heaven help me."

When they stepped outside and began walking, Ella was relieved that the window dressing at the first boutique they passed caught Claire's attention. She would rather make the phone call to Jackson later without an audience.

"Ella, you have to try on this dress. You have great legs, and you need to show them off."

She allowed her cousin to pull her to the boutique's door. Twenty minutes later, Ella stepped outside clutching another shopping bag with an above-the-knee little black dress to add to her growing wardrobe.

Claire continued about the dress. "It looks like it was custom made for you. Oh, we have to make plans for you to show it off."

Ella offered a non-committal, "We'll see."

"Reception should be okay out here. Make your call to Jackson."

Ella groaned. "I hate this —I'd like to get to know him, but still..." Her churning stomach testified to the anxiety over his invitation. It had been so long since she had spent time alone with a man.

"Patrick did a number on you. I get it, but pretty and talented has a shelf life."

"I thought I knew him so well. Was I the only one surprised when he broke it off?"

"Leave Patrick in the past where he belongs. Learn from it and move on."

"I'm not sure I want to risk getting hurt again."

"Look, it's not like you met Jackson through a computer dating service, your family knows him. We certainly wouldn't let him near you if we thought he was bad news. So make the call, I'm getting hungry."

Ella scrolled down her contact list and tapped on Jackson's name. Just when she thought she would get off with leaving a message, he answered.

"Jackson, hi. It's Ella."

"How's your day going?" he asked.

"Shopping away, putting a dent on my credit card." She stopped talking, not knowing what to say next.

"So, have you decided? Does a drive through Napa Valley sound appealing enough to say yes?"

"It sounds lovely, but—" Ella turned her back to her cousin as if it would keep her from hearing her next words. "Do you remember what I said about your phone?"

"I remember, phone in my pocket."

"Okay, I'd love to go."

"Great. I'll see you Saturday, say eleven o'clock?"

"Sounds good, see you then."

Ella returned her phone to her purse. As they walked to the restaurant, she struggled to keep up with Claire. Her energy level had plummeted with the morning's activities, and she was relieved when they stopped in front of Moretti's House of Pasta, only a block from the boutique. They arrived to find Jeremy waiting for them. Without hesitation, Ella dropped her shopping bags on a seat in the waiting area and hugged him fiercely.

"I wasn't sure when I'd see you." She turned to Claire and smiled. "How hard did you have to twist his arm to get him to leave work and join us?"

"Hey, I resent that," said Jeremy.

"We all know you're a workaholic just like Dad. You'd do well to remember that when you finally marry. Be sure to adjust your priorities accordingly." The hidden warning in Claire's comment hung in the air.

Ella missed the banter between her cousins. As to why she hadn't come home before now to the welcoming arms and comfort of her family, she couldn't say.

They spent the next hour catching up and walking a judicious path down memory lane, each in tacit agreement to steer clear of comments about Ella's parents. After paying the check, Jeremy said, "I hate to do this, but I have to get back to the office."

Ella stuck out her lip with disappointment. "Uncle Bill mentioned something about a promotion, and I have the feeling I won't be seeing much of you."

"I'm competing against two of my co-workers for the position. We'll have a decision soon. How long are you staying?"

"I'll be heading to San Diego week after next."

He took her hand and said, "I'll see what I can do. You know I want to spend time with my favorite cousin."

"As your favorite and only cousin, I'm going to hold you to it."

JACKSON TAPPED ON Bill's partially opened door, gaining his friend's attention. "Got a minute?"

He waved Jackson into his office. "Have a seat."

Jackson pointed to the pile of paperwork covering the Chief of Surgical Services' desk. "Are you sure?"

"Audits," said Bill. "My least favorite part of the job. What brings you by?"

"Returning this." Jackson dropped a brochure beside a stack of papers. He knew how lucky he was to have a boss that he could call a friend as well. Some of his former colleagues from Atlanta couldn't make the same claim.

Before Bill could respond, the phone rang. Placing the call on speaker, he continued to sift through the papers on his desk. "Dr. McMillan," he said, using his best professional voice.

"Hi, Daddy. Are you busy?"

"Never too busy for you."

Not one to beat around the bush, Claire got to the heart of the matter. "I'm worried about Ella."

"What's got you in such a state?"

"I can't believe you have to ask. Surely you've noticed her color's not good, and she's too thin."

Bill stopped his multitasking. "It does appear she's lost some weight but don't you think you might be overreacting just a little?" Bill rolled his eyes. Claire could be dramatic at times, particularly when her family and friends were concerned.

"Daddy, I saw her in her underwear while she was trying on new outfits. She looks almost anorexic, and we used to be able to shop all day." In a quiet voice, she added, "We only went to three stores."

"I think she's been pushing herself hard, especially this past year," said Bill. "Look, Claire, you're getting yourself worked up over probably nothing. Your mother has already mentioned to Ella about getting a physical exam while she's home. And I'm going to make sure she rests while she's here. So relax."

They talked a few minutes longer before he hung up. Turning his attention to Jackson, he said, "The conference brochure, what do you think? George Turner is giving a presentation on liver transplantation. He's an excellent surgeon and a great speaker. If you can work it out, his lecture alone would be worth the trip."

The phone rang again. "Sorry, my assistant had to leave early, I'll keep this short." He hit the speaker button again. "Dr. McMillan."

"Hey, Dad. I wasn't sure I'd catch you in, but I decided to give it a try."

"Jeremy, I haven't heard from you in a while. How's work?" Bill took off his glasses and pushed back his chair stretching out his legs.

"Work is fine. I had lunch with my girls today. What's wrong with Ella?"

"What do you mean?" Bill stood and began pacing in the limited area behind his desk.

"Well, I can't exactly say she's sick, but she looked tired and worn out. She hardly ate anything at lunch. Dad, do you think she has a problem? I mean she's as thin as some of the models Claire uses on her campaigns."

"She may have a few issues that need resolving, and I'm going to start working on them when I get home tonight."

"It's not just how she looks. We were together a good hour, talking about old times and not once did she mention Uncle Elliott or Aunt Linda. I'm worried, Dad."

After reassuring his son they would take care of Ella together as a family, he ended their conversation. He looked at Jackson. "I'm done for the day."

"Everything okay?" asked Jackson.

Bill shook his head. "Two calls about Ella. It's one thing for Claire to call, all worked up because that's Claire. But when I get a call from my son relaying the same concerns, I think I should be watching things a little closer." He rubbed his chin. "Ella told me she's been taking eight hundred milligrams of ibuprofen at a time for bad headaches lately."

Jackson wasn't hearing anything different from what he had observed while spending time with Ella. "As someone not so close to the situation, I'd say rest and some of Maxine's cooking may be all she needs."

"It's time for me to switch from uncle to doctor mode. We're going to have a frank discussion about this when I get home. Wish me luck."

"I think you might need it."

As they walked out of the office together, Jackson's stomach clenched, making him second-guess his decision to keep Ella's secret.

THE CALLING OF HER NAME pulled Ella from a drowsy state.

"Ella."

There it was again. She opened her eyes. Bill peeked around her bedroom door.

"Come in, Uncle." She pushed herself upright against the headboard of the bed.

"Hey, I just got home. How was your day?"

Ella stretched her arms upward above her head then covered her mouth as she yawned. "Shopping with Claire tired me out, so I decided to take a nap. I didn't mean to sleep this long."

"No headache?" he asked.

She patted the side of the bed, and he sat.

"No headache today." Pulling a pillow onto her lap, she picked at the fabric. "I should get up. I've missed precious practice time while I've been napping."

"I've been wondering about something."

"What's that?" asked Ella.

"Why did you agree to perform when this is supposed to be downtime for you?"

"Victor Ferrell was set for the concert and unfortunately broke his arm in a car accident. So I've been asked to take his place. I've played this concerto twice recently so it's pretty much performance ready. And I'm here in San Francisco."

Bill frowned.

"You're wearing your grumpy face."

"It's an easy fix. Tell me you'll change your mind and let the conductor find someone else to perform."

"I can't do that for two reasons."

He looked at her with suspicious eyes. "Why?"

"One, I gave my word to Pamela. Two, I feel a bond with that orchestra because I gave my first major performance with them."

"I remember that night. It was magical, the catalyst that changed your life."

"Exactly," said Ella.

"I thought this was supposed to be your time to rest. We both know you need it." He blew out a breath. "It'd be easier if I could call the shots. All I can do is support your decision."

Her uncle's concern wrapped around her like a warm, thick towel after a cold rain. A lump filled her throat. She nodded.

He stood and said, "So how about some dinner?"

Ella pulled her pillow up behind her head and leaned back. "I'm not hungry. I had lunch with *both* my cousins today. The restaurant was lovely, and the food was great."

"Oh? What did you eat?"

"I ordered a pasta dish and tea. I'm more tired than hungry. I think I'll stay in bed." Guilt over misleading him as to eating her lunch produced a sharp spasm in her chest.

"All right, baby. I'm going to find some dinner then go to bed. My day started pretty early this morning."

"Night, Uncle Bill."

As she heard the click of the door, Ella pushed back the covers. Her rumpled clothes gave her the urge to rummage through the dresser drawers until she found her worn and comfortable Eastman tee shirt and some pajama pants. While brushing her teeth, the realization came that it had been a long time since she'd had anyone ask about her day. Being on her own for so long had caused her to hold everything inside.

She should ask her uncle for help, should tell him about her pain. And she would. After the concert. Pinches of guilt made her stance on the matter shaky. Settling back into bed, she turned on her side and closed her eyes. It wasn't long before sleep followed.

Wearing a black dress, she sat between her aunt and uncle in the front pew at Grace Cathedral. Instead of listening to the speaker, she focused on the caskets in front of her. Two of them. A mahogany one covered with white roses, mums and snapdragons accented with greenery sitting beside a coffin of cherry wood. Pink and white roses and white football mums draped over the top. There were other sprays of beautiful flowers everywhere, but her eyes remained on the caskets. The speaker eulogized her parents with kind and loving words.

She was choking. Couldn't pull air into her lungs. Shooting into an upright position in her bed, she felt pain in her chest as she struggled for air. The nightmare had returned, repeating the horror that entered her life just because someone had been careless enough to text while driving.

Grabbing her knees and pulling them against her chest, she rocked back and forth trying to settle from the shock of going through it all again. The stability in her life had been taken away in mere seconds, and her life had never been the same since that time.

The LED readout on the clock glowed 3:33 a.m. Ella's breathing calmed. The familiar, sharp pains in her stomach kicked in. Taking her purse from the nightstand, she searched for antacids. Panic set in when she came up empty-handed.

Calm down and breathe. Music bag.

Ella lost no time heading to the stairs. Another attack of pain caused her to misstep. She tumbled down several stairs and finally grasped the handrail stopping her forward motion.

Bill came out of his room. "Ella?" He descended the stairs to stand in front of her. "Are you hurt?"

"I woke up and decided to go downstairs. Clumsy me, tripped over my own feet."

"Let me help." Bill took her by the shoulder and upper arm.

Ella gasped.

"Stop. What hurts?"

With a guarding motion, she placed her arm around her waist. She couldn't confess about her stomach pain just yet. The first thought that popped into her head came out of her mouth. "I think I turned my ankle."

"Let's get you back to your room." Uncle Bill eased her up the stairs and back to bed. He palpated her ankle. "Looks good, but you may have sprained it."

"I just turned it when I stumbled on the stairs."

"Why were you going downstairs this time of night?"

"I needed my music bag..."

"Okay. I'm going to make an ice pack, just in case. Stay in bed; I'll bring your music bag too."

Ella's body relaxed in response to his words. Her initial idea to keep her symptoms from her family was becoming a monumental task. Needing to focus on her upcoming performance meant dealing with the pain later. Until then she'd have to up her game to be a convincing actress.

JACKSON SWITCHED DIRECTIONS when he saw Bill at the nurses' station. He set his portable chart pad and coffee on the counter. "Good morning. How did your talk with Ella go last night?"

"Morning." Bill sighed. "I didn't get anywhere with her before going to bed or after she fell down the stairs during the night."

The older man's eyes clouded with concern, and Jackson felt a stab of guilt about holding back information his friend might be better off knowing. "Is Ella alright?"

"She claims she twisted her ankle when she fell. We iced it right away."

"You don't believe her?"

"She tried to pass it off as being clumsy."

Jackson raised an eyebrow indicating he knew there was more to be said.

"There's nothing clumsy about my niece. She was a competing gymnast for three years."

Jackson came to Ella's defense. "It was a tumble in the middle of the night. I think you're making too much of the incident. Was she limping this morning?"

"Sleeping when I checked on her. I could have woken her, but she needs the rest."

Jackson looked thoughtful. "You're probably right about the sleep. Maybe I should cancel our plans for tomorrow."

"You have plans with Ella?"

"We're driving up to Napa Valley for the day. But if she hurt her ankle—"

"Don't cancel your plans. She needs to do other things besides practice. Just keep an eye on her, please."

"Will do." Jackson opened his mouth to ask a question but closed it.

"You have something else to say?" asked Bill.

"I want to ask you something about Ella, but I'm hesitant. I don't want to overstep into areas that are none of my business."

"If you have a concern about my niece, don't be shy about it."

"The night I took Ella home from Maxine's, she asked me to keep my phone in my pocket. Yesterday she told me she'd go with me to Napa if I'd keep my phone in my pocket while I'm driving. So what's the deal? Did she have a close call texting and driving?"

The color drained from Bill's face, and Jackson wondered what can of worms he had opened. Bill put his hand on Jackson's shoulder, guiding him into an empty consultation room. He motioned for him to sit while he did the same. Taking a deep breath and blowing it out, he said, "The person that killed my sister and brother-in-law was texting when the crash occurred." He wore the pain of the memory clearly on his face.

"I'm sorry, Bill."

"There are days when I have to remind myself that my sister is gone. Ella hasn't involved herself with any of it, the lawyers or the house. I was hoping this trip home meant she's ready to deal with it all, but not a word."

"She's only been here a few days, and she's got this concert coming up. That's a lot to deal with."

"You're right; the lawyers can wait." Bill stood. "I should get started on morning rounds. Thanks for giving Ella a distraction."

"I'd say it's very little compared to what you and Maxine have done for me. You were a lifeline when I needed it. I don't think my life would be the way it is today without your friendship."

"Enjoy your trip to the valley."

"Thanks, we will." What was he in for? Offering friendship to someone stuck in her grieving. Something he had had such a hard time with himself. His breath caught in his chest at recalling the months of darkness and despair he had suffered.

If he offered his friendship to Ella while she struggled, would it bring up the dreadfulness he had finally managed to put behind him?

Chapter Four

Jackson navigated his car onto the Golden Gate Bridge. Beyond the bridge's end, they passed Vista Point heading north on Highway 101 toward Santa Rosa. The San Francisco skyline had disappeared miles back, exchanging the energetic hubbub of the city for the quiet, beautiful scenery boasting sights of mountains, trees, and fields. Green dominated the landscape before them, framed by a sky of never ending blue.

Ella settled back in the leather seat of the sports coupe and sighed. Such a small thing, but Jackson's heartbeat ticked faster at the contented sound. She seemed more relaxed than when they had started their outing to Napa Valley. A comfortable silence settled between them negating the need to keep a steady flow of conversation going.

He liked seeing her free from the tension always simmering below the surface. His eyes left the road, and he glanced in her direction. Ella sat tall, her back unyielding, no doubt from years of sitting at the piano. Her straight nose gave a regal appearance to her profile. Happy to be the one to offer her what he hoped would be an enjoyable day brought a pleasure that had been missing from his life for some time. A different satisfaction from when he made a patient's life better from a surgical procedure.

He broke the quiet. "Sorry about my early appearance this morning. I have this thing about being punctual. It dates back to my childhood. Regardless, you seemed anxious, and I hope it wasn't because of that."

She wrinkled her nose. "I've gotta work on my poker face. That was my performance anxiety showing. I could only practice an hour and a half this morning. Thinking about when I can practice hasn't been an issue for years, and now I have to worry about neighbors and noise ordinances. It's frustrating."

"Makes sense to me. It sounds like you have real issues, not like my squawking about my punctuality obsession."

The faint semblance of a smile appeared on her face. Jackson liked the way her dark hair fell to her shoulders curling at the ends. The pink on her cheeks, though probably artificial complimented her beautiful face.

"No harm done. By the way, you're a lucky man."

"I am?"

"Yes, because I'm a *very* punctual person; you have to be in the performance business. My schedule is often so hectic that most times I don't have the pleasure of leisurely travel. Just practicing, performing, and moving on to the next stop —

always expected to be ready. So this lazy pace is a nice change." The smile brightened and lingered on her face.

"So touring has been tough this past year." It was more of a statement than a question.

"My agent booked a few more stops than usual, but I didn't mind. I love performing, but I guess it's possible to do too much. And I haven't been sleeping well for a while, consequently the dark circles." She pointed to her eyes hidden behind her Burberry sunglasses.

He took her being upfront about the dark circles and dizziness as a positive thing. Hopefully, if other symptoms surfaced, she'd confess those as well. Maybe he should take her to the beach like Maxine had suggested and get her out in the sun. However they spent time together, he'd be keeping a close eye on the niece of his boss.

Ella angled her head, studying his profile. "You seem miles away. Where'd you go?"

Her words broke into his thoughts. His eyes left the road momentarily as he glanced at her and smiled. "Never left the car. Bill told me about the kid texting, the one who caused the accident that killed your parents. Now I understand your obsession with texting while driving. It hits closer to home when you know people who've been affected by it. When Bill told me, I made a silent pledge never to text while driving."

Strained words passed her vocal cords. "Thank you for that." And then she attempted a laugh. "I believe I might be at a disadvantage here."

He frowned. "Why would you say that?"

"I'm sure Uncle Bill has told you all about me. And if he hasn't, I'm positive Aunt Maxine has. I know next to nothing about you."

"Well, we'll have to do something about that." Jackson smiled, showing dimples. "Starting today."

The road curved as they sped along the stretch of pavement a few miles from Napa. "Oh look," said Ella, as two brightly colored hot air balloons appeared high in the sky. "They're magnificent, just floating toward the clouds, their colors so striking against the blue sky. Can we pull over?"

After maneuvering the car to the side of the road, he stopped the engine. In no time, Ella sprang from the car, twirling around like a child and breathing in the fresh air. "Everything is so lush and green."

The unending rows of grapevines accented by a small lake in the background and the rise of mountains behind it made a picturesque sight. But Jackson focused on the woman enjoying the view. "I have to agree, just beautiful."

"I've always wondered what it would be like to float across the sky in an open basket and if things below look more vibrant than when looking out an airplane's window."

Leaning against the side of his car, Jackson took in the sight of Ella enjoying herself, which made him glad she had agreed to come on the drive today. Bill's anxiety about his niece had been apparent and probably justified when he told Jackson about her fall down the stairs. Watching her now made it seem as though he'd been discussing someone else. "You grew up this close to wine country, and you've never gone up in a balloon?"

"One of my mom's friends rode in a hot air balloon that malfunctioned. The one time we took visiting relatives to Calistoga, she refused to go ballooning because of her friend, who by the way didn't get hurt. And she wouldn't let me go either. Talk about bummed."

"I have a few ideas on how to spend our day, but if you'd like to take a hot air balloon ride—"

"It's okay. I'd like to see what you have in mind."

He reached for the car door. "Let's go."

IT WASN'T LONG before they were driving down Main Street, matching the speed of traffic that moved at a relaxed tempo. Ella eyed a collection of unique shops, two galleries, a spa, and a Firefighters Museum as well as several restaurants. The shift in pace from her usual go-go-go routine affirmed her decision. This decisive move, deleting continuous touring from her life.

Jackson pulled into a parking space at the Riverfront Plaza and walked around the car to open Ella's door. He reached for her hand. "I think we'll start with a trip to that bakery on the right. I missed breakfast this morning. And since you spent your morning practicing, I'll bet you haven't eaten either."

Goose bumps popped on her arms. Then a yearning surfaced to remain physically connected to Jackson, whose interest in her seemed genuine. It made her realize how much she missed a man's touch, embrace, kiss.

Don't become involved.

Remembering the vow, Ella released his hand as they entered the bakery. The purpose for coming home was to resolve her medical issue and deal with the legalities of her parents' deaths. Thinking about them caused the knot in her stomach to tighten. She had to put those thoughts far away or risk ruining a day promising lightheartedness.

Ella focused on Jackson as he conversed with the woman on the other side of the counter. He was a few inches over six feet, with broad shoulders and a lean body. Well-defined biceps stretched the fabric of the gray Henley he wore. His friendly smile, authentic. She could use a friend. If Ella allowed Jackson into her life, would it be a negative or a positive? Maybe she was getting ahead of herself, and all he wanted was to spend a carefree day with his boss's niece. A wave of heat covered her cheeks. Surely, Uncle Bill hadn't asked Jackson to take her along. Her eyes shot to the right at the disturbing thought.

"Earth to Ella."

She looked up at him. "I'm sorry, what?"

Jackson pointed to the display case filled with delectable dainties. "What will you have?"

"A small fruit salad, please."

"You can't come to a bakery and order fruit." He looked at the woman attending to the register and said, "I'll have a bear claw and coffee. Come on, Ella. You don't want to hurt the owner's feelings."

"Fine." She pointed to a peach raspberry scone. "Instead of fruit, I'll take that and a bottle of water."

They settled at a table on the patio overlooking the Napa River. Boats moved sedately on the water, the leaves on nearby trees ruffled by a passing breeze. The bubble-wrap of serenity surrounding them caused a smile to surface. She wished she could hold on to it forever.

Ella surveyed the area. Most couples seated around them engaged in quiet conversation giving an ambience of intimacy. The low noise level caused a tiny, faraway alarm to sound in her mind. Intimate was the last descriptor she would've used for their outing today. Stopping the scenario from growing, she asked the first question to pop into her head.

"Have you ever spent time on the water?"

"Water as in..."

"I know you surf, but I mean like on a river or a lake?"

"One of my first memories is going to Lake Lanier with my parents. We had a boat, but my grandparents sold it after they died."

"That must have made you sad...for your grandparents to take that away from you."

"I don't see it that way. They're just not fond of the water as my folks were." He picked up his coffee cup. "Maybe it was just too hard for them."

"Did you like living with your grandparents?"

"It was a great alternative. I could have ended up in foster care with strangers."

Ella had been determined not to think about her parents today, but that was an unrealistic goal. They were never far from her thoughts. "I can't image what it would have been like if I'd lost my parents at such a young age."

"They did their best to take care of me." Jackson settled back in his chair, his gaze shifting to the water. "My parents and I used to spread a quilt on our lawn and look at the stars. It was one of my favorite things to do. They taught me the names of the constellations. My grandparents aren't stargazers, but they bought me a telescope. I guess they thought it might make me happy to continue to look at stars. I still have it. Sometimes I set it up and take a look at the sky." He paused to take a drink of coffee then leaned forward, his eyes searching her face. "What about you? Do you like the water?"

The alarm jangled a little louder this time. Ella silenced it as she lost herself in the blueness of his eyes. She wanted to learn things about him and vice-versa. "I was on a swim team when I was young. But if my dad had a weekend off from the hospital, we'd go hiking. I earned a few of my Girl Scout badges on those hikes."

Jackson set his cup on the table and squinted his eyes.

"What are you doing?"

"Trying to picture you in a brown dress with one of those badge holders across the front. And a brown beanie on your head."

"Wrong picture. Girl Scouts wear green."

"Are you sure? I remember the little girl next door wore one of those brown outfits. I thought she was a Girl Scout."

"Brownie, one step away from Girl Scout."

"Oh."

They finished their food in silence, and finally, Jackson asked, "What would you like to do?"

"Earlier you said you had some things in mind."

"I happen to know that just minutes away from here is a winding, wooded country road that leads to a winery where we can do a little wine tasting. There's also a gallery and a garden. What do you think?"

"Sounds great, I'm in."

The stunning scenery astonished Ella. The road lined with beautiful, old trees that arched over the pavement allowed only small rays of sunlight to peek through the clustering of leaves. She gasped with pleasure as the gardens surrounding the winery came into view.

The gallery, housed in a century-old stone building, captivated her attention. "It's picture perfect."

"Nice. I'll have to thank my source for the suggestion."

As they began exploring the first floor, a fascination with the caliber of paintings, drawings, and sculptures on display played on her emotions. She shared this part of her easily, like her performances. The complexities of her disappointments and especially her grief she kept coiled up tightly, holding it in check, revealing it to no one.

"I know from talking with Bill and Maxine that touring has taken you around the world. I bet you've seen some incredible things in exotic places."

"When my parents joined me we would take in the tourist spots. The last few years, not so much."

"Did the sightseeing get old?"

"No. My assistant encouraged me to see the sights as we traveled. After a few years, my agent was able to move my bookings from small cities to larger ones. I gathered a following, and after that, it was hard to be anonymous in public. I found myself spending more and more time in my hotel room. After my parents' deaths—" Ella stopped and pulled in a ragged breath. "Well, I had a hard time for a while just making my performances." She raised her chin, fighting hard to keep tears from forming at the thought of her parents. "But in the eight years I've been touring, I haven't missed a single performance."

Jackson pointed to a bench along a wall, and they sat. "That's some record."

"It certainly made it easier for Rita to set up a tour."

He took hold of her hand. "Ella, I don't know you as well as I'd like, and maybe it's none of my business, but I'd like to throw something out there for you to think about."

Though the tingling in her hand confirmed she'd have to work at allowing Jackson a friendship and nothing more, she left it where it rested. This simple act made her feel safe. The break-up with Patrick had been traumatic. Her bruised heart was beginning to heal when her parents died sending her into seclusion. She liked feeling safe. She liked the idea of Jackson taking an interest in her.

"Okay, I'm listening."

"If you're starting to think of yourself as a commodity instead of an artist, maybe it's time to shift your career goals."

"I won't deny that's how my agent sees it. But to me, I'm an artist first. Right now, performing is the highest priority in my life."

"You're how old, twenty-nine, thirty?"

"Thirty-one."

"Maybe it's time to shift your priorities." With their hands still entwined he stood and pulled her upward. "Come on, we've got more art to admire."

She allowed him to take the lead. When she had started her performance career, she'd never considered shifting to some other angle of the music world. How would she weave teaching with performance if she took the position in San Diego?

After surveying the remainder of the treasures the gallery offered, they found themselves walking through the garden toward the parking area. A palate of colors gave a stunning presentation of the grounds surrounding the building. Orange-gold poppies, the state flower of California, had a prominent place in the landscape's design. Mist coming from the mountain provided a dramatic backdrop, adding to the grandeur around them.

The ease of the day with an attentive man caused a sigh of contentment to settle in her chest. "What a beautiful place. This is the best I've felt in weeks. Thanks for inviting me today."

"Glad to hear it. I'm sorry we didn't have time for the wine tour. The gallery exhibits were more extensive than I imagined."

Concern alarmed when he mentioned wine tasting earlier. Ella wasn't sure her stomach would handle it. "No worries. It's been a pleasant afternoon."

"But the day's not over. It's a shame we've come to wine country, and we're leaving without tasting the winery's offerings. But at least we'll have some local wine with a late lunch."

"So we're not going home?"

"Not just yet. I've heard about a music room and bar downtown. I thought we could get a bite to eat before we head back."

A sign just inside the door boasted live musical performances in a variety of musical styles. The bar had more patrons occupying the bar stools than the area filled with tables and chairs situated in front of a small stage. The strains of music coming from the stage affirmed that the choice of the afternoon was jazz.

Ella settled back in the padded chair and once again attempted to calculate how long it had been since she had taken time to relax without an itinerary controlling her every move. The hostess handed them menus. She found it hard to concentrate on the list of savory items with the grinding in her stomach that had kicked in on the ride back to town. Had she remembered her pills?

Panic edged in as she dropped her menu on the table. "I'm going to leave the ordering up to you while I find the ladies' room. I'd like a glass of water along with whatever you choose for us."

Ella followed the sign directing her to the restrooms. She washed her hands then anxiously dug through her purse, expelling a sigh of relief when her fingers wrapped around a small bottle of antacids. Popping two into her mouth, Ella paused to chew the tablets. Pushing the door open, she swallowed and made her way back to the table.

She had found it difficult, even painful at times to consume certain foods and drinks. It seemed the list was increasing by the week. It took all her willpower not to flinch when she saw the bottle of Zinfandel on the table. Instead, she smiled and said, "So what did you decide on?"

"I ordered a chicken pesto flatbread pizza. According to the menu, it's handcrafted."

"Sounds good," she said, all the while hoping the garlic in the pesto wouldn't set off additional stomach pains. Ella settled back in her chair and sipped cautiously at her wine. The mellow sounds of the ensemble enveloped the room, allowing another layer of the wall she had built around herself to melt in the presence of the man who awakened feelings she had buried after the break-up with Patrick.

Jackson's fingers tapping on the table caught her attention. "Looks like you're enjoying the music," she said.

"It's pleasant. Living with my grandparents, I heard more than my share of the giants of jazz. Louie Armstrong, Count Basie, Duke Ellington. I'm sorry, Ella. If you don't like jazz, if it grates on your nerves, we can cancel our order and go somewhere else."

"This is fine. But I have to admit I'm more of a swing fan. Tommy Dorsey, Benny Goodman, Glenn Miller." A look of surprise on Jackson's face made her add, "Due to the influence of my grandparents and their record collection."

"Did you spend a lot of time with them?"

"Claire and I spent two weeks every summer in Sacramento with them. During our first visit, it rained for several days, and I guess they were running out of ways to entertain us indoors. They pulled out their big band collection and danced for us. We made them do it every summer after that."

A wistful urge took over, and she let a groan escape. "It was so much easier to be a kid back then than a grown-up now."

"Just because you're grown up doesn't mean the fun has to stop." He dipped his fingers in her glass and flicked some water at her.

Her mouth dropped open. "You did not just do that." She dunked her fingers in the water and returned the gesture and laughed. "We're even. And we should probably act like grown-ups now."

The waitress appeared with their food. Jackson lifted the glass from the table and handed it to the waitress. "Could I get a fresh glass of water for my friend, please?"

She liked this playful side of Jackson, certainly something that Patrick hadn't possessed. If he had, she'd never seen it. The easiness of the day was something Ella craved. Her life had become somber and businesslike without any release. It had only taken four days with Jackson to make her see she wanted her life to change. Would the change include Jackson?

AS THEY DROVE down the coastal highway toward San Francisco, Jackson admitted to himself he didn't want their time together to end. Satisfying quietness surrounded them, like the fulfillment he experienced after performing a successful aerial on his surfboard. Even so, he turned on the radio instead of engaging Ella in conversation. The soothing sound of a James Bay song came through the speakers.

They passed over the last mile of the Golden Gate Bridge. Jackson glanced over at the dozing brunette.

We should have returned earlier.

His subconscious had pushed the thought more than once during the day. Stopping at a red light, Jackson focused on Ella and hoped he hadn't complicated her medical condition by his selfishness.

When they arrived at Bill's house, he touched her shoulder. "Ella," he softly called. Her eyelids fluttered. "You're home."

Pulling her head upright, she covered a yawn. "I can't believe I fell asleep."

"No worries. We both know you have some issues to iron out — after the concert." Jackson left the car and moments later opened Ella's door.

Together they climbed the stairs. "Thanks for the best day I've had in a long time," said Jackson.

"You're welcome. I enjoyed today, too. Let me know if you're interested in hanging out again." She unlocked the door then turned to face him. "I think I'll sleep well tonight, and I can thank you for that. Goodnight."

As he backed out of the driveway, Jackson's thoughts remained on Ella. He exhaled. "I'm glad one of us will be able to sleep tonight."

THE INSTANT ELLA AWOKE on Sunday, her rejuvenation dawned like the first light. A smile captured her face. Standing and stretching brought with it a semblance of her old self. How could one day of relaxation bring such relief to the tension that had become her norm? Or did this peaceful solace come from spending time with a handsome, caring man? She sighed as her mind hit replay, recalling the last twenty-four hours.

Maybe they'd spend more time together. But shopping filled today's agenda, not a man's arena. Glancing at the clock, she hurried to shower and dress so she would be on time to meet Maxine and Claire. Refreshed from a good night's rest hopefully meant she'd be able to keep pace with her co-shoppers. Fatigue had been her reality in the last month, but today she sparkled with renewed energy.

As they walked into the first dress salon, Ella said, "I can't believe I didn't pull a dress for this performance before Dory sent my gowns to the cleaners."

Maxine squeezed her shoulder. "We'll fix this. Besides, with all your concerts and photo shoots, you can never have too many gowns."

The last shopping trip for a gown had been with her mother. Ella attempted a smile. "Glad to have your help today."

"I'm happy about it," said Claire. "You know how much I love to shop."

The trio spent the early afternoon hours scouring San Francisco for just the right gown. After searching in four stores without success, discouragement plagued Ella.

"I insist we stop for lunch," said Maxine. "I have a suspicion that neither of you girls ate breakfast." When Ella protested, and Claire chimed in, Maxine raised her hands for them to cease their objections.

"Claire, you may be engaged now, but that doesn't mean I'll tolerate you starving yourself to fit into a wedding gown. You don't need to lose weight, and we'll find the loveliest dress for your big day. We've narrowed it down to some beautiful choices, and now we have your maid of honor here to help you decide."

Maxine shifted her gaze to Ella. "It wouldn't hurt you to increase your caloric intake while you're home."

The women didn't linger over lunch. Taking only the time needed to eat the salads they ordered, it wasn't long before they resumed their mission. In a small shop on Fillmore Street, Ella took great pains to explain what she wanted.

The sales woman listened intently then said, "Come with me." She turned to Claire and Maxine. "Wait here. I want to see your reaction when she's wearing the gown."

Ella followed the woman to a small dressing room.

"This is my favorite part of the job, matching a customer with the right dress." She dug into her pocket and produced an elastic band. "Here, pull your hair up while I get the dress."

Taking a brush from her handbag, Ella followed through. Nervous energy had her pacing the limited area.

I miss you, Mom.

A while later, the duo returned. Maxine and Claire were engaged in conversation. When Ella stepped from behind the curtain, they gasped in unison. Encouraged by their reaction, she moved to the professional dressing mirror.

Their search for the perfect gown ended with Ella's first glance in the mirror. Her breath hitched as she touched the silver beading detail across the top of the bust, her eyes following the trail of beading throughout the skirt to the floor.

This must be how Cinderella felt when she put on her ball gown.

Ella had purchased many dresses over the years, but this one had to be special. If she asked him, Jackson might come to the concert, so she wanted this dress to be perfect. Ella turned and modeled for her audience.

"Simply stunning," said Maxine.

"Perfection." A tingling sensation skirted across the base of Ella's neck at her cousin's words.

The shop owner chimed in. "And no need for alterations."

Claire moved to Ella's side, her words offered in a low tone. "You're going to ask Jackson to the concert, aren't you?"

"I don't know." Why was she backing off now? Didn't she want to be Cinderella around Jackson if only for one night?

"What are you girls whispering about?" asked Maxine.

"I'm trying to convince my stubborn cousin to invite Jackson to the concert. Maybe you can talk some sense into her while I make arrangements to have this knock-out gown pressed and delivered to Dad's house."

"An excellent idea," cooed Maxine. "I've been trying forever to persuade Jackson to get out more. You'd be doing him a favor, Ella. But you must ask him soon. It's almost rude to offer an invitation just six days before an event."

"I'll think about it."

Chapter Five

Coolness hung in the air as the sun began its descent. Jackson paused before pushing the doorbell. Loud, dark chords and fast running notes spilled out the open window on the west side of the house.

Not wanting to disturb her practice, he sat on the top step mesmerized by the music. Another facet of Ella emerged, this one holding him in awe. To be able to take black notes on paper and turn them into such wonderment for those listening was a rare gift.

He liked the Ella he had seen on the trip to Napa. Far away from her piano, she had become approachable, even willing to share glimpses of her life with him. Hopefully, that would continue as they spent time together.

He found it interesting, this pull to a woman so different from Beth. His wife had been a nurse practitioner, and getting to know her had been comfortable. Their careers in common had allowed a natural progression into other areas of interest. They both believed in giving back, so they had volunteered at a local women's shelter. And Beth had adored the time they had spent on the beach while he surfed.

Ella, on the other hand, was a successful musician who poured her whole self into her career. It consumed her life. How could she survive the stress without counter activities to give relief from her fervent profession? He could help her with that. She seemed to enjoy their day in the valley. Maybe they could spend time on the beach, at a movie, or on a picnic.

Finally, there was a break in the sound. He stood and rang the bell. As he waited, it became apparent she might not answer the door. Jackson recalled what she had said about tuning everything out when she practiced. As he turned to leave, the door opened. Ella dabbed at her perspiration-covered skin with a small towel. Her usually pale face appeared white and fatigued. Shocked by her appearance, he didn't speak right away.

"Jackson, what are you doing here?"

"Following my boss's orders. May I come in?"

She stepped aside. "Of course."

"Bill had to stay late for a meeting and asked if I would check on you, to make sure you eat dinner. Hope you like Chinese," he said, holding up a bag.

"I love Chinese take-out. You can put it in the kitchen. I need a few minutes. Make yourself at home." She offered the invitation as she started up the stairs.

When she returned, she had changed into green crop pants with a white and green stripe top. Ella had twisted her hair into a knot on top her head. Some unruly wisps fell on her nape. His gut jerked. He was attracted to her. The urge to care for her swelled in his chest.

Jackson set the cardboard containers of food between the plates and utensils he'd placed on the table while Ella pulled two bottles of water from the refrigerator.

"Water okay with you?" she asked.

"Perfect." He wanted to ask how she was feeling; if she had experienced any new symptoms, but he didn't want to push her. He would have to rely on his medical instincts and observation, to gauge if she was merely exhausted or if there was something more going on.

After filling their plates, he spoke. "I was sitting on the steps listening to you practice. I'm impressed. Being so focused on medicine for the last decade I sometimes find myself a little lacking on the cultural side of things. You sound ready for a performance to me."

Her eyes lit up. "I'm. So. Excited. The Tchaikovsky piece is a stupendous concerto, very challenging."

Though she had changed her clothes, she had not been able to remove the visible effects of her practice session. "How long did you practice today?"

"Polish to perfection is my motto. I was up to three hours when you rang the doorbell."

Good grief, no wonder she looks exhausted.

"You look tired. I'm not sure you should be pushing yourself so hard."

"It's what I need to do. The piece will take about thirty-five minutes to perform with the orchestra. That'll be a walk in the park compared to the practice session I just had. You might as well change the subject. I have a routine I follow to prepare for my performances, and I won't be deterred from it. Not by anyone."

"Got it."

"There are other things we can talk about besides music."

"Okay. How about those Chargers?"

"Are you making fun of me, Jackson Hart?"

"Just changing the subject."

"Maybe I should call foul for changing the subject to sports when there's not another man within ten yards."

He should turn things around, maybe apologize. As Jackson shifted in his chair, he noticed the smirk on her face.

"I'll have you know before my life became captivated by the piano, my dad took me to sporting events. My favorite was football."

"So we can talk 49ers and Chargers. Awesome."

"But I haven't followed the game in years. With touring, there's simply no time." The conversation paused as she stared into space. She sighed and said, "No time."

"For?"

"Anything but music. It's been so long since I've been to the movies, I'm not sure I remember what the inside of a theater looks like." She rubbed the back of her neck. Her effort to smile didn't quite make it. "That was a silly thought."

"Not really, I know what you mean. I love surfing, and for several years while I was in med school and working through my residency, I had to let it go. Now I can work around my schedule and surf again. You told Maxine that you're going to catch up on reading and movies. Take it a step further. Make a list of things you've missed or never done and have some fun."

Ella pushed her plate aside. "Maybe. Do you always have such good ideas floating around in there?" She reached out and tapped the side of his head.

"Hey, I don't save all this brain power for just when I'm performing surgery."

Ella giggled. "Good to know you're not totally absorbed in your work, like me."

"You just need someone to bring balance to your life, at least in little doses. Let me help you check something off your list."

Her mouth turned upward into a smile. "For instance?"

"I'll take you to the movies."

Her teeth sunk into her bottom lip while she considered his offer. "I'll take the time to relax and go to a movie with you if you'll promise to come to my concert. It should be mind blowing. Just think about it, a whole evening of Tchaikovsky!"

He liked the way she could go from zero to sixty in a few seconds when she talked about music. An ache settled in his heart when he realized this was her passion. Would it be possible for Ella to be passionate about more than one thing?

A wide grin slid across his face. "It sounds like a deal to me." He stood and set the plates in the sink. "I'll get to spend two nights with you instead of one." A feeling of breathlessness caught his chest. For the first time since Beth, he wanted a shot at happiness again.

As they worked together to tidy the kitchen, he asked, "Will you have time for a movie this week, or will you stay in practice mode until your performance?"

"I'm afraid the movie will have to wait until after the concert. I can't stray from my routine. And I have two rehearsals with the orchestra."

She followed him to the door. "Be sure to report to Uncle Bill that I ate my dinner."

"I'll let him know." The urge to kiss her overwhelmed him. Holding his emotions in check, he leaned down and placed a gentle kiss on her cheek. "Goodnight, Ella."

AFTER CLOSING THE DOOR, she touched her cheek and wondered if she should allow herself time with

Jackson. Her primary objectives were settling her parents' estate and resolving her stomach pain. Then on to San Diego to figure out her future. Would it be wise to start something knowing she might end up residing eight hours away from here?

Sharing dinner at the kitchen table with him had been atypical. The end of a grueling day of practice was dinner alone in her hotel room, and maybe a Pay-per-view movie if she could stay awake. Spending time with him made her realize it wasn't just the physical intimacy she missed since Patrick, but the whole package. Could she one day have it all? Patrick hadn't thought it possible so he moved on looking for the woman who would give her whole self to him. She had allowed herself to shoulder the blame for their breakup. Maybe their relationship hadn't worked because he wasn't the right man for her.

Absorbed in her thoughts, the ringing of her cell phone made her jump. Seeing it was Claire, she pressed accept. "Let me guess — Uncle Bill asked you check in with me."

"What do you mean? The last time I talked to Daddy was Thursday."

"I don't mean anything. What's up?"

"I'm happy you're home. Now you can take on the usual maid of honor duties you wouldn't be able to do long distance."

"I'm happy to help, but I know Aunt Maxine has hired a competent wedding planner."

"I suppose she's got it together, or Mom wouldn't have hired her."

She caught the edge of anxiety in her cousin's voice. "I'm here. What do you need?"

"I don't know her, and I trust you. You've never led me astray. Well, there was that one time in middle school..."

"Claire, you have to let the Jeffrey incident go. What I knew about boys back then, as grandma would say, wouldn't fill a thimble." She wasn't sure she knew much more about men.

"The wedding planner is dogging me for a date to do a taste testing at the Wilmont Hotel for the reception food and wedding cake."

"Set a time for next week and get back to me. I don't have any other commitments after the concert."

"Will do. Can I help you with any pre-concert prep, even though I'm not sure what that would be?"

"You're sweet to ask, and that's why I love you. I've got it covered. Dory is flying in on Thursday. She'll have everything under control. Just be sure you're sitting in the audience Saturday night to cheer me on, okay?"

"I'll be there, and you'll finally meet Ed."

"That's great. Have I told you how happy I am for you?"

"At least once, maybe more. I'll see you Saturday. Night Ella."

"Goodnight."

Ella changed into her pajamas. Though she sank into bed thoroughly drained, her mind wouldn't shut down. Her thoughts jumped from Jackson to the wedding to the concert and meeting a new conductor. Then back to Jackson — the man who could make her leave her heart in San Francisco if she moved away.

ON THE NIGHT BEFORE the first rehearsal with the orchestra, Ella sat in the library practicing. Mello sounds floating in the air put her in a relaxed mood, so different from the Tchaikovsky she had been rehearsing for the last several days. Ella sensed her uncle's presence at the door of the library but finished the musical phrase before moving her attention from the keyboard.

"Hi," said Bill. "I thought you'd be playing away on Tchaikovsky, but isn't that Gershwin?"

"You're right. I don't spend practice time on my concert pieces this close to the performance. If I'm not ready by this late date, practicing won't help me now. But I do work on other things for the future."

"I have a question—"

Something about her uncle's eyes told her his demeanor had shifted to concerned parent. "All right."

He settled into his chair behind the desk. "Do you research the conductors or the managers you deal with before you meet them?"

A lump formed in her throat. She missed her dad and the part he'd played in making her world safe. "What you want to know is how safe am I around these men. Will they take advantage of a pretty, young woman?"

"Ella, you mean as much to me as Claire and Jeremy. I need to know you're safe."

"I don't spend time with them outside of practice and performance. So I've never had to address any issues of that nature. You can relax, Uncle Bill. All's well."

"How much do you know about this conductor, Alexander Fletcher? Have you done a Google search?"

"No, but I bet you have. Did you dig up any dirt?"

"Everything I read makes him sound near perfect."

"Then what's the problem?"

"No one is perfect. All I'm saying is be cautious."

She left the piano and hugged her uncle.

"I've loved hearing you play again, and I'm looking forward to Saturday night. All of us are. I'll let you get back to—" The doorbell interrupted his words. "Let me get that."

Ella started the last section of *Rhapsody in Blue*, stopping when she heard a knock.

"Jackson."

He paused at the door.

Even in nondescript green surgical scrubs, his good looks and model-like physic popped. The five o'clock shadow screamed rugged and sexy. His blue eyes scanned Ella from the waist up.

"What are you doing here?"

"I needed to make sure you're all right."

Her eyes widened as she put her index finger to her lips. She waved Jackson into the library. He leaned against the large desk, his hands holding the edges.

"So much for staying quiet. You can't say things like that with Uncle Bill nearby."

"I've been concerned about you since last night. You looked exhausted after your practice. And I didn't like your lack of color, then or now."

She put her hand up. "Stop right there. Take this conversation in a different direction, or you can leave, and I'll go back to practicing."

Quiet tension settled between them.

Now that Jackson was here, Ella wanted him to stay. She moved the conversation away from her. "Do you always leave the hospital in scrubs?"

"No, I change into my street clothes, but I had an unusual morning."

"Tell me about it."

"Trust me. You don't want to hear about this."

"I miss my dad's stories. Mostly they were funny, but sometimes they were sobering."

"Alright, you asked. Before I could change into my scrubs this morning, a nurse paged me to the medical-surgical floor. A postoperative patient had increasing abdominal pain. While I assessed her, she puked on the bed, the floor, and me. And then she said, 'I feel so much better now.'"

Ella rolled her lips inward to conceal the laughter waiting to erupt. When Jackson laughed, she joined him, the tension between them gone. "If I'd had my second cup of coffee, I would have missed the puking episode and come away a clean man."

Ella liked the fact that he could laugh at such a gross start to his day. "I'm glad you showed up clean." She wrinkled her nose. "I don't care for pungent odors."

"Then I'd say it's a good thing you don't work in the healthcare industry." Jackson cleared his throat. "Now, back to the other reason, I'm here. I know you have rehearsals this week with the orchestra, and you don't want distractions. But I'd like to drive you to the concert hall Saturday night."

The corner of her mouth turned upward in a lop-sided grin. "Wow, you've got confidence — calling yourself a distraction."

In one smooth movement, Jackson left the desk and settled on the piano bench beside Ella. The closeness of his body produced an undeniable heat. With his finger, he slowly traced the side of her face until it rested under her chin.

Shivers of delight ran down her arms when he lifted her face toward his. Feeling the pressure of his lips on hers, she closed her eyes. The slow, simmering kiss caused her heartbeat to gallop into a wild rhythm.

She pulled away, staying focused on his eyes. Watching as the blue irises turned dark. He captured her lips again, and she melted into his broad chest. The man could kiss and she obliged him with her participation.

When they came up for air, Jackson pulled in a breath and said, "I've wanted to do that for the longest time." He touched her shoulders lightly. His eyes searched her face. "I have a question."

"What's that?"

"Am I on your agenda?"

Ella had promised herself she wouldn't do this again. She needed time to regroup. Memories from her past breakup caused her heart to continue racing. "Maybe you should leave. I have to stay centered until this performance is over."

"What about Saturday night?"

"You have to know I'm attracted to you. I don't go around taking random kisses from men I barely know. But following my routine is paramount to my success. My assistant is arriving Thursday, and she'll put everything in place, including a car service to take me to the concert hall."

"When will I see you again?"

"After the concert." The disappointment in his eyes made her add, "Unless..."

"Yes?"

"If you'd like to stop by my dressing room before the concert begins, I can leave your name with the stage manager."

"I'll plan on it." Leaning over, he kissed her lightly on the lips. "I'll take my distracting self away from you, but I'll see you on Saturday."

After Jackson's visit, it was impossible to focus on her music. She left the library, the tingling from his kisses remaining on her lips. The hold music had on her life seemed to be loosening, allowing for other things and people to sway her.

And she wasn't sorry.

Chapter Six

On Wednesday evening, Ella arrived at Symphony Hall an hour before the start of rehearsal. Adequate preparation included getting the feel of the keyboard she would be playing. She had never seen a more beautiful instrument. The seductive pull of the Steinway made her hurry up the steps to the stage. She placed her hand on the closed lid with reverence. After propping the lid open, she took her seat on the piano bench.

Three-quarters into her warm-up routine, she stopped. A handsome man, late thirtyish with light brown hair parted on the side walked toward the stage from the house. He was wearing dark dress pants and a pale yellow polo shirt open at the collar. With one hand tucked in his pocket, and a lightweight black jacket tossed over his shoulder, an air of confidence surrounded him. He climbed the stairs to the stage effortlessly.

"Hello, I'm Alexander Fletcher. If you're not Ella Craig, you're a good imitation." He gave her a welcoming smile.

The challenge of gaining respect from yet another conductor had Ella standing to meet him head on.

"Mr. Fletcher." She held out her hand, pleased to note his handshake equal rather than one of dominance. Though she wanted his respect, he gained hers right away.

Releasing her hand, he shook his head. "Please, call me Alex."

Wanting to project an air of professionalism, she'd always addressed the conductors by their surnames. "All right, Alex." His name rolled off her tongue with ease. "I'm honored to meet you."

"The pleasure's mine. I'm glad we had this turn of events. Not so much a few weeks ago when our scheduled guest artist broke his arm. I have to say you have a much prettier face, and your playing is of the same caliber as Victor's."

Ella's cheeks heated, the blushing called to the high school girl deep inside. "Thank you." Hoping to take his attention from her face, she rubbed her hand against the polished wood of the piano. "I've been bonding with your magnificent keyboard."

Alex chuckled. "Our manager will be glad to hear that. He almost suffered a heart attack when he saw the price on the purchase order. But I insisted and got my way."

As if on cue, several musicians emerged from backstage and began setting up. A trumpet player blew some warm up notes. It wasn't long before the stage was alive with noise and musical sounds.

Ella stood and performed a few stretching exercises until Alex stepped on the podium. He rapped his baton on the music stand, and the noise began to die away. She reclaimed her seat at the piano.

"Attention, everyone! I'd like to introduce the guest artist who is saving us from scrapping the second half of our concert." With a grand gesture of his baton, he added, "Ms. Ella Craig."

The musicians applauded an enthusiastic hello.

She had never been a rescuer. The idea that she could save the performance for this group who had worked so hard made her chest swell with pride. Ella smiled. "Thank you. It's great to be here."

Alex rapped his baton once more. "Alright, time to work. Let's take it from the beginning."

It was always a challenge to meld with new musicians, but this was one of the things from which Ella derived satisfaction; to integrate her solo part with the orchestra and end up with a spectacular performance by everyone.

The rehearsal started out well enough. From start to finish without stopping, a run through of the first movement took twenty-three minutes. Ella's last performance of the concerto had come in at nineteen minutes for the first movement.

Alex placed his baton on the music stand. "Not bad. Now let's dig in and make it perfect."

Several minutes in, as the violin section plucked a bouncy pizzicato on their strings, Ella became aware of a light layer of perspiration on her skin. As she swayed from left to right to execute the melody across the entire length of the keyboard, lightheadedness emerged causing her to reinforce her concentration. She could tell they were falling out of sync, the first sign of a problem. Alex took that moment to stop and talk with an inflexible firmness to the cello section. Guilt tugged at Ella, knowing she was just as culpable for the disruption of the musical line.

Taking advantage of the pause in rehearsal, she pulled a handkerchief from her music bag. A wipe of her face followed by a long drink from the bottled water she brought refreshed her. Hopefully, it would last until the first official break.

Alex angled his baton in the air to begin again. After only a few stops, they came to the end of the first movement. A smile captured Ella's lips. She had been doing this long enough to know when she fit well with a group. They would perform proficiently on Saturday night. Ella's goal to inspire the orchestra to awesomeness was in progress by the time the musicians took a short break.

Alex walked over to the piano. "Care to share?"

"Sorry, I don't follow."

"Your smile. I agree, it's going to be a great concert."

A tingle rushed up the back of her neck, and Ella pulled in a breath. How could he have guessed her thoughts by a simple smile?

"I know we'll need to tweak a few things, but I feel it."

The odd exchange left her unsettled. "Excuse me, please. I need to go backstage before we start up again."

As she went in search of the ladies room, Ella considered the energy that had radiated from Alex during their exchange; the undertone of it as far from amorous as it could be. The spark was that of a kindred spirit. Being an only child, she had always craved the closeness of a sibling and had experienced it with both her cousins. But never from a random stranger. It had an enticing effect on her.

The rehearsal ended two hours later. Fatigue overwhelmed Ella. She struggled with her sweater. Alex approached and assisted her in a gentlemanly manner. "Do you have time for a coffee?" he asked.

She gathered her music. "I don't drink coffee, but I have time to talk."

They walked out the door of the auditorium. "There's a coffee shop on Van Ness. Do you think you can find something there to drink?"

Maybe a drink would revive her for the drive home. She pushed out a smile through her fatigue. "I'm sure I can."

He slipped into his jacket. "Great, it's not far. Would you like to walk?"

"That's fine with me." When they arrived, Alex volunteered to get their drinks while Ella claimed a table by the window. As she watched him, a comparison between Jackson and Alex formed in her mind.

Jackson — when she thought of him she sighed like a schoolgirl indulging in a crush. Ella couldn't help it. Jackson's physique, his manners, good grief — his sexy dimples. All of it brought about a desire to know him better. A way to enjoy her time in San Francisco with this heartthrob before moving on.

Alex, on the other hand, acted with professionalism in front of his orchestra. He had struck a chord with her like they could become best friends. Perhaps she felt that way because they were kindred spirits in the musical world. She'd never had a close male friend. Something about Alex made her believe it could happen. And she could always use another friend. Living the nomadic life she had chosen wasn't conducive to building friendships.

"One smoothie for the lady," said Alex, placing the drink in front of her.

"Thank you. What are you having?"

"An iced coffee." Once settled, he asked, "How do you feel things are going with the concerto?"

"Overall, I feel good about it."

"I hear a silent 'but.' Something bothering you?"

"There were a few tempo transitions that weren't smooth in the third movement. I have complete confidence we'll work it out at the dress rehearsal."

"This is what we'll do. Friday night we'll go over that section before we begin the run through of the complete concerto. Now, let's talk about something else, anything else except the concert."

Pent-up tension left Ella's shoulders. "Where did you study music?"

"My studies began at the Cleveland Institute of Music. I started out pursuing a performance degree in violin. But after a few conducting courses, I was hooked."

"From a performer to a conductor. I'm not sure I could give up performing."

"You just haven't found anything that's worth making a change for."

Ella sipped her smoothie. "Maybe. How long have you been with the San Francisco Philharmonic?"

"Two great years and counting. Your bio states you hail from here but have been away for quite some time."

"I left San Francisco for Eastman when I was seventeen. From there I started touring. I haven't been home for any real length of time since then."

"Are you home for good?"

His questions were becoming personal. Ella checked the time on her cell phone. "It's been nice talking with you, Alex. But it's getting late, and I should head home."

The walk back took a relaxed pace, and Ella was almost sorry when they arrived at her car. She slid in behind the steering wheel.

Still holding the car door, Alex asked, "May I drive you to rehearsal Friday evening? I'd like to get to know you better, and we can talk on the way and back afterwards."

"I'd like that."

"If you'll hand me your phone, I'll add my contact info. Then you can text me your address."

Her gut jerked at his suggestion to text, but something bigger pushed her to hand over her phone.

"All set." He returned her phone. Ella reached for the door and watched him give a small wave of his hand. Her stomach settled, and she smiled as she exited the parking lot into the flow of traffic. The pleasant evening brought to light how wound up into a knot she'd become during the last tour. Ella was sure being in a continuous tight coil of tension wasn't the way she wanted to live her life.

ELLA PEEKED OUT the window from the upstairs bedroom as Alex parked his silver Porsche with precision against the curb. When the doorbell sounded, she took time for a final look in the mirror. Ella descended the stairs as Dory answered the door.

"Hello, Alex. Thanks for the ride to rehearsal."

"My pleasure."

"Alex, this is my assistant, Dory. She has interrupted her time off to assist me for a few days. Dory, this is Alex Fletcher."

"It's nice to meet you, Dory."

"You, too."

"What do you think of my dress?" Ella turned in a circle. The light layers of material swirled around her. Thank goodness the floral print maxi dress had a self-tie sash. She had cinched it snuggly around her waist making it presentable.

Ella stopped in front of Alex. "I like to mimic the conditions of the performance as much as possible. That's why I chose a long dress tonight."

He smiled, exposing a perfect set of teeth. "You look nice."

Dory added, "Those colors are lovely on you."

The delicate blue-green print reminded Ella of shades of water like the clear, blue water of Portugal. A memory of a happier time in her life. From her subconscious, Jackson appeared in the water. Her skin prickled, and she reluctantly shut down the image.

"Thank you, Dory." She shifted toward Alex. "We should probably go."

As they drove away, Ella tuned into rising anxiety. Knowing she always had some apprehension about impending performances, she was confident it had nothing to do with Alex. The nerves were part of the package, and she accepted it. As Ella twisted the cloth sash between her fingers, she noticed Alex appeared completely relaxed. Despite the undercurrent of anxiety, Ella gave full attention to her new acquaintance.

"What will it be?" asked Alex, as he reached toward the stereo. "Classical, jazz, hip-hop, marches."

Ella grinned. "The many sides of Alex Fletcher? Let's listen to whatever you have loaded in your CD player now."

"Are you sure? It might surprise you."

"I'm not backing away. Let's hear it."

He pressed the button.

She rewarded him with a smile. "Handel's Water Music Suite. Nice."

"I think so. Although I don't mind marches, I'm not really into hip-hop."

"So, Conductor Fletcher, you're not a connoisseur of all musical genre?"

"Absolutely not. Making the assumption you read fiction, do you read all genres?"

"Touché."

"This is our time to get acquainted," said Alex. "Let's start with the basics."

When he didn't continue, Ella said, "Oh, you want me to start?"

He nodded.

"With the basics."

"Yes."

"I'm thirty-one years old, born and raised in San Francisco. At seventeen, I moved to New York with my mother to attend Eastman School of Music. I—"

"Wait, your mother moved to New York with you and your father stayed here?"

"Yes. Daddy had to stay to take care of his patients. Mom needed visual evidence of my adjustment to college life. She refused to rely on deciphering my phone calls to determine if I was okay."

"And your father went along with it?"

"My parents' only child and so young moving across the country — he didn't fight her on it. My mother rented an apartment, and I lived in the residence hall. The second year, she spent more time in San Francisco than New York. When I needed a weekend away from campus, I went to the apartment. Mom and Dad had a place to stay when they came to visit. It worked."

They pulled into the parking lot, and Ella's mind went immediately to the rehearsal ahead. Determined to work out the tempo snags in movement three, she drew in a deep breath.

Alex parked his car in the spot reserved for him. He turned to Ella and said, "Everything, including the Allegro con fuoco, will be fine."

He was doing it again. Reading her thoughts.

Alex continued, "And if not, better to have it happen tonight in dress rehearsal than tomorrow night at the performance."

She gave him a weak smile. "I'd prefer everything be perfect both nights."

There was an air of excitement as the musicians took their places in preparation for the run through. Parts one and two sounded performance ready, but a cracked bass drum head forced Alex to stop their progression. Interruptions were avoided at all costs during dress rehearsals, but the unexpected was always a possibility. The orchestra members took a break while the necessary repair took place and twenty minutes later, the rehearsal resumed.

Alex had been right. The third movement played out smoothly, and the rehearsal ended without mishap. While her ride tended to some last minute details, Ella gathered her music and closed the cover over the keyboard. Tonight's kick-ass practice had transformed her pre-rehearsal nerves into bubbly exuberance for tomorrow night's performance.

As they pulled away from the concert hall, Alex spoke up. "I thought the third section went well."

"Yes, it did. Let me put your mind at ease. I'm ready for tomorrow night."

"I'm not worried, Ella. The subject of the concert is considered closed. Are you hungry? We could stop and get a bite to eat."

Exhaustion shouted from every part of her body. She leaned back against the seat. "It's sweet of you to offer, but I'm thoroughly exhausted and need my bed."

"Okay. Would you like to listen to more Handel?"

"Sure."

After listening for a bit, Alex asked, "Why did you come home to San Francisco?"

"I agreed to stop on my way to San Diego, specifically for this concert. A personal favor for my manager. Visiting with family is a bonus."

"Your explanation comes across like you want to be anywhere but here."

"I have my reasons."

"Okay."

Alex pulled into the driveway and escorted her up the stairs.

Ella unlocked the door. "Thanks for the taxi service tonight. I've enjoyed our talks."

"It doesn't have to end tomorrow night."

He's nice.

She smiled. "Good to know. But I'm not only here for a short time."

And I want to spend it with Jackson.

"Right."

Ella opened the door and stepped inside. "Goodnight, Alex."

If Jackson were saying goodnight to another woman, would he be thinking about Ella as much as she was thinking about him now?

Chapter Seven

Saturday arrived. Ella purposely did not set her alarm clock the night before. She thought it best to wake up on her own after her body had achieved the amount of rest it needed. She studied her reflection in the mirror while brushing her hair. This past week had been very full, preparing for the concert and getting to know Alex. She liked him, and she thought the feeling was mutual. Then there was Jackson. Just thinking about him stirred up butterflies in her stomach.

She wandered downstairs and found Dory in the kitchen. The smell of coffee was inviting, but she couldn't chance her stomach rebelling with pain if she drank it.

"Morning, Dory. Did you sleep all right last night?"

"I should be asking you that question." She placed a breakfast of yogurt and fruit in front of Ella, as this was their routine before a performance. Light, small meals throughout the day.

Ella regarded the small-framed woman with salt and pepper hair. Doreen Goddard was the epitome of a big surprise in a small package. She appeared modest and reserved but could spring into action or act like a big, bad wolf if the need arose.

Ella took a bite of fruit then waved her spoon in the air. "At first I was angry with Rita for expecting you to be here for this concert. But truthfully, I'm glad."

"I wouldn't want to be anywhere else."

"You don't think I could handle even one concert on my own?"

"I didn't say that. I just don't have anywhere else I need to be."

"You've spoiled me. I don't have to worry about a single detail when you're around. It's so different now from when I started out. I had to do it all and perform, too. I hope you never feel I take you for granted."

"Let's hope not. Now eat your breakfast, then practice."

After Ella finished her food, she proceeded to the library and warmed up her fingers and mind with scales and arpeggios. She picked random sections of the concerto to spot-check her technique. Then she pulled out the Gershwin piece and practiced for another hour. Fatigue staked its claim, making her arms and legs grow heavy.

A long soak in the tub became a necessity instead of a luxury. Before Ella knew it, the car service had arrived. Dory assisted the driver with loading her things into the trunk, and they were off.

A tingle of exuberance passed through Ella. It had been a month since her last concert. Taking the stage, the excitement from the audience, the satisfaction of a well-executed performance. She'd missed it all. Then add to that an escalating thrill because Jackson would be in the audience tonight. Those were the kinds of feelings she needed to explore so she could figure out her future.

Upon arriving at Symphony Hall, Ella made a detour by the dressing room before heading to the stage area. It was a comfortable space with a sofa and a few chairs for visitors. Floral arrangements added color and beauty throughout. She moved around the room touching and smelling flowers, her excitement undeniable.

"Aren't they lovely, Dory?"

She plucked the card from between the petals and read, "So glad the wait is over. We've missed hearing you play. Love, Uncle Bill and Aunt Maxine."

Ella moved to the arrangement of roses, lilies, and poms, their varied colors blending harmoniously. They were from Jackson. Her mouth curved into a smile and her heart began pounding as she read the card to herself.

Looking forward to tonight.

She had been preoccupied the last few days with Alex and practice. She needed only a few more hours of concentrated focus and then she could turn her attention to Jackson and what the evening would bring.

She sat at the dressing table while Dory organized all the paraphernalia they had brought. She noticed the small flower arrangement on the corner of the table and pulled the card from between the stems.

"Who is that one from?" asked Dory.

"I'll let you guess. It says 'Keep me in the loop.'"

"I'd have to say Rita."

"And you'd be right. I guess that's about as heartfelt as she can get."

Dory's lips formed a faint trace of a smile. "She does a great job staying in professional mode 24/7."

"I don't know why she's that way, but that's something to ponder another night. I'm going to check out the stage."

Ella took her seat at the grand piano and began playing scales. When she decided her fingers were ready, she played the beginning and end of each section of the concerto. Feeling satisfied with the warm-up, Ella stood to leave. Turning around, she nearly ran into Alex.

"Hi," he said. "Ready for tonight?"

She smiled. "Ready as I'll ever be. Just heading to my dressing room to start my hair and makeup. Dory should have everything set up by now."

"I guess I'll see you in the second half. Would you like to go out for a late dinner tonight? I know a fabulous place not far from here." He grinned. "I won't make you walk, I promise."

"Alex, I appreciate the offer, but I have plans for later tonight." She moved toward the back of the stage. "Good luck with the first half of the concert."

As she walked away at a moderate tempo, Ella wished for the night to proceed in slow motion. Even so, tomorrow would come. And she'd have to make good on the promises she'd made to herself.

And Jackson.

JACKSON'S NERVES WERE ALL OVER the place. Damn it; he wasn't a fifteen-year-old boy going on his first date. Still, he took extra care as he shaved. Leaving a telltale sign that his hands had been anything less than steady as he cleaned up for the evening was not the way he wanted to greet Ella. It had been four days since he had seen her.

Four. Long. Days.

Little exposure to classical music brought concern he might not take to it. This thing that was such a monumental part of Ella's life. What if he couldn't stand it? His grandmother's voice echoed in his mind.

Stop putting the cart before the horse.

Traffic was heavy on the drive to the concert hall, but that was good. It gave his nerves time to settle before heading backstage to see Ella. The stage manager let him pass, directing him to her dressing room. Jackson raised his hand to knock and stopped, his hand sliding away from the door. Was he going to do this, act on his feelings for Ella? The last four days of missing her had come with a battle. Could he get past the unreasonable guilt that stabbed at him for desiring another woman? Logically, he knew Beth would want him to be happy. It wasn't his heart that needed convincing, but his head.

Before he could raise his hand again, the door opened, and a woman said, "Can I help you?"

"It's all right, Dory. That's my friend, Jackson." She waved him inside. "Dory's stepping out to take care of a few details. You can keep me company."

He paused long enough to say, "Hello, Dory."

The older woman nodded a silent greeting and went on her way.

Ella pushed the door closed. "I'm glad you decided to stop by."

Message received. She wants to spend time with me.

"Traffic's heavier than usual tonight. I know the concert's starting soon, but I wanted to come by and wish you luck."

Pointing to a chair, she said, "Please, have a seat."

His eyes remained on her, memorizing every inch of her face. In the back of his mind, he could hear his grandmother telling him it was rude to stare, but he couldn't stop.

"I know the makeup is a little heavy, but it's necessary with the lighting. I'll take most of it off after the performance before I leave the building."

Her words made him blink. "You're not dressed."

And it's getting hot in here.

"It's too early. I'll stay in my robe for another hour. I'm sorry, this is making you uncomfortable."

"Not really, just took me by surprise."

"The flowers you sent are lovely. Thank you."

"I'm glad you like them. So, what happens now?"

"Well, in a few minutes you'll leave to find your seat, and I'll stay here and try to relax for the next hour. Then usually the conductor stops by during intermission, and before you know it, it's time for me to take the stage."

"So how do you relax?"

"I usually have a cross-stitch project going. It's one of the things I don't have much time for. I work on a project while I wait. I hate to say it, but I think you should probably go find your seat."

They stood and moved toward the door. The smell of strawberries clung to Ella's hair. Jackson wanted to pull her close and get lost in the scent. Instead, he pushed out a breath and said, "So is this when I say break a leg?"

She laughed. "I'm not superstitious, so no. I've put my time in, and I'm ready for tonight. But you could tell me to enjoy myself while I'm performing because it's all about joy, not only for the audience but also for me."

"All right then," he said as he took her by the shoulders. As she looked up at him, her eyes shining, his pulse doubled. "Enjoy yourself," he said. "And I'll see you after the concert." He kissed her lightly on the top of her head and walked out the door. If it had been another time or place, he would have gone for her lips.

ELLA SCANNED THE PRINTED PROGRAM. It boasted a stellar line-up of Tchaikovsky titles. The orchestra opened with *Marche Slave* then continued with *1812 Overture. Symphony No 4 in F minor* closed out the first half of the concert, taking the audience to intermission.

Nerves that Ella usually held in check before a performance bounced around, causing her concentration on her cross-stitch piece to stray. Rechecking her cell phone for the third time in ten minutes, she blew out a breath.

"Time to get dressed," she announced to her assistant. Dory followed behind the folding screen and assisted her into the exquisite gown. Ella took the time to adjust and smooth the soft material; she wanted to look perfect. A knock punctuated the silence.

Dory opened the door, and before she could utter a word, Alex said, "Hello, Dory. It's good to see you again. Is Ms. Craig ready?"

Ella called out from behind the screen. "Alex, come in. I'll be out in a moment. I heard parts of the other pieces. It sounded fantastic."

"Thank you. I was pleased with it."

Ella stepped out from the partition.

"And with your performance, I'd say the audience is surely getting their money's worth tonight. Aurally and visually. Ella, you look incredible. Are you ready?"

Ella appreciated the compliment but had hoped Jackson would have been the first to admire her new gown.

"Thank you, and yes, I'm ready." He held out his arm. She hooked her arm around his. "I'll see you in a bit, Dory."

THE ORCHESTRA MEMBERS WERE WARMING UP when Jackson and the others returned from intermission. Positioned near the front of the stage, Claire, Ed, and Jeremy sat to Jackson's right; Bill and Maxine on his left. A prime spot where they could watch Ella as she performed.

The first half of the concert had brought relief. It allowed Jackson to lose his anxiety about sitting through an evening of classical music, pretending to enjoy it. So far, it had been engaging. He'd consider doing this again, especially if Ella was part of the deal.

The tuning process ended with the concertmaster taking his seat. Anticipation produced a silence across the audience. Ella walked out from the back of the stage through the middle of the orchestra followed by the conductor. Jackson's breath caught in his chest.

The sight of Ella in the Jovani gown Maxine had described during the intermission caused a sudden jerk in his gut. Kate Upton had nothing on Ella who bowed and shook hands with the concertmaster. The audience's applause died away as she seated herself at the piano.

Jackson remembered to breathe. He fixed his eyes on Ella, ignoring the orchestra and their conductor. The concerto had a strong, compelling beginning. Ella's hands moved across the entire length of the keyboard. Her body swayed, as if in a fluid state, from right to left repeatedly as the sounds moved from low to high and back again.

Large monitors anchored on each side of the stage gave another dimension to the performance. At times the camera focused on the conductor, who used his whole body to entice the orchestra to do his bidding. Jackson wondered what impression he'd made on Ella.

The camera adjusted to capture Ella's hands as the tempo shifted to full speed. She struck the keys with strength and accuracy. Not one note out of place that he could tell. Watching her fingers keep pace with the music was almost surreal. The amazement must have shown on his face. Maxine leaned over and said, "She's wonderful, isn't she?"

"I'm astounded," he whispered. "It's like riding in the front seat of a rollercoaster." He relaxed as the full orchestra engaged and Ella's participation in the piece ended for a time. She reached inside the open piano and produced a handkerchief. After wiping her hands, she replaced it inside the instrument.

The tempo had slowed, and the volume decreased when Ella reached for the keys. Now she hovered over the keyboard as a light, playful sound began. The melody bantered in an echo between the flute and piano and then between the oboe and piano. No sooner had Jackson settled into the soothing sound than the composer shifted gears and the volume of the Tchaikovsky piece grew. There was a flurry of Ella's fingers at the keyboard as she commanded the sound to rise from the piano.

The camera shifted to Ella's face, her concentration undeniable. Jackson agreed that she did get in the zone when she performed. He leaned toward Claire and said, "Does she know she makes faces when she plays?"

"She's seen videos of herself performing, but I don't think Ella realizes it at the time. She's sealed away in her world of music."

The rollercoaster ride resumed with the crescendo of sound and increase of tempo. Jackson watched in amazement. Ella's head and body jerked in sync with her hands as she pounded the piano keys, exuding strength and power that surprised him. Especially given the paleness she had sported since returning home.

The second section ended. Alex held his baton in the air as the orchestra paused. He glanced at Ella and gave the downbeat for the start of the final movement. The last seven minutes of the performance. A powerful sound and sight. It appeared Ella put her all into the finale. Chills ran up and down Jackson's arms. As he left his seat to join the audience in a standing ovation, Jackson searched for the words to later express to Ella how her performance had touched a part of him he didn't know existed.

EUPHORIA USUALLY DESCRIBED Ella's state of mind after a performance. She had given the Tchaikovsky piece her all, but tonight the exhilaration took a back seat to the exhaustion that claimed her entire body. She rose slowly from her seat, hampered by arms and legs of lead and accepted a kiss on her cheek from Alex. She turned and bowed to the audience. The applause continued as she shook hands with the concertmaster and acknowledged the audience once more. As she retreated through the orchestra to the backstage area, Alex followed behind her.

"I can tell the applause isn't going to stop until you take another bow." He gave her elbow a light push.

As she retraced her path through the orchestra, pain pummeled her stomach as if shouting *ENOUGH*. Suspicion niggled at the back of her mind. She had waited too long to seek medical attention. Stepping between the violin players, she reached the piano as a smothering heat engulfed her, the sound around her fading. Before she could bow, blackness swirled around her as she crumpled into a heap on the stage floor.

Chapter Eight

Jackson thought he had seen a misstep. Something wasn't right as Ella returned to the stage. So really, he wasn't shocked when she sank to the floor. His medical instincts kicked in as he pushed past Maxine and fled to the stage. Recognition of the stage manager came to mind as he hurried past him, saying, "I'm a doctor."

Bill's voice hovered in the background. "Can we get the curtain pulled? Push those chairs back." The orchestra members retreated, giving them room.

Jackson knelt beside Ella's lifeless form on the stage floor. Touching her neck, he palpated her carotid artery, surprised at its rapid beat. Her colorless skin set off an internal alarm.

He rubbed her cheek and spoke in a crisp voice, "Ella, wake up. It's Jackson." He gently shook her shoulders until her eyes flickered.

"How's her pulse?" asked Bill.

"Too fast. I don't like it. Ella," he repeated. "It's Jackson."

Her eyes opened. "Jackson?"

"I'm here, Ella. You fainted."

She attempted to move her upper body, but he stopped her.

"Jackson, please, this is embarrassing."

"Let me help you." After assisting her to a sitting position, he rose. Reaching around her waist, he pulled her from the floor. When she bobbled unsteadily, he gathered her into his arms. "I think we'll do it this way."

He glanced at the stage manager. "Which way to the dressing room?"

"Follow me."

Dory held the door open as Jackson hurried into the room followed by Bill. He placed Ella on the sofa.

"Is she all right, Dr. McMillan?" asked Dory.

"I'm okay," said Ella. "You can direct your questions to me."

"Of course. What happened?"

"I'm not sure. I felt weak and hot. Then the sound around me disappeared, and everything turned black."

"You fainted. What have you eaten today?" asked Jackson, his voice efficient and unemotional.

Dory stepped between the sofa and Jackson as if guarding a child. "She had yogurt and fruit for breakfast. About an hour before we left the house, she had some pasta and vegetables."

Ella's assistant remained in protective mode. Jackson relaxed his shoulders and stepped back.

"Maybe she's hypoglycemic," said Bill. "Dory, find us some juice or soda, not diet."

"I'll check with the stage manager."

Jackson pulled a chair beside the sofa. His heart raced, pounding at his chest. He should have insisted she see a doctor the day they met. What had he allowed to happen because of the delay? He didn't like what he saw; colorless skin covered by a fine film of perspiration. "How are you feeling?" he asked.

"Mortified. I've never done anything like that before — and in front of a full house."

Aw, baby," said Bill, "Don't feel that way. You're not going to lose any fans over a fainting spell."

Jackson watched as the older physician reached for her wrist, feeling for her pulse.

Dory raced through the door. "No juice, but I got soda."

Ella slowly shifted into a sitting position. Doreen held the can out to Ella, who pushed at it as if it were a snake. "Wait. Let me take off my dress first. I don't want to spill anything on it."

Dory motioned to the men. "Turn around or wait outside while I help her out of the dress."

In no time, Ella was wrapped in her robe and settled on the sofa. Jackson turned and scrutinized her face as she took a sip of cola.

"It'll take all night to get your blood sugar up if you keep sipping like that."

"I don't usually drink soda."

He stared her down. Ella turned the can up, taking a long drink. She leaned toward Jackson, her shoulders moving as she took in two big breaths.

Jackson instinctively moved toward her, unsure of what was happening. Without warning, her face contorted. I'm going to be sick."

Dory tossed a towel at Jackson while she said, "Hold on, I'll grab the trashcan out of the bathroom."

Without warning, Ella yanked the towel from Jackson while pushing the soda can at him. She held the towel to her mouth and vomited blood.

A significant amount of bright red blood. It scared him. Not the doctor who knew how to react in an emergency. But the man inside who had opened his heart to this woman now in crisis. The blood, coupled with a rapid pulse confirmed internal hemorrhage. He'd bet his career she had an actively bleeding ulcer.

He stood and turned to Bill. "She needs IV fluids."

"The sooner, the better," said Bill. He slid into the chair beside the sofa. "Dory, call 911." He turned to Ella. "How's your stomach, do you have any pain?"

Jackson could see the panic in her eyes as Bill pressed on her abdomen.

Ella put a hand on her uncle's arm. "That hurts, please stop."

Alex stepped through the partially opened door. "Ella, I was worried—" He stopped when he saw the towel covered with blood. "You're not all right. What can I do?" he asked.

Jackson took a step, his movement intending to drive Alex back to the door. "The situation is worrisome, so we called for an ambulance. You can direct them back here."

"I'll stay with her," countered Alex. "She's my guest artist, my responsibility."

"She needs us more right now."

"And why is that?"

"Because we're doctors." Pointing to Bill, he added, "And he's Ella's uncle." Jackson's tone intensified. "So if you want to help, get the EMTs in here ASAP."

Ella's small voice reached his ears. "I feel sick again."

Jackson darted over to the sofa as Bill lifted the trashcan for her and bloody emesis left her mouth. She leaned back again against the couch and closed her eyes.

Jackson cradled her hands in his. "Ella, stay with me."

Commotion at the door drew his attention. Relief flooded through Jackson's body as the EMTs hurried into the room, making the space tighter.

"We've got a possible bleeding ulcer. Let's get some IV fluids going," said Bill. "STAT."

The medical technician wrapped a disposable cuff around Ella's upper arm. "BP is 84/39, heart rate 146."

Within minutes, the other technician said, "I could only manage a small gauge needle, but your fluids are going."

"She'll need another IV site," said Jackson. "We can try for a larger bore catheter after she's hydrated."

With quick, smooth motions, Ella was transferred from the sofa to the gurney and the four men surrounded the stretcher as they exited the building. A gaggle of photographers and Alex huddled near the back exit. He squeezed Ella's hand when the gurney stopped momentarily. "Ella, I need to finish up here with the reporters and then I'll come to check on you."

She nodded and closed her eyes.

Jackson glared as he watched the exchange between them. "Let's move," he said and jumped into the back of the ambulance. A police officer closed the doors and thumped on the window. The ambulance pulled away with lights flashing and siren blaring.

BUSTLING ACTIVITY FILLED the emergency room cubicle. Ella opened her eyes and blinked at the harsh, bright lights above her. The brilliance advantageous for assessing trauma victims.

"She's awake."

A familiar voice had her head turning to the left. The sight of Jackson at her side produced a wave of relief.

"Ella, you're at the emergency room. They're taking good care of you."

Depleted of energy and confused for a moment, she murmured, "Where's my uncle?"

"He's nearby, talking to someone that's going to help you."

"I'm sorry—"

"No need for sorry. They have some questions for you, so I'll step out for now."

A nurse pulled a portable computer to the bedside and began asking questions. Someone on her other side drew tubes of blood and inserted another IV. Her vital signs were continuously monitored, the beeps a constant background noise. At random intervals, the sound disrupted causing the nurse to check the numbers on the monitor screen.

As each person finished their task, they left the room. Finally, Ella was alone. Nausea claimed her attention. The unrelenting squeezing pain in her upper abdomen had her clutching the emesis bag the nurse had left at her side. What had she done to herself? She should have sought help while touring or should have come home sooner for treatment. Panic cut through her nausea. Seeing all that blood had been scary. Could this have been avoided if she'd paid closer attention? Acted sooner? She vowed she'd never do anything this foolhardy again.

Bill whisked back the privacy drape and hurried in with another doctor.

"Ella, this is Ken Arnold. He's going take care of you. I'll let him tell you his plan."

The man approached her and said, "Hi, Ella. We suspect you have a bleeding ulcer and the way we deal with that is performing a procedure call endoscopy. I'll place a small tube with a camera down your esophagus into your stomach to see what's going on. If you have a tear in your vessel, we can repair it while we're in there."

Ella touched the left side of her head. "Why is my head hurting?"

"Let's have a look. Dr. Arnold's fingers passed over a knot on her scalp. He stepped aside so Bill could feel it as well. "We might have another problem."

"What is it?" asked Ella.

Bill pulled a penlight from his pocket. "I want you to follow the light with your eyes."

"Okay." Her eyes followed the light.

"Now, squeeze my hands." Again, she complied.

"Did you hit your head when you fainted?" asked Bill.

"I don't remember."

Bill turned to his colleague. "She needs a CT scan. What should we do first? It's your call."

"CT scan if we can do it now on the way to the procedure room. If not, I think we need to go ahead with the endoscopy to get the bleeding under control."

"No problem, I'll make the CT scan happen now."

"While you do that, I'll post the endoscopy. Just a reminder Bill, while Ella's with me, you take some time for a large cup of coffee, preferably on another floor."

"Uncle Bill?"

He took her hand in his. "What is it, baby?"

"I'm not a baby. I'm an adult, and I'll be okay while you drink your coffee. The last thing I need is for you to be standing over Dr. Arnold and make him nervous while he's working on me." She met the challenge in his eyes. "Promise me you'll go away and drink coffee."

His gray eyes softened. "Promise. But there's something you need to realize."

"What's that?"

"I'm always going to look out for you."

AT HALF PAST MIDNIGHT, Jackson sat alone in the third-floor doctors' lounge. The coffee he had poured earlier remained in his cup, the steam having disintegrated a while ago.

A chill swept over him as he pictured Ella in the GI lab going through a serious procedure, her life in jeopardy. Jackson pushed a hand through his dark hair with jerky motions. The evidence of internal bleeding at the concert hall had rattled him. The guilt for not having persuaded her to seek medical treatment sooner weighed on his chest. An eerie sense of déjà vu made the tiny hairs on the back of his neck bristle. A familiar fear flooded his heart just like before. When Beth had died.

The beep of the card reader on the opposite side of the lounge door caught his attention as it opened.

"I wondered where you went," said Bill.

Jackson's hands hugged the table as he half stood, the anxiousness churning inside his chest. "Any news?"

Bill motioned for him to sit. "You know this could take a while." He rinsed out the coffee pot and set up for a fresh one. As the dark liquid dripped into the carafe, he joined Jackson at the table. "You seem worried. Could it be you've fallen for my niece?"

"I like Ella, like spending time with her." The first woman since Beth to make him want more than his medical career.

"Yet you seem pretty upset about something out of your control."

Jackson jumped up, almost knocking over his chair, and he began pacing like a caged animal.

"She'll be okay. I trust Ken Arnold with her life."

Jackson stopped. His hand slapped the side of the refrigerator. "I should never have kept my mouth shut. I should have made her tell you."

"What are you talking about?"

"The day Ella came home, she almost passed out at the airport. Later that night, when I drove her home from Maxine's place, she asked me to keep quiet about her symptoms until after the concert."

"You knew she had symptoms of a bleeding ulcer, and you did nothing to help her?"

"She never mentioned abdominal pain when I questioned her. I was trying to see things from Ella's point of view."

"How dare you decide what's right for my niece? That was a lousy judgment on your part."

"I'm sorry."

"Thanks to you, she's bleeding and in serious condition that you could have prevented. Maybe I should question your assessment skills, Dr. Hart."

Before Jackson could reply, Bill stood and stomped out of the lounge.

Why had he done it? Why had he kept Ella's secret? She had convinced him she needed the time to prepare for the concert. Once he had looked into her eyes as she had pleaded with him, he was a goner. It wasn't until now that he realized the strength of Ella's hold on him. He had given what she'd requested, even to the detriment of her health and Bill's opinion of his medical integrity.

THE SOUNDS CUT into her peaceful sleep. Ella wasn't ready to open her eyes, so she left them closed as she tried to identify the noise around her. There were monitors beeping and alarms sounding and people nearby talking in quiet voices. Something was pushing her to open her eyes. She blinked a few times, finding it hard to focus. The bright light made her want to retreat to her former state.

"Ms. Craig, you're awake. That's good."

She turned her head and saw a man in green scrubs with a matching cap covering his hair. The doctor from the emergency room. What was his name?

"How are you feeling?" he asked.

Ella opened her mouth to speak, but nothing came out. She tried clearing her throat.

"Just relax. I'll have the nurse bring some ice chips."

The nurse pressed a cup half filled with ice chips and a plastic spoon into her hands. When the ice melted in her dry mouth, she couldn't recall a more welcoming sensation.

"Thank you," said Ella.

"The procedure went well. I found the bleeding and fixed it. Your recovery will take a while, but you'll be good as new. You're going to your room now, and I'll be by in the morning to check on you. We'll talk more about your recovery regimen then."

The stretcher maneuvered through the corridor smoothly. Ella would have to congratulate her uncle on the Cadillac-quality ride. Staring at the lighted ceiling made her head hurt. She closed her eyes and kept them that way until transferred to the bed in her room. Someone touched her arm.

"Ella, it's Aunt Maxine. Your uncle is here, too. Wake up darling."

"Not asleep, just sleepy." Ella worked at pushing her eyes open.

"I told William I wouldn't stay long. I just needed to see for myself that you're okay. I'll be back tomorrow to check on you." She kissed her niece on the cheek. "Thank you, William. Call me if there's a problem tonight, and I'll come back. I'll send everyone home on my way out. Goodnight."

Bill squeezed her hand and placed a light kiss on her cheek. "Night, Max."

When her aunt was gone, Ella said, "So what's my story?"

"You had a bleeding ulcer that had eroded through a vessel. Dr. Arnold repaired it. We've given you two units of blood to replace what you've lost." You'll have to spend some time healing, but that's the way it is with every surgery. Your conductor friend reviewed the videotape at the end of the concert. It showed you did hit your head on the edge of the piano when you toppled to the floor of the stage."

"That explains my headache. I hope it won't last long."

"About that...you have a concussion. And it could take longer for you to heal from that than from your surgery."

"How long are we talking?"

"There's no prescribed amount of time. Every case is different. It could take as little as six weeks or as long as three or four months. We don't know."

"But I have an interview next week."

"We're not going to talk about that tonight, but you need to realize if you can't meet your obligation due to health reasons, it won't be the end of the world."

"But it's not your world we're talking about, is it?"

"Ella, I can't have you getting worked up, so please just settle down and rest."

"I have a feeling that sums up my immediate future. Where's Jackson? I need to thank him for taking care of me."

Bill snorted. "You don't need any more visitors tonight. You can see him tomorrow. The nurse will wake you every two hours to monitor your concussion, so I'm afraid you're not going to get much sleep. When I come by tomorrow, we have some talking to do." He kissed her on her temple. "Love you, baby."

"Night, Uncle. Thanks for taking care of me." As bad as things were, they could be worse. She could have collapsed on tour and had no support system at her side. She was grateful for her family. And Jackson.

THE KNOCK ON THE DOOR of her hospital room pulled Ella from the edge of sleep. Attempting to sit up made her stomach clench, intensifying the pulsing in her head. She leaned back against the pillow.

Claire hesitated at the door. "Okay if I come in?"

"Sure, unless you're going to make like a vampire and take more of my blood."

"I'm in advertising, remember? You won't see me walking in with a caddy of needles, tubes, and bandages." Claire pushed a chair next to the bed. "Mom is fretting about not being here with you. She may be the boss of her company but still has to keep her customers happy. You can expect to see her this evening."

"Thanks for the heads up. Not sure I'm up to Aunt Maxine's effervescence."

"I assured her I'd leave work early and stay with you for a while, but I know my mother. She'll have to lay eyes on you to know you're okay. How are you doing?"

"I don't feel like running a marathon."

"Who are you trying to kid? I'm the only one in the audience, and I know you don't run."

"Right. Will you cut me some slack if I tell you my head hurts?"

Claire touched Ella's arm lightly. "I'm sorry. Do you want me to get your nurse?"

"No, I'll wait it out for a while. Distract me."

"How?"

"Let's talk about your wedding."

"No thanks. All Mom talks about is the wedding. I know; we'll discuss the new men in your life."

"What about them?"

Claire leaned forward as though she was about to expose some deep, dark secret. "Daddy said after you fainted, your orchestra conductor showed up in your dressing room. When he said he would take care of you, Daddy thought Jackson was going to pounce on him."

"That's silly. Jackson's not the pouncing type."

"Face it, Ella. You don't know Jackson all that well, and you just met Alex. We should analyze your men."

"How can we do that if I don't know them?"

"We'll size them up by their cars."

"What?"

"I'm in advertising, right?"

"Yeah."

"In my business, we analyze our customers by the color and type of car they drive. It helps us identify their personality type and guides how we approach them."

"You're kidding."

"Nope. What colors are we working with?"

"Silver and dark blue."

"Silver for Alex and blue for Jackson. Am I right?"

"Yes, how'd you know?"

"Silver gives off a metallic gleam; an indicator of someone who is sophisticated. His status is higher than most, and he's not afraid to show it. Silver's linked to things that are new, modern, cutting-edge. It's the color of security and style."

"Wow. You can tell all that from a color?"

"Yep. Does any of that fit your conductor?"

"Maybe some of it. Alex is not *my* conductor. Tell me about blue."

"The owner that chooses dark blue is confident, credible, and authoritative. What kind of car?"

"SUV."

"He is dependable and trustworthy. Dark blue is a solid, happy color. I'd say that captures some of Jackson's traits. Tough choice since neither guy sounds like a slacker."

"No contest. Alex is great, but when I'm around Jackson..."

"Your body reacts a certain way?"

"For the first time since I arrived home, I wish I weren't going to San Diego, partly because of Jackson."

"This is great. I was beginning to think you'd never find anyone that you'd—"

A knock on the door stopped Claire's words.

"Come in," said Ella.

JACKSON STEPPED INSIDE carrying a vase of flowers. "Hi, Ella. Claire." He walked across the room and placed the lovely arrangement on the bedside table. "You look better today."

"More flowers?"

"You didn't get a chance to enjoy the ones I sent yesterday and hospital rooms always need some color."

"Thank you."

Claire stood. "I need to be going."

"You've only been here a few minutes."

"Don't let me chase you away," said Jackson.

"Sorry. I've got that thing to do. Great to see you again, Jackson." She squeezed Ella's hand. "I'll call you tomorrow."

Before either could react, Claire was gone. Ella pointed to the chair. "Can you stay a while?"

In answer to her question, he sat. "You were out of it last night. How are you doing?"

"I don't feel like running a marathon."

"Probably not. Do you run?"

Ella smiled. "My cousin just reminded me that I do *not* run."

"With everything that's happened, I didn't get the chance to say how phenomenal you were last night. I'll sum it up in two words. Blown. Away." What a remarkable person. Ella possessed beauty and talent, but also sadness he wanted to help wipe away.

Looking toward the window, she murmured, "Thank you."

"Are you okay?"

Slowly she directed her gaze at Jackson. "I owe you an apology. I shouldn't have asked you to stay quiet. I used the concert as a way to hide from my problem. I've been doing that the last few years."

Her green eyes appeared dull. Not unusual for an ill person, but he missed their usual brightness. "The only thing you need to face right now is rest and sleep."

"There's nothing to keep me from it. Uncle Bill says I'll be here a few days and when I get home it could be weeks before I fully recover from my concussion."

"Maybe now you can relax and enjoy being home."

"What I need to do will not be relaxing or enjoyable. But I intend to follow through."

"Your parents."

"Yes, facing what I've put off for two years."

"The pathway through grief is different for each person. You just have to find your way."

"After Mom and Dad died, I withdrew from everything but my music. I took the easy way out instead of facing my grief."

"I'm sorry it made you sick."

"A hard lesson, but I've learned from it."

Jackson took her hand in his. He studied her fingers as he entwined theirs together. Long, slim fingers with short trimmed nails. Fingers that moved effortlessly across a keyboard; that pressed piano keys with precision and purpose.

"If you want to talk or play your music or run off to Napa Valley again, I'm your man. Just tell me what you need."

She focused on their hands. "I dreamed you were sitting by my bed last night."

"It wasn't a dream. I couldn't leave until I knew for sure you were okay after the endoscopy." He brushed his fingers against her hair. Ella closed her eyes at his touch and smiled.

When she opened them, she groaned. "You're out of focus."

"How's your head?

"It's been hurting since I woke up. I hoped it would go away."

"I should leave and let you rest."

"I guess I'll ask for that pain medication now." Ella pressed the call light then adjusted her covers. "I'm glad you came. Thanks again for the flowers."

"I'll come back. Feel better." Jackson stepped into the familiar hallway. No matter how complicated his patients' medical issues, his professionalism made caring for them doable. Watching Ella as a patient called his emotions into play, making this a difficult task. He needed to find a way to make up for his part in her situation, and right now, he didn't know how to do that.

Chapter Nine

Home from the hospital for a week, Ella rested on the sofa in the living room. Her shoulders slumped as she released a sigh.

"What has you so out of sorts today?" asked Dory as she tucked the lightweight comforter around Ella's legs.

"I want to play my piano, to do anything but lay around." The culpability resting on her heart leaked out in her words. "I'm the reason you're not on vacation like you planned. Instead, you're here tending to me like I'm a sick child."

"I wouldn't wish to be anywhere else. Someone needs to be here while Dr. McMillan's at the hospital. It won't be for long. You'll be up and about before you know it."

"I put this off too long. I chose not to get help when I should have, and now I'm paying for it."

"Too bad about the concussion. I know it will be difficult for you to only rest and be away from your piano."

"When will Uncle Bill stop treating me like a child? I can stay by myself."

"If that's how you feel, you should tell him. If you want me to leave, I will."

Guilt stabbed at Ella's heart. Dory remained because she care about her. "He has a valid point, but you never heard me say that, right?"

Dory smiled. "Not a word. Any requests for lunch today?"

"I'm not hungry. Maybe later."

The doorbell rang. Dory slipped quietly out of the room. "Dr. Hart, it's good to see you."

"Thanks. You, too. Is Ella sleeping?"

"She's resting on the sofa. I'm sure she'd love some company."

Jackson followed Dory into the living room. "Hi. How's your day going?"

"My day's not going anywhere. I've been parked on the sofa all morning." Ella moved from her pillow, her upper body wobbling in protest. She closed her eyes, drawing in a breath. "My head is spinning."

"Relax, Ella. Moving more slowly should help."

His tone had a soothing quality, useful for a physician. But it didn't push away her impatience. "How long is this going to keep happening? I'll be so rusty by the time I sit in front of my piano, "Chopsticks" may be the only piece I'll be able to play."

Jackson settled into the chair across from the sofa.

"Dr. Hart, I'm making chicken tortilla soup for lunch. If you stay, perhaps Ella will act the gracious hostess and eat with you."

"Please, Dory, call me Jackson. So, the patient is stubborn. I can't say that's a surprise."

Ella narrowed her eyes. "If you two are going to gang up on me, then I'll turn over and go to sleep."

"I'll be in the kitchen if you should need me," said Dory.

"Come on, Ella. You're smart enough to know you need to eat even if you don't want to. While I'm doling out advice, let me say this; it's hard when you lose control to an illness. Be patient and allow yourself forgiveness."

Ella willed her body to relax. "I suppose you're right. I'm just so tired of it all. I want my life back."

"You'll get there if you do what you're supposed to."

She folded her arms across her chest. "I don't have much choice. For now, my neurologist is in charge. He's the one with the timeline."

"Cut him some slack. There's no routine fix to fit all patients. Everyone heals at a different rate of speed. And head injuries aren't all the same. Look at this as a well-deserved vacation. With lots of free time."

"But I'm not free. My body is holding me prisoner from life. I can't do much of anything right now."

"Have you watched all those movies I brought you? I can bring you more."

"I don't want to watch movies."

"Ella, you're going to have to be patient and let your body heal."

"Easy for you to say."

"In the meantime, you can think about all the things you want to do. We'll make that list we've talked about."

A heaviness settled in her chest. She picked at an invisible piece of lint on the comforter.

When she didn't respond, Jackson asked, "Do you want to talk about it?"

"I suppose at the top of the list should be the other reason I came home."

"Your parents."

She looked up, her eyes watery. "I need to tie up the legal issues of my parents' deaths and decide what to do with their physical assets. I'm not sure I'm strong enough to handle it by myself."

"You're not alone. Your family will help you."

Ella focused on Jackson's face. "Will you give me a hand? You've been through this before when your parents died."

Jackson stood and shoved his hands in his pockets. "I was a child. I didn't have anything to do with the disposition of my parents' estate."

"I realize that. My thoughts were you could be there as a friend, for emotional support."

"What do you need me to do?"

"I want to go to the cemetery, but not alone."

Ella recognized the vacant stare in his eyes. The look when someone's thoughts are anywhere but real time. Was it wrong for her to ask him? He *had* buried a wife. "Jackson?"

He drew in a deep breath. "I'll go with you. When you're better."

"YOU CAN GO IN, Ms. Craig." The gray-haired assistant placed the phone on its base.

Ella knocked on her uncle's office door before stepping inside. "Hi, Uncle Bill." She walked to where he sat behind his desk and kissed the top of his head.

Without preamble, he said, "How did your appointment with the neurologist go?"

"I'm surprised you didn't have him call you as soon as I left his office."

He rose and waved toward the sofa across the room. Once seated, he said, "You know that wouldn't be ethical. Even William McMillan, Chief of Surgical Services has to abide by HIPAA rules. I'd like to know how you're doing."

"He hasn't released me yet." A smile spread across her face. "But, I've been given the all clear to play my piano again. Not full force, but delicately in small increments of time."

"You've been up-front with him about any problems?"

"I've learned my lesson. Falling out in front of a full house because of my stubbornness was a wake-up call. I'm not keeping any secrets. Can you say the same thing?"

"What does that mean?

"I get unhappy vibes when I bring up Jackson's name."

The intercom's buzzer sounded. "Dr. McMillan, Mrs. Johnson is here."

"Great, send her in."

Terrific, we'll have to revisit the Jackson issue later.

Bill stood and walked toward the door. "Doris, come in. I'm glad you had time to stop by today."

"I didn't want to miss my chance to meet your niece."

He led her to a chair by the sofa and Ella stood. "I'll go. I don't want to be in the way of your meeting."

Bill placed a hand on her shoulder to signal she should stay. "Nonsense, Ella. Meet Mrs. Doris Johnson. She's the head of our volunteer services."

Ella smiled. "Hello."

"I'm delighted to meet you, though I feel like I know you. Your father always talked about your tours and what you were doing. He looked so forward to the trips he and your mother would make to visit you."

A lump constricted the space in Ella's throat, stopping any response she might have managed, so she smiled instead.

Bill spoke up. "Let's sit. I was hoping Mrs. Johnson would be able to stop by while you were here. She's in a quandary about a donation the children's unit has received. I thought you might have some suggestions." He signaled with his hand toward the volunteer.

"Well, dear, I was telling Dr. McMillan that the children's wing has received a piano. We don't want it sitting in the common room catching dust and are trying to figure out how best to use it. I'm sure it was a well-intentioned donation, but money is so much easier to accept. What do you suggest we do with it?"

"You could sell it; that would bring the cash you'd rather have."

"Indeed it would, but this is a sensitive matter."

Bill leaned forward. "Meaning we don't want to hurt the benefactor's feelings over this donation."

"Because they might not donate in the future," said Ella. "So, find someone to play for the children. They could come in a few times a week, and everybody will be happy."

"Ella, don't you see. Your good news today could be the answer Mrs. Johnson is looking for."

The head of volunteer services sat with a look of confusion on her face. Ella echoed it in words. "I don't follow."

"You've suggested she find someone to play the piano, and you got the green light today to practice again, in short clips. It's perfect all the way around."

Excitement crept into the older woman's eyes. "If you could spare the time to start a program for our patients, we would search for a volunteer replacement. The music would give the children something to look forward to, especially our long-term patients."

"I need to think about it. Give me a few days, Mrs. Johnson, and I'll get in touch with you."

"Thank you, Ella." Turning to Bill, she said, "This turned out more positive than I had expected." She pulled a yellow post-it-note pad from her pocket and scribbled on it. She ripped off the top page and shoved it in Ella's direction. "I'll be waiting for your call." She stood and checked her watch. "Look at the time." She moved toward the door, Bill following her. "I've got another meeting. Goodbye."

The intercom buzzed. Bill rested his hip on the edge of his desk and pushed the button on the phone system. "Yes, Shelia?"

"Mrs. McMillan is on line one."

"Thanks. I'll take it." He pressed the speaker button. "Hey, Max. Is everything all right?"

"Sure, fine. I have a save the date for you, and I wanted to get it on your calendar now."

"What's so important?"

"Jackson's grandparents are coming to town next week, and we're all going to dinner. Is your evening free a week from Wednesday?

"I'm not sure I can go."

"Don't tell me you're scheduling surgeries in the evenings now."

"That's silly, of course not."

"William, you will go, and before we step through the door of the restaurant, you're going to tell me what's going on between you and Jackson."

"There's nothing to tell."

"I refuse to discuss this over the phone, but there will be a discussion. I'm hanging up now. Goodbye."

So, Aunt Maxine has noticed the strain, too. And it sounds like she plans to do something about it.

Raising his eyebrow, Bill replaced the receiver on its base and sighed.

A grin slid across Ella's face. "How's the love thing going with Aunt Maxine?"

"Not so good today." Bill settled into his chair.

"I got that."

"Enough about Max. I'm so glad you're going to play for the kids."

"The way Mrs. Johnson was talking before she left makes me think maybe I've been suckered."

His eyes confirmed her suspicion. "Uncle Bill, you set this up. Please, don't tell me you donated a piano—"

"Nonsense, there's a benefactor, and the kids love any activity that gets them out of their beds. When you gave me the news that you can play again, it was a spontaneous thought. Initially, we were going to pick your brain about coming up with a program of some sort."

"I hate doing nothing. It would give me something to look forward to, just like the children. I guess I'll head home and get to the planning. See you tonight." She stopped at the door and turned back. "Try not to get too upset with Aunt Maxine. With Claire's wedding just weeks away, it wouldn't do for the parents of the bride not to be speaking to one another."

JACKSON ROLLED OVER and punched his pillow. A week had gone by since he'd promised to accompany Ella to the cemetery. His way to make up for holding back. For not pushing her to see a doctor immediately when she'd admitted to her symptoms. To erase the part he shared in her collapse and illness. A sense of foreboding over making good on his promise caused his stomach to churn.

For a second night, Jackson couldn't sleep. After leaving Ella with a pledge of support, memories of his time with Beth had sprung to life. His wife and the bittersweet memories of their life together were front and center of his thoughts tonight. The trips they had taken, their quiet time at home after a busy day at the hospital. Even images of them making love floated before him when he closed his eyes to sleep. Why was this happening? He didn't have a clue. He did know it made the thoughts about spending time with Ella feel like he was cheating.

For a second night, Jackson left his bed and dressed. He walked to his car, knowing a drive up the coastal highway was the only way to clear his head. He just didn't know how far he would have to drive.

Chapter Ten

While stirring the lemonade ingredients in a crystal pitcher, Ella stopped momentarily and touched her stomach. It was hard to believe the pain was finally gone. Why had she waited and endured such suffering? The answer lay in the fact she was still running from her parents' deaths. Now willing to face her grief, Ella had punctured the relationship developing between her and Jackson. Asking for help that he wasn't willing to or couldn't give.

It had been eight days since she had foisted Jackson's support. And yes, she was counting. Dory had left a few days ago, and then Ella had received another call from Alex. He didn't have a problem expressing how much he'd like to see her, so she had extended an invitation for him to visit. In contrast, Jackson's only response to the two phone messages she'd left was a short text stating how busy he'd been at the hospital.

The doorbell jarred her thoughts. She opened the door and found Alex holding a picnic basket in one hand and a portable boom box in the other. A fleeting thought that she wished it were Jackson caused a pinch of guilt to stab her chest as he flashed a bright smile at her. Alex was a thoughtful man who was proving to be a good friend.

"Hi. I'm glad you're here."

Lifting the basket, he said, "Surprise, I brought lunch. Hope you're hungry."

"I wasn't expecting lunch."

"That's what makes it a surprise."

She smiled.

See, thoughtful.

"Eating is at the top of my lists of favorites again. I just made lemonade."

He stepped through the doorway. "Where would you like this?"

"It's a gorgeous day, let's take it outside on the patio."

"While you set out the food, I'll get the lemonade. Should I bring plates?"

"No plates, I've got it covered."

Ella returned with the pitcher. "How did you know I love picnics?"

"I didn't, but I have an insight to touring. Not all glitz and glamor. No time for picnics either. So I figured it was time for one."

She watched him empty the contents of the basket. "Looks like you have a feast stashed in there."

"Sandwiches, pasta salad, fruit — and I brought you some chocolate truffles. You can save them for later if you like. Is there an outlet where you can plug in the CD player? I'm not sure if the batteries are charged or worn."

Ella sighed, a sense of contentment settling over her as she plugged the CD player into an outlet by the French doors. "All set here."

He pulled out a chair. "Come have a seat."

Ella filled her plate and began to eat. She took a sip from her glass. "This is nice, Alex. Thank you."

"My pleasure." He reached out and placed his hand on her forearm. "I'm glad you're feeling better."

When she didn't respond, he leaned back and said, "So, what are your plans? Are you going to stay in San Francisco?"

"For now. My neurologist has yet to release me from his care. Even then it depends on…"

"On what — or who?"

Dear, Lord. I'm just not interested in him in a romantic way.

Ella laid her fork aside. "Alex, I've enjoyed the time we've spent together, but…I value you as a friend."

"Because of the doctor who took care of you after the concert."

"I'm sorry, I—"

"Ella, honey, I don't want to date you."

Her muscles tensed. A yellow flag of caution popped into her mind.

Remember the nut case in Brussels.

"I'm not sure how to respond to that."

"Let me try to explain. When you came along, I sensed a strong chemistry between us. Although asexual, we clicked from the beginning. I'm an only child and most of my life I could only imagine what it would be like to have a sibling. We established a solid musical connection by the end of our trip to the coffee shop, and I had this sense of completeness. Like I had found the piece of me that's been missing."

A sigh of relief spilled from her lungs.

"I hope I don't sound like a crazy man. You're a beautiful woman, but that's not what draws me to you."

"You had me thinking *crazy* for a minute." She smiled. "We're good."

"You didn't answer my question. Are you going to stay in San Francisco?"

"My parents died here. Maybe I'll find peace if I work through the mess I left behind two years ago."

"And if you can't?"

"I'm looking at other options." In an attempt to shift the conversation from her problems, Ella pointed to the boom box. "Are you going to turn that on or did you bring it just to balance out the picnic basket you were carrying in your other hand?"

Leaving his chair, Alex said, "Now's a good time." He pushed the power button and returned to his seat.

Pleasant sounds in a slow tempo escaped from the CD player. "Are you going to tell me anything about the music?"

"Can't you just listen and enjoy?"

She closed her eyes. "Beethoven."

"You have a good ear. It's Beethoven's *Violin Romance No. 2.*" They sat in silence for several minutes as the strains of the violin came through the speakers.

"Wonderful technique and the tone, it's as beautiful as anything I've ever heard. Even with the limited ability of the speakers."

Alex's mouth turned upward into the slightest of smiles.

Her eyes became wide with comprehension. "You're playing; you're the artist."

He nodded. "Correct again."

"Is there a significance to the recording? Why did you decide to play it for me today?"

"It's my last violin performance. I gave up playing so I could move on to something just as wonderful, but different."

"When you started conducting."

"That's right. There are many ways to use your talent, Ella. You should guard against crushing your musical spirit since touring is out."

"What does that mean?"

"Plan, think of options."

"Are you ever sad when you listen to your old recordings? That you stopped performing."

"No, and I think it's because I love what I do. Coaching musicians to bring music to life — it's a stupendous high."

"That's the way I feel about my playing. So how could I ever stop?"

"There's no reason to. Other alternatives include performing without the downside of touring."

Ella pushed her plate away. "Okay, I'll play your game. Name some."

"You could teach, impart your knowledge to gifted students, and still perform."

"What else?"

"Not everyone can afford live concerts. You could become a recording artist. In fact, I've been mulling around a project that I think you'd be perfect for. Wouldn't it be nice to settle down, to have a place to call home?"

And now they were back at the crux of the matter. Accepting her parents' deaths. Should she test the waters of this newly formed friendship with Alex? She had tried with Jackson, and she had broken them, or so it seemed. Ella hadn't heard from him since she asked to lean on him for strength. No, she would use her family to fortify her when the time came to talk to lawyers and dismantle her childhood home.

"Ella?" Removing the twisted napkin she had been tormenting, he took both her hands. "You seem distressed."

She squeezed her eyes tightly enough to push back brimming tears. Ella opened her eyes as a declaration that she was ready to address the unfaceable. "There are things I need to do regarding my parents…"

"Let me help you." He smiled at her. "I always wanted a little sister. Professionally, I think you're an industrial-strength performer. Look at the success you've become. But personal matters are different. The pain can pull you down to the point you need a hand to help you stand. A hand to give you strength."

Having someone walk this path with her would be a wise move, undoubtedly easier. A tempting offer from her new friend. "I've put everything into my career because, at one time, that's all I wanted."

"What do you want now?"

"To come home. My career will work itself out, but I have to give my all to find peace over Mom and Dad."

"Let me help you."

She looked up at him. "How do we start?"

"Tell me about this mess you haven't dealt with."

Ella swallowed and focused on her fingers. "I haven't been to our house since the funeral. It's mine now, but I can't bear the thought of going there."

"Okay, we'll start with the house. I'm not going to push, but you need to work up some courage to face it. In the meantime, how about an afternoon at the beach? I'll bring an umbrella and plenty of sunscreen."

Ella laughed, and it felt good. "Okay. I think I'm going to like having a big brother."

JACKSON SAT IN THE DOCTORS' LOUNGE taking a short break with a stronger-than-he-liked cup of coffee. Work was his saving grace. He might not know how to navigate his relationship with Ella, but he could care for the sick. Since his last visit with her, Jackson had poured his full attention toward patient care, leaving no time or energy for anything or anyone outside the hospital. His personal life was beginning to mirror his life after Beth's death. The thoughts about his wife brought his sorrow over her passing simmering to the surface, and he had to work hard to push it back so it wouldn't consume his life as it once had done.

Ella was a different matter. There was guilt where she was concerned. Guilt about keeping her secret, making him partly responsible for her collapse and internal bleeding. Guilt about ignoring her. He hadn't been by to see her; wasn't taking her calls. He had to make a move or risk losing the relationship that was starting to bloom between them.

An older colleague joined him at the table. "I'm looking for Bill. Have you seen him today?"

It was rare that they spent any time in the same space since Ella's diagnosis. "Sorry, no." Before he could stop it, a sigh escaped.

"Bad day, Dr. Hart?"

Jackson shook his head. "Could be better."

"How so?"

"Life could be better. I had a fifty-eight-year-old man on my OR table this morning. He needed a straightforward splenectomy."

"Was there a problem?"

"Not with the procedure, but before suturing the incision, I took a routine look around. There were suspicious spots on the pancreas — probably cancer. It's crap! The man has his spleen removed because someone T-boned his car, and now he may have cancer."

"You're looking at this the wrong way. If it's cancer, you caught it early, and your patient will get the treatment he needs to survive. If you hadn't seen it, he'd come in later with symptoms and the diagnosis would no doubt be stage-four pancreatic cancer. He'd be looking at barely enough time to get his affairs in order. Be sure you spin it that way when you tell him what you found."

"Thanks, I'll do that."

"Wish I could stay longer, although not for this pathetic excuse for coffee." He tossed his cup in the trash. "I've got to scrub for an appendectomy. See you later."

"Later." Jackson absentmindedly waved his hand in the air. His thoughts returned to Ella. He had attempted to call her earlier that morning, but before she had a chance to answer, he'd hung up.

Discomfort had claimed him as he thought about accompanying Ella to the cemetery. To say the goodbye she had been unable to utter at her parents' funeral. It was the right place for Ella to start, to break down the wall she had placed around herself. Was it possible to spin it in a positive direction as he would do for his patient with cancer? She had asked for his support. Absent from his vocabulary were the words to tell her no. He would keep his promise. Jackson picked up his phone and tapped her number.

TWITCHY MUSCLES CAUSED ELLA to close her eyes and pull in a calming breath as Jackson drove under the cement arch of the entrance to the cemetery. His out-of-the-blue phone call yesterday had made her heart pound as they agreed on a meeting time.

When she opened her eyes, she realized they had picked a good day. The sky was clear, an advantage to showing off its spectacular shade of azure. Thick green grass, neatly manicured grew between the hundreds of grave markers. The sight seemed to go on forever. Many gravesites boasted colorful flowers, a testament to the fact that most visitors to the cemetery didn't come empty-handed as she had.

Ella guided him around the gravel path to the location they sought. "Stop here," she said in a somber voice. Her eyes fixated on the giant sequoia thirty feet away. Jackson opened the door and offered his hand. She took it and stood, pulling in a deep breath.

"I'm proud of you for coming today," he said.

"Did you think I was going to renege?"

"I wasn't sure. You need to say goodbye so you can move on, but I know how hard this can be." He advanced, and she followed, her feet progressing from gravel to grassy ground that slightly inclined as they moved ahead.

Sauntering in silence, Ella studied the names on the markers. She halted in front of the shaded headstones that bore the names of her parents and took hold of Jackson's arm for support.

"It's so different from last time. No tent or chairs. No caskets." She sank to the ground, putting her level with the headstone. Another task she had left to her aunt and uncle, and they had done well. A tasteful upright companion marker of black granite with a simple border of oak leaves. Her father had loved the outdoors. Engraved across the top were the words *"Together For Eternity"* and her parents' names and dates below. An ache settled in her chest. "I'm glad this huge tree shades their plots. It's peaceful — I didn't expect that." She plucked a blade of grass from the ground.

Jackson squatted beside her. "I'm going to take a walk over to the pond, give you some privacy."

She looked up at him, but no words came.

"Take your time, Ella. I'll meet you at the car." He squeezed her shoulder and stood, his retreating footsteps silenced by the grass.

Rather than look at the letters composing her parents' names, she focused on the backdrop of mountains in the distance. Her eyes admired the landscape as her head performed a slow, quarter turn first to the left and then to the right.

Ella had expected tears, but other than an occasional sob rising from her chest she was surprisingly calm. "I miss you, Mom and Dad."

Immediately, her eyes scoped the area again, making sure she was alone with her spoken thoughts. She had never pictured herself as one to visit a cemetery and speak with family members passed on to the afterlife, but it had its merits. You could pick the day and time you wanted to visit. You could say anything without judgment, and indeed no response.

"I want to come home, but I can't imagine living here and never seeing you."

She remained on the grass, sitting like a statue for some time. Inhaling and exhaling, the only movements she made. Closing her eyes, images of family time clicked by like a slide show as she focused on her parents. A half sob escaped. Ella pulled in a big breath, and the fragrance of roses filled her nostrils. The pink roses mixed with pink gerbera daisies and some purple flower she couldn't identify sitting between her parents' headstones provided a momentary distraction. Who had placed them here? It never occurred to her that anyone came to visit.

"I tried not to miss you, made myself sick. Got to figure out what I should do with our house — I don't think I can live there." A breeze flitted through the grass, and calmness claimed her. Closing her eyes, she raised her face to the sky and smiled. At that moment, staying in San Francisco surrounded by family seemed doable. A sigh of contentment escaped her throat. It was time to grow new friendships. And she didn't want to leave Jackson.

Ella pulled a pink daisy from the arrangement and stood. As she walked away, Jackson came toward her. He put his arm around her shoulder.

"You okay?" he asked, as they walked.

"Working on it. Thanks for being here for me. It means a lot."

"You should allow your family to help you, Ella."

"I plan to do that. Take me home, please."

JACKSON HELD IT TOGETHER long enough to make it outside after dropping Ella at home. Rushing for the door of the SUV, he stumbled against the vehicle while pulling in big gulps of oxygen.

His heartbeat galloped as memories of the aftermath of Beth's death came pouring out with a vengeance. Jackson thought he had tucked them away so tightly they'd never resurface. That it was the only reason he had been able to move on with his life.

His racing heart slowed as he started the engine and backed out of the driveway. He had been ready to start a new chapter of his life with Ella. The fortress he had built around the memories of Beth had cracked and was now crumbling around him. Although the pain had lessened, dealing with it was not what he wanted. But he had offered Ella his support, and now the only thing left to do was prepare himself for the possibility of sinking back into the awful pit of gloom that he had worked hard to overcome.

Beth had occupied a good portion of his daily thoughts for several days now, and Ella was the reason. He had worked so hard to bury those memories. The guilt about spending time with Ella had increased. The only way to make it disappear was to cut out the source. That meant turning away from the woman who had captured his heart the day he'd met her.

AT PRECISELY ONE O'CLOCK, Ella met Doris Johnson at the nurses' station of the pediatric unit. The staff took a moment from their duties to join them. "Here's the ray of sunshine I promised you," said Mrs. Johnson, presenting Ella as eloquently as Vanna White showed off her letter board. "Ella will get settled while you assemble the children. I'm excited, let's get started."

The nurses and techs dispersed to gather the children while the head of volunteer services led Ella to the piano. The large area decorated with bright and cheery colors added to her discomfort. Uncertainty about entertaining a room full of kids caused Ella's insides to quiver. She had never done a performance geared to children. Insecurity pelted her like a heavy rain with no end in sight. When the hand wringing started, so did the self-lecture.

Get hold of yourself. They're just children. Sick children.

Drawing in a breath, she placed her fingers on the keyboard and began playing. Ella bit her bottom lip hoping what she had prepared would be satisfying to the patients.

The closing of the door signaled everyone was present.

Time to start.

Ella's heart raced as she stood and cleared her throat. "Hi. How is everyone?"

Dumb question, they're patients in a hospital.

A jumble of sound reached her ears. Excitement touched her heart. She had a chance to make one or more of these little ones' day better, the goal needed for a focal point. Ella had stressed about entertaining a mixture of ages. The young faces ranged from toddler to maybe thirteen, which brought relief, toning down her anxiousness. She'd prepared the perfect program.

A swell of confidence prompted her to begin. "Is there anyone here who likes to sing?"

An overwhelming response had Ella believing this could be fun. "Okay, start singing if you recognize this song." She began playing "If You're Happy and You Know It." The room filled with noisy, happy voices and the rest of Ella's anxiety melted away.

The allotted time passed quickly. Ella turned away from the keyboard and smiled at the children "That's all for today."

Cries of "awww" filled the room. "Before you go, I'll play a song from one of my favorite Disney movies." Ella looked at Mrs. Johnson for approval and received a nod. "It's an old one, so you may not know it. Maybe the grownups can help me out." A chorus of giggles brought satisfaction to Ella. She had met her objective.

Placing her hands on the keyboard, she began with four measures of introduction. Ella began to sing the lyrics to "Beauty and the Beast" in a crystal clear voice.

Others chimed in, a mixture of the children and adults. There was applause when she finished followed by groans as the staff began gathering the children to leave.

"Are you coming back?" shouted a child from the doorway.

"I'll come back if you promise to sing with me again. I'll choose a different Disney movie next time."

"Yay, I love the *Frozen* song," shouted the last child to be escorted out of the room.

Ella gathered her things, a smile filling her heart. The audience had been different from her usual patrons, as well as the goals. Who knew she would find satisfaction from singing with kids?

I did a good thing today.

THE FOLLOWING AFTERNOON, Ella settled into the leather seat of Alex's Porsche. It seemed apprehension had become a constant in her life.

"Are you ready to do this?" he asked.

It was as good a time as any. Ella's life these days moved in slow motion compared to life on the touring track. And Jackson was suddenly absent, stating he was busier than usual at the hospital. "Part of my anxiety has to be the anticipation of going. Let's just do it. I might not even make it to the front door, but I'm ready to try." The roiling of her stomach confirmed her insecurity over the matter.

Alex pulled a CD from a storage case. After inserting it into the console, he put the car in gear. As they drove away, Ella leaned her head back, sighing as strains of "Air on the G String" filled the car.

"I thought you could use a little Bach."

"It's nice. Thank you."

"We'll take this as far as you can today. We can always come back and try again."

"You're a good friend." Jackson could take a lesson from Alex. After their trip to the cemetery, it seemed he had dropped off the planet.

Alex took her hand and squeezed it. "There's nothing I wouldn't do for my adopted little sister."

When they arrived at the house on Filbert Street, Alex parked at the curb, cutting the engine. "Ready?" he asked again.

Ella nodded then reached for the handle, pushing the car door open. Alex met her as she stood. Instead of moving toward the front door, she walked to the left and stopped at the bushes her mother had encouraged to bloom each year.

"Mom loved her gardening. The area behind our patio was always colorful and fragrant. After a trip to Scotland, she focused on making the garden as beautiful as those we'd seen in Edinburgh." Ella changed directions and stopped. "I want to do this—"

"I have a suggestion. Change your mentality about this from all or nothing to snippets. Take it only as far as you can today; then we'll leave." Alex offered his hand. Ella reached for it.

When she paused at the front door, Alex prompted, "Let's just open it. You can decide if you want to take a peek and leave or step inside to stay for a while."

She pulled the key from her purse and gave it to Alex. After inserting the key, he turned the doorknob.

"Keep in mind the house has been closed up for a long time. It's not going to be the same as you remember it."

Ella drew in a deep breath and nodded. "Okay."

He reached for her hand as he opened the door. They looked inside.

"I don't understand."

Chapter Eleven

For mere seconds, Ella imagined she had traveled back more than a decade, but this was real time. Curiosity superseded any misgivings about stepping into her childhood home. She moved slowly around the foyer, staring and touching. No dust particles were floating in dim, stale air. No furniture covered with sheets. The light came shining through clean windows. It looked like home.

"I don't understand," repeated Ella. "It's like someone lives here." Her hand flew to her mouth. "Someone lives here. We need to leave." Urgency carried her feet to the door.

"Wait." Alex walked back to the porch and rang the bell. There was no response. He stepped inside, shutting the door. "Let's have a seat and call your uncle."

Ella obeyed and moved to the living room, taking a seat on the sofa. She pulled up her contact list on her phone and waited for her uncle to answer.

"Ella, baby. What are you up to today?" asked Bill.

"I'm sitting in my living room. It's clean, smells great. I don't understand it because I was expecting the total opposite."

"I thought you would tell me when you were ready to go to your house or I would have said something."

"Tell me now. Is someone living here?"

"Baby, no. When I had the piano moved, I also had it tuned. The tuner remarked about how dusty the strings were, and it got me thinking. So I had a cleaning service come in and clean top to bottom. I wanted to make things easier for you. Are you alone there? I could try to get away for a while."

"I'm with Alex. Can we talk later? I plan to stay for a bit, but I don't want to take too much of his time."

"Sure. I'll see you tonight."

Ella slid her phone into her purse. She closed her eyes and shook out her hands. Relief settled over her.

"You okay?"

"Yeah, just something my dad taught me to do when I was nervous. 'Close your eyes and shake it away, El' he'd say. Wow, I'm only here a few minutes, and I'm eleven again."

"What did your uncle tell you?"

"No one lives here. Uncle Bill had a cleaning service come in. He thought it would be easier for me if he had the house cleaned."

"Thoughtful of him. Where do you want to start?"

"I think I'll go to my room."

Ella moved slowly up the stairs, her body sluggish. Pushing aside denial was not like flipping a switch. It was advancing step by step from one mindset to another that would hopefully improve the quality of her life. Free her to make decisions that could take her life in a new direction.

Alex followed a few steps behind. She was glad he was giving her space. Literally. Enough room should she change her mind and turn to run back down the stairs and out of the house. Ella continued upward because the professional side of her always persevered in the difficult and she was trying her best to have that attribute flow over into her personal life.

Reaching the top of the stairs, she audibly exhaled, as though she had climbed to the top of a mountain. Since the collapse on stage, her life had been all about inclines. Pushing hard to move onward and upward. She made a sharp left around the banister and continued to her room at the end of the hallway. The door stood ajar. She gave it a push.

The room looked just as it always had. White furniture against lavender walls. Tall bookcases flanked a full-sized bed covered with a purple comforter. Fluffy pillows rested against the headboard. The posters of NSYNC and Backstreet Boys hung on the wall they had occupied for years. A pink, thirteen-inch TV from her mother's college days rested on her desk. Sensory overload caused

Ella to move to the bed and sit. "Have a seat, Big Brother."

Alex situated the chair between the desk and the bed. "So, you were a typical teenager before you turned into a performing machine. I like seeing this glimpse of your before life."

She gave a weak smile but didn't reply.

"Is purple your favorite color?"

"It was when we painted my room. I haven't needed a favorite color for the past decade. All the traveling, you know."

Alex lifted the small TV off the desk giving it a once over from front to back. Favorite TV show?"

"Gilmore Girls. Yours?"

He placed the TV on the desk. "When I was a teenager? Never missed an episode of The X-Files."

"So, you were just an average teenager, too?"

"All the way. I had my friends I hung out with, got into scrapes with. Had a girlfriend, went to prom. All the usual stuff."

Her body relaxed as they talked. Ella was glad she had taken Alex's offer to help her with all she had faced today. She owed him big time. "I don't want to wear out your big brother services, but I'd like to spend some time in my parents' room. Alone, please."

He stood. "Take your time. I'll be in the living room."

Ella nodded, and he left her bedroom. Her legs became jelly as she walked to the opposite end of the second floor. The door to her parents' room stood ajar, just as hers had. She touched it and then tapped on it several times, using a bit more force each time until her view was unobstructed and the room was before her.

Her breath caught in her throat, her eyes watered. Her parents' presence was strong. She stared at the bed where she had spent Saturday mornings snuggled between her parents as they read and she played with her Care Bears or sometimes they turned on the TV and watched a limited amount of cartoons with her.

Ella removed the pillows and scooted to the center of the bed, leaning against the headboard. She wrapped each arm around a pillow and closed her eyes.

The best hugs had come when she scampered into their bed during a storm at night when it was dark and scary. They would tell her to hold on and soon the storm would be over. They told her the time after the rain was precious because it made everything brighter and cleaner.

And then she remembered the advice her father had given after her breakup with Patrick. He had said, when the pain of her loss had decreased, she should analyze the relationship. Look at the pros and cons and use that information to decide what qualities she wanted in a man and how she wanted her life to be with that person. She had barely emerged from losing Patrick when her parents had died, and life came to a screeching halt.

She stepped forward and crossed to the right. Sitting in a chair by the fireplace was a familiar thing. She had spent many times here talking with her mother about any and everything. She hoped one day she would be able to dole out advice, to solve problems for someone who needed her guidance, for that was one of the things she loved about her mother. And she wanted to be seen as a reflection of Linda Craig.

Ella drew in a deep breath with the realization that her mother would never have pushed her feelings aside for two years. She would have tackled the job of mourning with the insistence that she would get through it and move on, richer for having experienced this obstacle of life.

She had fallen pitifully short of mimicking her mother, but she could sense a resolve in the matter. Ella moved to the windows and peeked out. Her heart sank when she saw the disarray of the garden. Her mother's handiwork needed reviving, so whoever bought the house should have a love for beautiful flowers.

Ella had taken the second step in letting go. A release of pent up emotions and she was free. Her eyes fell on the picture frame that had always been a constant on the bedside table. Ella remembered it was the last thing her mother saw at night and the first thing in the morning. Picking up the frame, Ella hugged it to her chest and smiled. Now she was ready to leave.

ELLA SAT AT THE PIANO writing in a notebook. She gripped the pen with her teeth and placed her hands on the keyboard and began playing. A knock on the doorframe of the library interrupted her process.

With a raised eyebrow, she asked, "Home a little early, aren't you?"

"Just wanted to make sure you're okay. How are you?"

"Look at me. I'm making plans to play for the children. Did you think you would come home to a crying mess of a little girl?"

Bill pulled a chair beside the piano "No — I don't know. I want you to be all right, and I'll do whatever it takes for that to happen. What made you decide to go today?"

"Alex offered to take me. He made me realize I needed to see my house. One more step in moving on."

"How'd that go?"

"Scary at first, but positive overall."

"I would have gone with you. But I guess you were in good hands."

"Alex has become a good friend. Thanks to him, I'm ready to sell the house."

Giving a snap of his fingers, Bill said, "Just like that?"

"I think you're partly responsible for my decision today."

A pensive look settled over Bill's face. "Me, huh?"

"Yes. Seeing the sparkling clean rooms made me realize someone should be living there. It's a fabulous house, and it needs a family. It'll take some muscle to clean it out." A lump formed in her throat. She swallowed hard. "I'll need lots of help to deal with the personal things. It'll be rough, and I'll need my family with me."

Bill leaned over and wrapped his arms around her shoulders. "You got it, baby."

IT HAD BEEN SIX DAYS since Jackson had stood outside the closed door of the pediatric activity room. There were benefits to operating on children he hadn't realized. Like hearing about a volunteer coming to play the piano for them. Or learning that one of his patients' father worked for the TSA.

He had listened as Ella played for the kids and sang with them too. She had a voice of gold, not surprising at all. Ella oozed musical talent, but it was the woman, not the talent that pulled him to her. He'd vowed to stay away. But, like the Sirens of Greek mythology drew the sailors to crash their ships on the coast, Ella exerted a force that seized him. The fact he wasn't strong enough to keep his promise induced frustration.

"Any minute now." Jackson blew out several breaths as he paced while waiting for the arrival of his grandparents. Interesting how caring for a twelve-year-old with a ruptured appendix made it possible for him to be waiting here instead of baggage claim. When he had contacted the patient's father, a TSA official at the San Francisco International Airport, his only intention was to have someone check on his grandparents. Maybe persuade them to use wheelchair assistance. He had not expected a personal escort to the gate so he could do the assessing.

Jackson watched his grandparents step through the door of the jet-way. Irritation that had been building for the last few days over their impromptu trip died away. They greeted him with hugs and kisses. The reality of how much he had missed them hit him squarely in the chest, causing him to hang on to their embraces a little longer, a little tighter.

He pointed to the two wheelchairs sitting side by side with personal assistants behind them. When Eugene Hart set up a protest, he stopped him cold. "No discussion on this one, Granddad. This airport is huge, so you're going to ride beside Gram without any grumbling. I'm not going to wear you out just getting you to my condo."

Jackson was glad he had decided on this course of action. His grandmother looked the same as always, but his grandfather looked older and thinner.

"Maxine and Bill want to take us to dinner while you're here. Maxine said there was no way you were coming to town and not meeting them."

"That's nice. We're looking forward to meeting them, too. Right, Gene?"

"Sure, I suppose. Any good fishing around here, Jackie?"

"I don't know. Maybe we can figure that out together. But then we'd be leaving Gram alone. We can't do that."

"Nonsense. You two make your plans. I'll find something to do while you're gone. I have my quilting project with me."

"It's late afternoon. We should stop on the way home and get something to eat. What would you like?"

"Honey, you know we're not picky. Just pull in somewhere, and we'll find something," said Gram.

Carrie's Kitchen, located on the Bayshore Freeway, had a reputation for a varied menu with excellent service. His grandparents had no trouble finding something they liked.

After taking their orders, the waitress walked away. Gram took Jackson's hand. "We waited too long to come for a visit. We know you were busy your first year settling in, but when you didn't come home last year—"

"I came to Atlanta last year."

"You're not becoming forgetful, are you Lo?"

"I remember he barely had time to say hello before he was saying goodbye." She stared Jackson down. "So, we decided to invite ourselves, and I'm glad we did. Something's not right. I don't see the sparkle that used to live in your eyes. I thought if you had a fresh start, surely it would come back."

"My life is great."

"Maybe his life is all work, no play. Jackie, you shouldn't live that way. You need both. What about that piano player you've been telling us about?"

"Gene, that's personal. If Jackson wants to tell us about Ella or any other women in his life, well that's up to him."

Jackson shifted in his seat. "There's nothing to tell."

"Valerie's moved back home with her mom. She's such a sweet young woman and still single. You should come for a visit. It might do you both good."

"I'm really swamped now, Gram. I can't take any time off."

"Maybe soon?"

"We'll see."

With Gram pushing the happily ever after agenda, Jackson steered the conversation in a different direction. "I'm glad you'll meet Bill and Maxine while you're here. They helped me a lot the first year. Now we're good friends."

"I see you're tanned. Been out in the sun surfing again?" asked Gene.

"It's a different kind of surf out here, Granddad. I think it's more challenging than the east coast. Maybe my rusty surfing skills have me thinking that way. So you see I do more than work. I even took a trip up to wine country last month."

"I'm sure we'll find something to do."

This hour of reconnecting brought focus to Jackson. He had not given his grandparents consideration in the scheme of things. They missed him; he could see that a mile away. He made a silent vow to visit once or twice a year from here on out. One day they would leave this earth, and he didn't want 'should have' regrets.

"Got any ideas of what you'd like to do while you're on the West Coast?"

"I want to visit Grace Cathedral. Maybe take a cable car there," said Lois.

"Are you sure, Lo? It won't be like riding the trolley cars in the forties and fifties. Atlanta is pretty much a flatland compared to San Francisco streets."

"Oh, come on Gene. Just hang on tight and have a little fun."

Jackson grinned. Sometimes his grandmother had to pull her husband along, but when it was over, he always admitted to having an all right time. "What about you, Granddad?"

"Have you been to Alcatraz, Jackie?"

"I haven't seen much of the tourist stops, but Alcatraz would be at the top of my list. So that's your pick?"

"Now, Gene, we discussed this. You can't be climbing terrain that is steep and hilly."

"You've been reading up on the tourist spots. No worries, Gram. They have transportation that runs from the dock to the prison building and back. You can even go with us."

"See Lo; he's got a plan. Now Jackie, if you'd spend some time on figuring out what or who would make you happy, your grandmother wouldn't have to fret about you so much."

Chapter Twelve

Jackson stood when Bill and Maxine approached their table on the patio with the view of the bay. The waterfront seafood restaurant at Fisherman's Wharf had been Maxine's idea. He and his grandparents had arrived not five minutes earlier. His jaw clenched when he noted six place settings at the table. Jackson wasn't prepared to spend an evening with Ella; preferred that his next encounter with her be without an audience.

There were things he wanted to say.

But she wasn't with them. The stiffening hair on the back of Jackson's neck settled into place. He continued to stand while Bill held Maxine's chair. She looked up at her ex-husband and smiled. "Thank you, William."

Bill took the cue to claim his seat. Jackson copied his actions. Finishing the introductions, he looked up and his breath caught in his chest.

Ella stood fifteen feet away in a peach-colored halter dress that showed off her sun-kissed skin to perfection.

She made it to the beach.

Ella headed toward the table. Absorbed in her movement, the irritation he'd felt minutes before shifted to a tingling desire. Jackson wanted to touch her skin, to caress and kiss it. Somehow, he was on his feet when she reached them.

"Hello, everyone. Sorry to keep you waiting. I had to take an unexpected phone call."

Captivated, he continued to stand without moving.

Bill rose and held Ella's chair. As they found their seats, the waiter appeared for their drink orders.

Jackson's toe tapped a silent rhythm in his shoe as the irritation returned. Who was responsible for Ella's presence? She was not the type to intrude uninvited. This dinner was supposed to be a friendly meal bringing two sets of strangers together with him being the common denominator. He had planned on a pleasant evening, but how was that possible with tension settling into his neck and his mind on high alert to keep his present dilemma under wraps around their families.

While waiting for their food, Jackson's thoughts drew him away from the conversation. When Maxine had suggested this dinner, he had been apprehensive. He feared the strain between him and Bill at the hospital that would inevitably leak over into their social interactions. He didn't want to have to explain all about it to his grandparents.

Add Ella to the mix, and the evening held the potential for a minefield explosion. He looked past her golden tanned skin. The dress revealed slender shoulders and just enough cleavage to tantalize. Jackson pulled his focus from her chest to her face. Her eyes cut from side to side then she looked down. She was just as wary of being in attendance at the dinner.

His ears caught Bill's voice, and he tuned into the conversation in progress.

"Mr. Hart, Jackson told us you worked in aviation for a few decades."

"Yes, sir. I gave Lockheed Martin thirty-three years of my life. And some of them were my best years. My Lo here can vouch for that." He patted her hand, and she squeezed his.

"Mrs. Hart, did you work when you were raising Jackson?" asked Maxine.

"I had retired from teaching a few years before we lost our son and daughter-in-law. When Jackson came to live with us, I became a substitute teacher. It gave me a flexible schedule, but more importantly, it reestablished the connection I had lost with my students when I retired. Given the blessing of raising Jackson, we needed that connection with the younger generation."

"What a lovely thing to do."

Gram smiled at him. "I'd do anything for Jackson."

Gratitude mingled with love squeezed Jackson's heart as he kept steady eye contact with the woman who had been his loudest cheerleader. "Thanks, Gram. Same here."

Gram reached across the table and touched Ella's hand. "We were sorry to hear about your illness and a concussion on top of that. Jackson told us what an amazing performer you are. Maybe we'll be lucky enough to hear you in concert one day."

Ella sought Jackson's eyes. "You said that?"

"Just telling the truth."

Gene said, "Do you have plans to continue touring?"

"I have decided to change the course of my career. I just haven't figured out all the pieces."

"Having patience is one thing, but sitting on the sidelines and watching life go by is no way to live. Sometimes you just have to reach out and grab on to something. If it's the wrong thing, you'll know it before too long. My point here, trying something is better than doing nothing."

Jackson flinched at his grandfather's words.

"I seem to be embarrassing my grandson with my overflowing words of wisdom, so let's move this conversation on to new subject matter. I'd like to make a suggestion."

"What's that?" asked Bill.

"Could we use our first names? I like casual better than stuffy if it's all right with everyone."

"I agree," said Maxine. "I'll save stuffy for my clients."

Lois addressed Ella. "That color is beautiful on you, Ella. But I have to ask — have you been spending time on the beach or in a tanning salon?"

"I've been getting reacquainted with the city. And I recently spent a day on the beach."

"I hope you remembered your sun block," said Maxine.

Ella clasped her hands and pulled in a breath. "Yes, I did."

"I spoke at length with Claire yesterday, and she didn't mention any trip to the beach."

"Probably because she wasn't with me."

"Oh, Ella. If you'd called, I would have spent some time with you. The thought of you doing things alone makes me sad."

"I wasn't alone, Aunt Maxine. I was with my friend, Alex."

"That nice orchestra conductor?"

"The very one."

The conductor? She's spending time with him.

Jackson's stomach hardened. He passed annoyance and went directly to jealousy.

Bill spoke up. "Max, you're getting sidetracked from our guests." He turned to Jackson's grandparents. "Maxine mentioned you arrived on Monday. Have you seen any of our city?"

"Jackie took us out to Alcatraz yesterday. That was some tour."

"I wasn't sure how I'd like it, but it was incredible," said Lois. "I loved hearing about the history and the view around Alcatraz is beautiful."

"What else are you planning to see?" asked Ella.

"I wanted to see Grace Cathedral, and Jackson took us there this morning."

"The intricate stone and wood carvings are amazing," said Gene.

"And the peace when we stepped inside. So remarkable how we left a loud and fast-paced San Francisco outside and entered tranquility. The stained glass windows and artwork are breathtaking." Lois smiled at her husband and covered his hand with hers.

The yearning for the kind of devotion he saw in his grandparent's eyes sent a pang through Jackson's chest. He'd lost the chance to build such loyalty with Beth, and he'd messed up big time when he decided to stay clear of Ella. He wanted an opportunity to see if she felt the same about him, but wasn't sure she'd give him a shot. Maybe there was no reason to find out since she was seeing someone else.

"Lois, I'll be antique shopping for one of my clients on Friday. Would you like to come along?" asked Maxine.

"I love antiques, but I don't want to give up my time with Jackson."

"I understand, maybe the next time you visit."

"This is perfect," said Jackson. "Granddad and I can take that fishing trip we were talking about, and you won't be alone while we're gone. Works out for everyone."

Gram leaned forward making eye contact with Ella. "Will you go with us?" she asked.

"I'm not sure. Umm, I'd have to check my calendar."

"Ella, truly there's no reason you can't go. The wedding details are up to date, you don't volunteer on Fridays, and you're not on tour. So give it up and say yes."

She raised an eyebrow. "Yes."

Maxine laughed. "Ella, we're not asking you to walk the plank, just look at antiques. Besides, if you're out and about, you won't be tempted to tie yourself to your piano for hours. Which you're not supposed to do yet."

Gene spoke up. "Bill, we seem to be leaving you out. Do you prefer antique shopping or fishing?"

"I haven't fished in years."

Jackson caught the look of aggravation Bill threw his way.

"But I won't be able to join you, can't take time off from the hospital."

"Surely you can take one day out of your schedule," said Maxine.

"Our daughter is getting married in a few weeks, and you talked me into that cruise to decompress." He made quotation marks in the air. "Sorry, Gene. Maybe we can plan a little better on your next trip here."

"Gonna hold you to it, Bill. I hear there's a historic ships collection somewhere along the pier.

Can I talk you and Maxine into going with us to check it out after dinner?"

Jackson protested, "Granddad, it's been a long day."

"If you're tired, you can go home."

"On hindsight, I should have driven," said Ella. "I'm sure looking at some ship collection could be fascinating, but I've had a full day, so I'll pass on the tour. You all can look at old boats, and I'll wait on the pier."

"What's the problem? We'll get a taxi back to Jackie's place, and he can take you home."

Bill pushed his plate toward the center of the table. "Thanks for the offer Gene, but—"

"We'd love to," said Maxine. "And there's no need for a taxi. William and I can take you home."

"Then it's settled. We older folks will look at ships, and the kids can see themselves home," said Gene.

Oh, God. Now, what do I do?

ELLA SLID INTO THE PASSENGER SEAT as Jackson held the car door. His manners were one of the things she liked about him. He didn't do it to impress; it was just a part of him.

"Could they have been any more transparent?" she asked as he settled into the driver's seat.

Jackson fastened his seatbelt. "Yeah, that wasn't awkward at all. Don't worry, though. Traffic is light. I'll have you home in no time."

"Fine," retorted Ella.

The first sight of him tonight had made her heart race as little pulsations of pleasure skittered through her body. She had focused on Aunt Maxine while walking, feared she might falter if her gaze remained on him. Spending her evening exclusively with him; that's where she wanted to be. But apparently, Jackson didn't hold the same sentiment. Since their trip to the cemetery, he'd stayed away from her. And tonight he had directed few words her way. It was as though they were standing on opposite cliffs, a huge chasm between them with no way to come together. How had this happened? And why?

Her tone softened. "Could you help me understand something?"

"What's that?"

"Why you don't want to be my friend."

Jackson pushed at his right temple. "Will you take a drive with me?"

"You didn't answer my question."

"I want to try to explain some things. Do you trust me, Ella?"

Any doubts she'd had about him melted away at the sincerity of his words. "Yes, Jackson, I do."

"When I was new to San Francisco, I'd drive up and down this highway to clear my head. There's a spot I'd like to show you."

Several miles later, Jackson pulled down a winding road facing the ocean and stopped the car. He pulled a blanket from the car's trunk. They followed the path down to the beach and spread out the blanket.

Ella had gotten her wish. "It's deserted out here."

"I'm surprised because this location is a great spot for stargazing and the fog band is covering San Francisco."

They settled on the blanket. "What does fog in San Francisco have to do with the stars up the coast?" asked Ella.

"The fog blocks the sky glow from the city. The sky here is clear making the stars shine like fire. The limited light from the crescent moon makes it easier too."

"All right, Dr. Hart. Here's your chance to *shine*. Point to the stars. Tell me what you see."

"Okay." He directed her attention to the right quadrant of the sky and said, "Up there — that's Ursa Minor, also known as the Little Dipper. Only seven stars." He pointed to the night sky as if tracing them. "Four stars compose the bucket and three outlines the handle."

Scooting closer he slid his arm across her back to guide her arm to the opposite side of the sky. "And over there is Ursa Major or the Big Dipper."

Ella's heart pounded. His clean scent surrounded her, the heat from his body undeniable.

She turned her head in his direction, welcoming their closeness. Jackson stroked the side of her face, coaxing her toward his lips.

As they connected, her eyes slid shut. Lost in the kiss that seemed to last forever, she melted against Jackson's solid masculine form. Finally, she pulled away breathless; mesmerized by his face in the starlit night. Olympic physic indeed.

And could he kiss.

She wanted to understand what had them moving in opposite directions so she could stop it, prevent it from happening again. "How did things get so messed up between us?"

Jackson's hand fell from her shoulders. "I screwed it up when I decided the best thing for me would be to stay away from you."

"Let's be honest here. I put you on the spot. If I'd never asked for your help…"

"I had a hard time when Beth died. Don't know if I would have recovered if it weren't for my grandparents. They gave me time to grieve, then began to pull me back from the darkness of my life. They were smart enough to know when to stop sympathizing and start pushing so I could have a life again."

"I'm glad they were able to help you."

Jackson shifted until he faced her. "It began with the thought of going to the cemetery. You needed me, and I wanted to support you. Beth began to occupy my mind. A lot. Remembering the days and nights after I lost her — I didn't want to go there again."

"I called a couple of times, but you never answered. I didn't want to push. Now I understand. I'm sorry I asked you for something you couldn't give."

Jackson planted his palms down on the blanket as he hung his head.

She put her hand on his arm. "It's okay. I'm getting there. I've even been to my house."

He looked up. "How was it?"

"So different from what I expected. I felt peaceful when I left. Ready to let go."

"I'm sorry you had to go alone."

"I couldn't do it by myself. Alex went with me." Ella studied the frown on Jackson's face. "He's a good friend."

Jackson picked up a small seashell and threw it across the sand. "I see."

Why is he insecure?

"Alex is a great guy, but you shouldn't be jealous of him."

A boldness she would never have claimed as part of her personality overtook her. "I'd never do this with Alex." She placed her hands on his face and pulled him close, touching her lips with his. The kiss began soft and sweet. Jackson shifted and grasped her shoulders, the kiss morphing to fully charged. Desire blazed as heat shot below her belly. The sensation caused her to shudder.

Jackson pulled away, his breathing labored. "Although I like your dress, it's not appropriate for this night air."

He rubbed her arms and pulled her close. She rested in the haven of his arms. Jackson Hart was a man worth risking her heart for a lifetime of love. Ella snuggled into his chest. "The sky is beautiful tonight. Let's stay a few more minutes."

He tugged on the blanket and pulled the end around them.

Tilting her head upward, Ella stared at the sky. "If I had to come up with a positive outcome from my illness, I'd say being here for Claire's wedding is a good one." She looked at Jackson. "San Francisco is feeling like home more every day. I sometimes wonder if San Francisco would be a better fit than San Diego."

Jackson caught Ella's lips in a sweet kiss. "We should go. It wouldn't do for the maid of honor to get sick and miss the wedding."

"Will you be there?"

"I received an invitation. I'm not sure I'll use it."

"Why not? I'd like to see you all dressed up."

"Things are strained between Bill and me. I don't want your family to feel anything but happiness, so I think my staying away will help with that."

"What kind of problem are you having with Uncle Bill?"

"Sorry, I can't talk about it. Hey, you're shivering. Time to go." He pulled her from the ground.

As Ella helped fold the blanket, she made up her mind that she'd get to the bottom of the tension between Jackson and her uncle. Aunt Maxine would be the perfect ally to make that happen.

Chapter Thirteen

Ella leaned against the piano while looking at the patients in wheelchairs and on floor mats. Stationed throughout the area were medical personnel watching after their charges.

The audience of children quietly sat as she explained programmatic music. "It is music that suggests a sequence of images."

Blank stares.

I'm no good at this.

Ella took a deep breath and tried again. "You know, ideas in your head. I'm going to give you a short example, but you have to do your part. Use your ears to listen while you close your eyes to imagine what the music is trying to tell you. Let's start with a story I bet everyone knows. So you can see how this works. Am I right, does everyone know *Little Red Riding Hood*?"

The children talked excitedly as their little heads bobbed.

Settling at the keyboard, Ella played passages that mimicked the characters in the story and showed the children how music could teach their minds to visualize the story.

"Okay, now that you know what we're doing, I'm going to ask my Aunt Maxine to join us."

Maxine came forward and stood beside the piano. "Hello, boys and girls. I'm glad Ella asked me to help out today."

"She's going to read the story of *Peter and the Wolf*, while I play the piano. Before we start, let me introduce the characters and play each theme for you."

When the story ended, the nurse in charge stood. "All right. Time to return to your rooms."

Ella raised her voice over the protests. "Hey, everybody. I watched a Disney movie this week that I've never seen before."

She'd had no idea what the *Frozen* song was the child had asked for at the end of their last session. A little research on the Internet enabled her to grant the little one's request.

"If you know this song, sing it with me as you head back to your rooms." She immediately began playing and singing "Let It Go," and the children joined in enthusiastically. The sound thinned to Ella's lone voice as the last of the children left the room. When she had learned this song for today, some of the lyrics had called to her.

Ella was pleased that she was doing something positive for the kids. She just hadn't expected to get a personal message about letting go. As she gathered her music into her bag, Maxine approached.

"Fantastic job. I didn't realize until I saw the happiness on the kids' faces how much they need a diversion from their illnesses."

"Thanks for helping today. I'm pretty happy myself. I've missed playing the piano. Do you have time for coffee?"

The waiting area next to the activity room was empty, so they helped themselves to a cup and sat down.

"Jackson's not coming to the wedding. He says he wants it to be a happy day for our family and if he comes that won't be the case. Do you know what's going on between him and Uncle Bill?"

Maxine dropped her cup of coffee in the trash. "I have a good idea. Come with me."

Ella didn't speak as they wove their way through corridors, and down the elevator to Uncle Bill's office. Sometimes it was best just to let Aunt Maxine have at it.

Maxine strode past Bill's assistant. "Is he busy?"

"Dr. McMillan has a meeting in ten minutes."

"What I have to say won't take that long." Maxine knocked on the door before turning the doorknob, pulling Ella into the office with her.

"What is wrong with you, William McMillan?"

"Max-—"

Ella looked from her uncle to her aunt then closed the door.

"I witnessed the distance between you and Jackson when we had dinner with Gene and Lois. Do you know he's not coming to the wedding because of you?"

"If he's not coming, that's on him."

"That's bologna, and you know it. You haven't stopped blaming him for Ella's episode after the concert. I just thought you were blowing off steam at the hospital that night."

Ella stepped forward. "What are you talking about?"

"While you were in surgery, Jackson told your uncle he knew about your symptoms. He was blaming himself for allowing you to wait for medical attention."

Ella faced her uncle. "Lying in the emergency room, it became apparent *I* had messed up. *I* should have come home sooner. My blunder has nothing to do with Jackson."

"No, it concerns your uncle." Maxine moved into his personal space. She dug her index finger into his chest. "You're using Jackson as a scapegoat."

"That's ridiculous."

"William, I know you better than you know yourself. You feel guilty about Ella's illness. After we had lost Elliott and Linda, I remember you saying you should catch up with her on tour and make sure she was okay, but you never did. You believed the emails and phone calls that all was well. And then she came home ill. Guilt smothered you, but you pushed it away. Then you used Jackson, so you wouldn't have to face yourself."

"Stop it!" Slumping into his chair, he rested his elbows on the desk, holding his head. Silence surrounded them. Finally, he looked up. "I'm sorry, Ella. I should have done a better job looking after you."

"How could you do that to Jackson, Uncle Bill? I've always known you to be a fair person. Why would you do that?"

The voice on the intercom interrupted. "Dr. McMillan. Your appointment is here."

"Thanks, I need a minute. Get in touch with Dr. Hart. Tell him to meet me in my office in an hour."

"Yes, sir."

He looked at Ella. "Your aunt's right. Once again, I've put my work before family. It was easier to blame Jackson than myself. I'm sorry." He stood and walked the women to the door. "I'll take care of this Max, I promise." He hugged her. "Thanks for giving me a good kick in the rear. Ella, I'll see you at home."

Ella struggled to process the new information. Was Uncle Bill partly responsible for the rift between her and Jackson? She had to figure a way to change things between them.

Because she now realized Jackson was the man for her.

JACKSON SAT IN THE RECEPTION AREA of Bill's office. He'd been surprised by the phone call summoning him to a meeting. The fact he would see Bill for a showdown today never entered his radar. He pulled at his necktie to release the confining object from his neck.

The door opened. "Come in, Dr. Hart."

The greeting offered did not bode well. Jackson obeyed. Once the door closed, they were chest to chest. He stood over Bill's five-foot-eleven-inch frame by a good four inches.

"Have a seat," said Bill as he stepped behind his desk and sat, putting distance between them."

"I'm glad you called. There's something I wanted to tell you, just haven't gotten around to it."

"Because I'm your boss, I'll go first."

"Sure."

"I wasn't fair to you the night Ella collapsed. I wanted to place the blame anywhere but where it belonged."

"Don't you think blame is the wrong word? Ella is partly responsible for ignoring her symptoms, but there were extenuating circumstances."

"I'm not talking about Ella; I'm talking about me."

"You? You're going to have to back up and run over that again."

"I'm at fault here. It took a visit from my ex-wife today to straighten me out. For me to realize I used you unfairly to hide my complicity in the matter."

Jackson shook his head. "I had a part in this, too."

"Yes, you did. Any guilt you have about your inaction is on you."

Bill stood and walked around the desk. "What you probably don't know is I felt guilty that night, too. I didn't do a good job looking after my niece. I made a promise to my sister the day we buried her. And I failed."

The older man propped his hip at the corner of the desk and placed a hand on Jackson's shoulder. "I'm sorry I misdirected my anger at you."

Jackson looked up at the man who had aided in giving back his life and said, "Accepted."

"Good, now what have you wanted to tell me?"

"I've received a few offers to practice elsewhere, away from San Francisco."

"Are you planning to leave us?"

"No, but I'm not sure I would have given the same answer last week. I've never wanted to leave here, but the strain has made things difficult."

"I'm glad that's settled. One more thing; you're coming to the wedding. That's the issue that brought everything to a head today with Max."

"I haven't decided about that."

"Claire would be hurt if you didn't show up."

"I doubt that. Claire will be absorbed in her big day. She won't notice if I decide not to attend."

"Then don't hurt my niece. Ella was with Max today, and she wanted to know what I had done that was keeping you away from the wedding. Please, don't hurt her."

"I'll think about going."

Jackson left the office and blew out a breath. On the one hand, Bill had apologized, lifting the tension simmering between them since the night Ella passed out. On the contrary, he had given him a warning. Jackson had no intention of hurting her, had not meant to do that when he'd turned away from her. After their night at the beach, he believed they were moving toward a mutual desire, wanting more than friendship. Even so, the need to tread lightly cautioned his mind. He had unintentionally hurt her once, and it hadn't been pleasing on his end either.

His course of action was clear: move things forward and hope for the best. He pulled his cell phone from his pocket. As he waited for Ella to answer, his pulse quickened, remembering the kisses they had shared on the beach last night.

"Jackson, hi."

"Go to dinner with me."

"I know you just had a meeting with Uncle Bill. How'd that go?"

"We cleared the air. So, you'll let me take you to dinner?"

"Yes, take me to dinner. When?"

Closing his eyes, he let his head fall back as the remainder of tension left his body, along with the breath he'd been holding. "I'm not free until Friday. I've been working extra shifts lately."

"Friday's good. You can text me the details later."

"See you Friday."

Text me the details later.

Things were getting better for her. He frowned as he realized he hadn't been the one to help her grief issues. Did it matter where the help came from as long as it came?

On a more positive note, Jackson was sure he hadn't imagined it. Ella was interested in moving forward.

Chapter Fourteen

The excited buzz of pediatric patients welcomed Ella into the activity room of the children's unit. Their smiles and enthusiasm warmed her heart. Volunteering while a more permanent solution emerged lifted her spirits.

Settling at the piano, she said, "You're going to hear some program music today, and we'll finish with a song from a Disney movie. Now, who remembers what program music is?"

A girl seeming to be about ten years old waved her arm in the air. "I do, I do."

Ella nodded at her.

"It's music that helps you follow a story, and you can close your eyes and see it in your head."

"Excellent. Today we're going to do things a little differently. I'm going to play some songs from a piece called *The Carnival of the Animals*. We'll listen to five of them. The music should remind you of a swan, a cuckoo, a kangaroo, a lion and a hen. I'll start, and when you think you know which animal the music sounds like, you can shout it out."

The exercise had most all the children joining in with enthusiasm. Ella noticed three patients in the back of the room in their beds. They were possibly too ill to sit in wheelchairs. Their inclusion in music time told Ella the children needed this. They may not be as energetic as the other patients may but the smiles on their faces told her selling this piano for cash would have been the wrong move. Money couldn't buy their smiles.

"How many of you have seen *The Little Mermaid* movie?" Their joy made her smile. "It's one of my favorites. Everybody, sing "Part of Your World" with me."

Since her first visit, Ella's state of satisfaction had grown to euphoria. She owed gratitude to Alex for guiding her to see there was more to life than what touring offered. She glanced around the room at the beaming faces, listening to the sweet voices. Too soon, their time ended.

A nurse stepped forward. "I'm glad you all had fun, but it's time to go back to your rooms and rest."

Ella tried for a poker face at the fussy reactions and moans of disappointment. More staff moved in to assist the small patients. A little girl with long red hair sat quietly in her wheelchair while she waited for help. There was a sadness about her that drew Ella to her side.

"Hi, I'm Ella. What's your name?"

"Natalie."

"It's nice to meet you, Natalie."

"I liked the music you played."

"What was your favorite animal?"

The small patient squinted and pulled her lips together. "Mmm, I think the kangaroo. If I close my eyes, I can pretend that I'm hopping beside him."

"Even better, the next time you're outside playing you can leap around and pretend the kangaroo is beside you. I bet you've missed playing outdoors while you've been here."

"Not really. I don't go out much. I can't walk or play with the other kids since the accident. I'm here to have an operation to fix my leg, and then I'm gonna learn how to walk again."

"How old are you, Natalie?"

"I had a birthday last month, and now I'm seven." The girl smiled.

Ella smiled back. "I bet you'll be walking in no time."

The smile left Natalie's face. "My mom says not to hope too much. It might not happen."

"Oh. Is it okay if I hope for you, that everything will go well with your surgery?"

"Would you?"

"I sure will. And you can think about the little mermaid. Ariel wished hard to be part of a different world, and it happened to her." Ella looked up at the nurse, then back to the child. "Looks like it's time for you to go. I had fun talking with you."

The red-haired child gave a small wave, and a smile appeared on her face before the nurse guided the wheelchair toward the door.

Ella returned to the piano and gathered the music, placing it in her bag. Hearing a familiar voice, she looked up. Alex stood at the back of the room with a man she didn't know. Her face brightened as they walked toward her. "Alex, what are you doing here?"

"My friend's in town for the day, and he wanted to meet you. I remembered you'd be here this afternoon. Ella, Scott Kahil."

She held out her hand. "Hello, Mr. Kahil. It's nice to meet you."

"Ms. Craig. Is your afternoon free? Can we buy you a coffee?"

"Wide open. I'll say yes to your offer only if you call me Ella."

"I can do that. Is there any place in the hospital where we can get a decent cup?"

"The Bistro has a gourmet coffee area. It does a good business."

After settling at a table with their cups, Ella said, "Alex, why have you gone to the trouble to surprise me with a visit?"

"Not very subtle am I?"

"Ella," said Scott, "I've been abroad for the last month. When I returned to work last week, I heard you missed your interview at the conservatory.

"How do you know about that?"

"Sorry, I teach there. Alex and I studied music in Cleveland together. We were due for a visit, but honestly, I wanted to know if he had any information on how you're doing in regards to your recovery. We could use someone of your caliber to join us at the conservatory. I guess Alex agrees because he offered to introduce us.

"That's it?" asked Ella.

"In a nutshell," said Alex.

"Believe me, if I had a week, I'd use every hour to persuade you to become a part of our exceptional school."

Alex pushed his cup around in a circular pattern. "About time for that interview or have you decided your future is in San Francisco?"

"You could visit for a few days with Alex," Scott said.

Ella turned toward Alex. "Why would I interrupt your summer to have you accompany me on a trip to San Diego?"

"Alex is the clinician for a summer honors orchestra of high school students from around the state. He'll practice with them for three days and end the clinic with an evening performance. It would give you time to see our campus as well as the interview. And he could help you explore the city in the evenings."

She anchored her eyes on Alex.

He grinned. "Say yes, Ella. We'll make up for some of the time you spent alone on tour."

"Well, the best I can do right now is say I'll think about it."

"Think fast," said Scott. "The clinic starts next week."

Ella recalled pieces of the afternoon conversation as she put the finishing touches on dinner. She smiled when she heard her uncle's footsteps on the hardwood floor followed by his voice.

"I smell something good."

"In the dining room, Uncle Bill."

"Wow, look at you. Cooking and everything."

"We'll see what you think after we eat. I'm a bit rusty when it comes to the kitchen, but I wanted to give it a try. You've been good to me. I wanted to do something for you."

They sat and began eating. After a few bites, Bill said, "This is great. Thanks, baby."

"I'd have to work at messing up a salad. The lasagna was more of a challenge."

"Can't wait. I missed lunch today, so let me warn you, I could eat a horse."

When they finished their salad, Ella served the lasagna.

Bill took a bite and moaned. "Delicious. Tastes like you spent all day in the kitchen. Please don't tell me this came from a box."

"Made it from scratch. I do remember some of the things Mom taught me."

"Is it getting any easier — remembering your mom and dad?"

"I guess I'm not working so hard at trying not to remember. Does that make sense?"

"Is that what you've been doing for two years? Trying not to think about them. That's an impossible task. You need to let your happy memories comfort you. I still cry for my sister, but I love remembering her even through my tears."

"It's a rollercoaster. Some days are better than others. I find distracting myself helps. Like playing for the children at the hospital."

"That was today? Darn, I wanted to come by and watch."

"Come next Tuesday. Tell your assistant to put it on your calendar."

"Let me make myself a note." Bill pulled his phone from his pocket and made the notation.

"I met the most adorable little girl today. She's going to have an operation on her leg. It doesn't sound like her mother is thinking positively about it."

"It's a shame. I know about that patient. Her mother could use an attitude adjustment."

"Is she going to be all right? She'll be able to walk after the surgery?"

"Baby, you know I can't discuss her or any other patient with you. So let's talk about something else."

"I just want this so badly for her."

"Ellaaa." He drew out the last syllable of her name.

"Okay. Mmm... I'm thinking about going to San Diego for a few days."

"What's in San Diego?"

"I met a man today—"

Bill stopped the forkful of lasagna heading to his mouth and let it drop to his plate. "Hold on. You're not going anywhere with some man you just met today."

Ella opened her mouth to speak, but Bill pressed on. "You may be an adult, and you can tell me all day long you're going to make your own decisions. But I will not allow you to traipse off to a city hours away from San Francisco with some man you met today!"

An alarm went off in Ella's head as she watched her uncle become red-faced while he spoke. "Uncle, please calm down. You didn't let me finish."

She watched his heaving chest settle along with his breathing. "Let's try this again. I met a man today, a representative of the Windom Conservatory of Music. He encouraged me to visit the campus for a few days when I interview."

"Are you sure about this? Have you ever been interested in teaching?"

"My whole focus till now has been on performing. Alex has helped me see I many other choices. You could say I'm exploring my options. If it makes you feel any better, Alex will be with me."

"Is he looking the school over, too?"

"No, he's working with a group of high school students from around the state for a few days. They'll end their time together with a concert."

"I'm not ready for you to take on a new job and leave us again."

"Don't have me packing my bags just yet. I'm not sure about anything at this point."

ELLA TOUCHED HER ABDOMEN, the butterflies flagging her attention, reminding her of the news she should share with Jackson. One last glance in the mirror confirmed she'd made the right choice. She wore the above-the-knee little black dress acquired during the shopping trip with Claire. The one that showed off her great legs. Descending the stairs, she heard voices, then silence.

"Ella." Jackson gave her an appreciative once-over.

She continued to the bottom of the stairs. "Hi," she murmured.

"Looks like you two are all set. See you in the morning, baby." Bill kissed her on the cheek before exiting the foyer.

Jackson reached for Ella's hand. "Ready?"

She smiled. "All set."

She had eagerly waited for tonight, but now the butterflies stirred, going another lap in her stomach. Was the cause Jackson's presence or her news? She had to tell him about the trip to San Diego, and the possibility of taking a position at the music school.

Shyness overtook her. "I didn't know where we're going. Is my dress all right?"

"It's perfect. You're perfect."

The short ride to Restaurant Amara didn't give the opportunity for in-depth conversation. Once they were settled and perusing the menu, Ella still couldn't shake the uneasiness moving within. Now that they were contemplating moving their relationship to the next level, was she prepared to complicate things for a job five hundred miles away?

Jackson tapped her menu. "What looks good?"

She focused. "I'll have the lamb chop."

The waiter approached with the lobster tempura Jackson had ordered at first glance of the menu. "Have you decided, sir?"

"Yes, my friend will have the lamb chop, and I'll have the prime rib. Also, would you bring us an appropriate wine?"

The waiter nodded.

"Thanks." He turned to Ella. "I'm going to dig in. One small apple was the only lunch I managed between surgeries today."

Ella placed a piece of the appetizer on her plate. "So, a busy day."

"It wasn't that bad. It made the time fly by, and now I'm here with you."

She smiled. "I'm glad you want to spend time together."

He laid his fork on the table and reached for her hand. "I think you're remarkable and I don't want to waste another minute dancing around feelings. I want us to spend time together. To see where things might go."

Ella squeezed his hand and disengaged. Taking a bite of lobster, she struggled to swallow. She had to disclose about the trip to San Diego. Making him aware Alex would be there too might create a counterpoint of dissonance much like a Schoenberg musical composition. If he was ready to invest some serious time into getting to know her, how could he properly do that if they lived hours apart?

The waiter arrived with their food, and she decided it was best to allow Jackson time to eat before she mentioned the trip. She waited patiently as the waiter poured their wine.

"The music is lovely."

Jackson raised his eyebrows. "My mind isn't in the music."

Tongue-tied and knowing she was blushing from the heat on her cheeks didn't help her situation. The best way to get through dinner was to let Jackson do the talking. She waited until he swallowed a taste of prime rib and said, "Tell me about your surfing." And that was all it took.

Fifteen minutes later, Ella found herself laughing at his stories and the tenseness that had earlier overtaken her stomach eased away. Alex was right. She needed to investigate new opportunities.

Her heart was telling her this man could be a huge part of her future. She had to be up front about everything with Jackson. Hadn't the last two years proven that? Hiding her feelings from the people closest to her, and even herself had been destructive. She wouldn't go there again.

Still, she kept quiet on the drive home. Waiting until they were out of the car, Ella turned when they got to the steps. "Sit with me. I have something to tell you."

They settled, but the words stuck in her throat.

Jackson wrapped his arm around her shoulder. "A grave countenance. It can't be that bad."

She gave a tentative smile. "I wanted to share some news with you. I'm going to San Diego next week."

"Following Maxine around while she shops for a client? The trip will be good for both of you. It'll give her a reprieve from thinking about wedding details, and she's missed you."

"No, not with Maxine. I'm going to the Windom Conservatory of Music, to look the school over. They have an opening for an Artist in Residence."

"The operative word being residence. You'd move to San Diego?"

"That's correct. Just going to see the campus and discuss the requirements of the position. I'm leaving Wednesday and returning on Sunday."

"Four days. Must be a large campus. Better pack those DVDs I gave you, so you'll have something to occupy your evenings. Have you been cleared to drive that distance?"

"I'll be flying. With Alex. He's doing a music clinic with high school orchestra students, and they're having a closing concert on Saturday night. I told him I'd stay for the performance."

His arm dropped from her shoulder. "And what is he going to do for you in return?"

A slow anger sent her back teeth grinding, a habit she'd had trouble arresting in the past. "Alex is going to show me around town after his rehearsals are over. I've said it before, but I think it bears repeating. You don't have to be jealous of him. If the thought of me spending a few days away with a friend is difficult for you, then I guess you should leave."

"It's not difficult." Jackson stood. "I'm leaving because I don't want to say something I'll regret later."

"You do that." Ella stood and hurried up the stairs, never looking back before she unlocked the door and slipped inside.

Their exchange had not gone the way she had hoped. Maybe there was a part of them that wouldn't mesh, wouldn't be good for a long-term relationship. The fact he didn't seem to believe her when she told him he shouldn't be jealous made her wonder if there were other things he didn't accept.

She collapsed on her bed emotionally exhausted. At this point, the touring track was looking attractive once again. She rolled onto her back. What would her mother do? The fact that she couldn't ask her brought the sting of tears, which led to a bout of crying.

The next morning, Ella awoke with a dull throbbing in her head. The hurt from Jackson's departure pressed on her heart. Handling things differently last night would have brought a better day, but this was new ground. She had no experience dealing with men and their egos.

Ella downed two acetaminophen tablets followed by a long drink of water. After dressing, she headed downstairs to her piano, and the relief it would bring from playing. The doorbell rang.

He came back.

Hurrying to the door, Ella drew in a cleansing breath ecstatic she had another chance to make Jackson understand about Alex. She pulled on the doorknob. Her joy immediately deflated.

"Aunt Maxine." Her aunt's first visit to her ex-husband's house since Ella returned. Her stomach clenched. "Is something wrong?"

She leaned in and kissed Ella's temple. "No, dear. I'm meeting William to finalize the details of our cruise."

As if on cue, Bill came from the kitchen carrying two cups of coffee. "Ella, I didn't know you were awake."

"I'll leave you to your planning. I'm going to practice."

"Hold on. Join us in the living room. I have something to tell both of you."

Her uncle's demeanor made the tiny hairs on her arms stand at attention.

They all sat in unison.

"I have some distressing news."

Her heart raced. Had Jackson been in an accident after he left last night?

"Gene Hart suffered a heart attack yesterday."

Ella pulled back in shock. "He's not—"

"He survived," said Bill. "I don't have any details about his condition."

"What can we do to help?" asked Maxine.

"Pray that he'll get through this. Jackson should be in Atlanta by now. He'll update us when he knows something."

Why did it feel like her life was about to spiral downward?

Chapter Fifteen

J ackson's heartbeat quickened along with his steps as he pushed through the doors of the hospital. He'd managed to remain calm from the time he'd received the phone call from Valerie, during the redeye flight to Georgia, and on the taxi ride from the airport.

The anxiety to know if Granddad was okay took on a ferociousness that had him taking long strides to cover the distance from the hospital lobby to the cardiac ICU. Jackson rushed into the waiting room. The dimly lit area had a half dozen people occupying seats in various stages of rest. Intermittent flashes of light darted from a muted wall-mounted TV in the corner of the room. His eyes adjusted to the low level of light.

As he scrutinized the group, his eyes fell on Gram. She sat in a chair with her head against the wall, her eyes closed. He took a seat beside her. Shock followed by a pinch of guilt flowed through him as he noted how much older she looked since he had seen her a few weeks before. Knowing his grandmother, she probably hadn't left the hospital since she'd accompanied her husband in the ambulance eighteen hours ago.

Gently, he touched her arm. "I'm here, Gram."

Her eyes popped open, and she shifted forward. "Jackson! How — you shouldn't have come."

He glared his disapproval.

"I was going to call you this morning."

Her words belied what Jackson could see on her face. The tension in her shoulders fell away as he hugged her tightly. She did want him here.

"How's Granddad?"

"The nurses and doctors all say the same thing. He's stable but needs surgery. Dr. Haimes would like to do it as soon as possible, but your grandfather hasn't signed the consent form."

"When can we visit?"

Gram eyed the clock on the wall. "Twenty-three minutes. Can I get you some coffee while we wait?"

He began to protest and stopped. The look in her eyes told him she needed something to do. "Coffee sounds great. Thanks."

She stood. "It'll feel good to stretch my legs. I won't be long."

He had been grateful for the phone call from Valerie, his grandparents' neighbor. Gram needed him as badly as he needed to be in Atlanta. Resting elbows on thighs, his hands massaged his head. In less than twenty-four hours, his life had become a jumbled mess. Why had he let jealousy cloud his time with Ella? He'd walked away like a sulking kid.

He sighed. He'd have to think about that later. Granddad was his focus now.

It wasn't long before Gram returned. Jackson took the coffees from her while she settled into a chair. He handed her a cup of the hot liquid. "Have you been here the whole time?"

"In the ambulance, I told Gene I wouldn't leave him. And I haven't."

"Well, now you can. We're going to visit Granddad together, and then I'm taking you home to get some proper rest."

She opened her mouth to speak, and Jackson put his hand up to stop her.

"No arguments. We're in this together, and we'll look after each other." He lifted his plastic-coated coffee cup. "Thanks for the coffee. I needed it."

Another glance at the clock and Gram said, "Time to check on Gene."

Jackson followed her to the double doors of the ICU.

She picked up the phone. "Eugene Hart's wife and grandson to see him." The automatic doors swung open to let them enter the world that held precious lives lingering between life and death.

Jackson put his arm around Gram, allowing her to lead him to the third cubicle on the right. She stopped in the hallway to hug him. "Glad you're here. I'm going to say good morning and leave you two alone. I want to check on some of the other visitors I've met while I've been here."

Gram moved to the bedside and placed a kiss on her husband's cheek. His eyes opened in response. "Morning, Sunshine."

"Look who showed up on our doorstep." She moved aside allowing Jackson to advance.

"Jackie, you came."

Jackson leaned down and kissed the top of his grandfather's head. "Sure I came. There's no way I'd let you two go through this without me."

"Gene, I'm going to check on Mrs. Long. She's so worried about her husband she forgets to eat. I'll make sure she has some breakfast while you visit with Jackson. I'll be back later." She squeezed his hand before walking out the door.

"One of the many reasons I love her, always thinking of others."

"What about you?" asked Jackson as he drew a chair close to the bed.

"What about me?"

"Are you thinking about Gram? Why are you dragging your feet about a surgery that will most likely give you more years with the woman you love?"

"I was waiting for you. I didn't want Lo to be alone, especially if something goes wrong. So now I'm ready. Tell that doctor he can schedule the surgery."

"Good, that's what I wanted to hear. We need to figure what triggered your attack, so you can avoid it, and hopefully not have this happen again. What were you doing when all of this started?"

"This is ridiculous. The doc will fix my heart, and everything will be all right."

The face that defined stubborn stared at Jackson.

"Granddad, answer the question."

"I was resting when the pain started."

"That's all, just resting. What were you doing before that?"

Silence followed Jackson's question. The older man's lips drew into a taut line.

"You know, Granddad, at your age there are probably some things physically exerting that you should give up. You wouldn't want to worry Gram. Are you still doing yard work?"

Granddad's face turned red as he measured out his words. "I was making love to my wife. I don't *care* what you or any other doctor thinks. That's something I'm not giving up."

A flush of heat pushed from Jackson's neck upward. He opened and closed his mouth.

Oh, crap.

"Do you hear me, Jackie?"

"You can discuss this with your doctor." Jackson stood. "I'll let him know you'll have the surgery. Rest up. Recovery is work."

He stepped out in the hallway and shook his head.

Note to self. Another reason family shouldn't treat family.

After leaving word for Dr. Haimes about the surgery, Jackson moved with purpose through the familiar corridors of the hospital. How could he come home, even for an emergency without stopping in to see his teacher and mentor?

Stepping into the reception area, he approached the woman behind the desk. A new fixture to the office. Dr. Williams' former assistant must have finally retired. Pulling his professional demeanor front and center, Jackson said, "Good morning, if Dr. Williams is in, I'd like a few minutes of his time. Would you let him know Jackson Hart is here?"

The middle-aged woman gave him the once-over and smiled. "Have a seat, Mr. Hart. I'll give Dr. Williams your message."

"Thanks." He took her suggestion and settled into a chair. He scrubbed his hands over his face, hoping to erase the exhaustion from traveling overnight as well as the information he'd just learned from his grandfather. The door opened, and Dr. Williams walked out.

"Jackson, what the devil are you doing in Georgia? Have you decided to leave the West Coast and come home?"

His mentor clasped his shoulder, producing a sensation of comfort. "My grandfather suffered an MI yesterday. I just arrived this morning."

"I'm sorry to hear that. Come in." He pointed to a chair. "Have a seat. How's he doing?"

"He's stable in the CICU but needs surgery. He finally gave the green light this morning, so I hope his doctor will post the surgery soon."

"The sooner, the better. If there's anything I can do, don't hesitate to ask."

"Thanks, I appreciate that. I couldn't come to town without stopping in to say hello."

Jackson stood and began pacing. His ex-boss allowed him time to think without conversation. Stopping, Jackson looked up. "I never took the time before I left to thank you for all your support after losing Beth. For telling me it was okay to move on literally and emotionally."

"I'm glad I was able to help. How are things in San Francisco?"

"Great. I like the hospital and the people."

"Something in your voice keeps me from being convinced you mean that."

"No, it's true." Jackson pushed his hand through his hair and reclaimed his seat. "I had a lot of time to think about my grandparents on the flight to Atlanta. I'm selfish. Living a life of contentment in California without any thought as to how they're doing."

"What's going on Jackson?"

"I think I should consider moving back. Granddad is seventy-six, and Gram is seventy-two. I should be here to take care of them. Do you have any openings for an aspiring general surgeon?"

"Let's take this one step at a time. Let your grandfather get through his surgery. Then we'll talk again. I'm glad you stopped by. My door is always open."

"Thanks for your time, Dr. Williams. I should get back to Granddad."

JACKSON JOINED GRAM in the modest living room. Seeing the phone against her ear, he turned to leave. She waved him back. He faced the triple windows above the sofa. The beauty of the tree-lined street caught his attention for a moment before he took in the rest of the room. The décor wasn't as sophisticated as Maxine's townhouse. And it wasn't as large as Bill's house. But it was home. A substantial Craftsman-style house that he'd been privileged to share with his grandparents. His lungs expanded fully, pride settling in his chest.

"I'll see you in the morning, Gene. Don't be stirring up any trouble for the nurses tonight. Love you." She disconnected the call and looked up at Jackson.

"How's Granddad?"

"Feisty as ever. I predict he'll be discharged in a few days just as Dr. Haimes suggested this morning."

"I hope he's aware it won't be a cakewalk when he comes home."

"He knows I'll be enforcing the rules, but then I've always done that. How about you? Looks like you have something on your mind. Come sit and talk to me."

Jackson settled into the chair beside the sofa. "What would you say if I told you I'm thinking of moving back to Atlanta?"

"I'd ask what foolishness has gotten into you."

"I'm serious. Dr. Williams has offered me a position at Emory Hospital, and I'm considering it."

"Is Ella planning to relocate to Atlanta?"

"Ella has nothing to do with it."

"She should since you're in love with her."

"*Love?* Wow. I *might* have feelings for her, but it's not love."

"Don't you want a wife and children? You shouldn't trade the possibility of love for us."

"Ella has other plans. She's considering a position at a music conservatory in San Diego."

"So it's easier to run home to Georgia than stay and fight. I guess maybe you're not in love with her after all."

Jackson pressed his eyelids with his fingers. His hands fell into his lap. "I thought maybe you and Granddad missed me. And I should be closer than twenty-five hundred miles."

"So you think we're getting too old to live alone, do ya?"

"Let's just say I'd feel better if I could get to you sooner than later if something happened to either one of you. This weekend is a perfect example."

"You should spend your time pursuing Ella and give her a reason to stay in San Francisco."

"I don't know what I'm going to do, but I need to decide soon. My patients are in limbo about their treatment. I've left the surgery service short staffed.

"If you were back there right now, how would you go about making your decision?"

"I'd take a drive up the coast to clear my head. The only driving I can do here is the 285 Perimeter around Atlanta. It wouldn't be a fast drive, or relaxing."

"You're better off taking a run in the park. Go on, get some air."

He closed the front door behind him and stepped out into the oppressive heat. He'd be drenched in sweat and needing a shower by the time he made it to the park. Jackson turned back to the air-conditioned house. A voice spoke up.

"Hi there, stranger."

He looked to his right. Valerie sat in a big, white rocker under the twirling blades of a porch fan. "Come have a seat," she called out.

Jackson walked across the grass and took the steps two at a time. He sat on the rocking chair beside her.

"How 'bout some lemonade?" she asked, pointing to the side table.

"Sure, thanks."

She poured a glass and handed it to him. Jackson held it to the side of his face and closed his eyes. Lowering the glass, he let the cold liquid flow into his mouth.

"Ahh. You have the right solution to a stifling evening."

"How's everything next door?"

"Granddad's getting better every day. Gram won't admit it, but she's worn out. Thanks for calling me."

"You needed to know. I wasn't sure when Lois would call, so I did it for her."

"How are things with you?"

"I miss painting. Haven't quite decided what to do with myself."

He reached over and touched her arm. "I'm sorry. When Gram told me about your accident and the nerve damage to your hand — well, it was hard to hear."

"Thanks." Taking the pitcher of lemonade from the table, she refilled their glasses. "Mom needs me, and the distraction from my *situation* is a good thing."

"Have you gotten a second opinion about the nerve damage?"

Valerie stood, walked to the porch railing, and looked out at the picture-perfect scene before them. "Second opinion. Third opinion. I've finally realized I have to face the fact I won't paint again."

"Let me make a few calls."

She spun around to face him. "No!" Drawing in a deep breath, she splayed her hands in front of her. "Thank you, no. You're sweet to want to help, but I can't hear it again from another physician. It's not good to wish for something beyond your reach." She returned to her seat. "I'm glad Gene's recovery is going well. Does that mean you'll be going back to California soon?"

"Yeah, probably in a few days. But it might be just to pack up and move back to Atlanta."

"You're coming home? Why? Every time Lois shares news about you, it seems everything is good."

"Granddad's heart attack got me thinking. They're getting too old not to have me close by."

"Mom checks in with Lois daily, and if they need something, I usually step in to help."

"That's great, Valerie. I appreciate it, but I need to be the one taking care of them. Just like they took care of me when I needed someone."

"What about that woman in San Francisco? When Gene and Lois returned from their visit, she was all excited about Emma or whoever. So excited you'd found someone that makes you happy."

"Ella is a friend, and I'm not sure it'd go past that."

"Then you can't come home."

"Why not?"

"You have to find out if your connection to her could become something more. You deserve that, Jackson."

"I'm not sure things will work out with Ella. I do know I need to be near my grandparents. So, I'm moving home."

"Men, sometimes you're dense."

"What does that mean?"

"There's no reason for you to choose between love and family. Convince Ella life isn't worth living without you. Make her *want* to come to Atlanta."

"Did my grandmother plant you out here to stop me on my way to the park?"

"No setup. But glad I'm here to contribute a woman's opinion about your dilemma."

They stood and hugged. Returning to the house, Jackson found Gram reading in the living room.

She set her book aside. "Did you have a good run?"

"I didn't make it to the park. Valerie was outside and invited me over for a visit."

"How nice."

He squinted. "You didn't have anything to do with Valerie just happening to be outside."

"Jackson, that's ridiculous."

"Just remembering Valerie's first summer home from college. You tried your best to throw us together."

Gram smiled. "Well, you were shy back then. You needed a nudge. But then you met Beth, and you were fine."

A pang assaulted his chest causing him to pull in a quick breath.

"Oh, honey," said Gram. "I had no idea just hearing her name still tears you up. Maybe if her parents hadn't taken her back home to Nashville, you would have had a place to visit her."

"Like our visits to Mom and Dad's grave sites?"

"Those visits were good for us all. I remember how you would carry the flowers from the car and place them oh-so-carefully against the headstones."

Jackson leaned his elbows on his thighs and held the sides of his head. Straightening he said, "Those trips to the cemetery became a part of our routine. They just seemed natural. It was different with Beth. Her death slashed my heart into so many pieces..."

He paused. The old wound not so deep now. He whispered, "I wasn't sure I would ever heal."

Gram stood. Moving to his side, she rested her hands on his shoulders. "I'm not sure you have."

He shrugged. "I made the change you and Granddad insisted I needed and buried myself in my work. Life's been easier the last year, but lately, memories of Beth have surfaced."

Gram sat in the chair next to Jackson and took his hands in hers. "Perhaps you haven't said goodbye. Maybe that's the answer. If you've locked Beth's memories away hoping never to think about her again well, that's not right. You had a wonderful life together, and you should be allowed to think about those times without it tearing your heart out. Let her go, Jackson, but keep the memories. She's part of who you are today."

He swiped at his eyes. "How do I do that?"

"Her bones are resting in a Nashville cemetery. Maybe her spirit is lingering nearby."

"You think I should drive to Tennessee?"

"What's a four-hour drive if the trip gives you what your heart needs?"

"I guess disconnecting here and not taking Beth home with her parents has had consequences. I'll think about it. Thanks, Gram. I've missed our talks."

"So have I, and I'll only say this once. You could call more often." She smiled and stood. "I'm going to bed a little early tonight. I think the last few days are catching up to me." As she walked to the door, she turned and chuckled. "My age is showing. I forgot to tell you Ella called while you were out. When I saw her picture on your phone, I answered it. We had a nice talk."

His posture perked up. "What did Ella say? Did she leave a message?"

"She wanted to know how we're all doing. I gave her an update. Goodnight, dear."

"Night, Gram."

As soon as she was out of the room, Jackson grabbed his phone to check for a text message. Nothing. Had she called just to get the status on Granddad? Bill could have relayed that information to her. No, she wanted to talk. As much as it confirmed their connection remained intact, it would also make it that much harder to leave San Francisco.

Too early for bed, he picked up the remote and turned on the TV. The thoughts running through his mind wouldn't allow him to focus on a Netflix binge tonight. He clicked the power button and rose.

Jackson closed his bedroom door and lay crosswise on his bed, the fatigue of the past few days weighing heavy in his body. But his mind was alert with thoughts of Ella. She had said more than once she might remain in San Francisco. And now a move to San Diego was a possibility that could separate them permanently.

Rolling over to the edge of the bed, he pulled the nightstand drawer open and retrieved a picture frame from its hiding place. His favorite picture of Beth stared back at him.

Ella's arrival into his life had caused the numbness to subside, had made him come alive with a desire for more than a thriving practice at the hospital. She could bring a healthy balance to his life. But only if he let Beth go. Since her death, he had progressed from anguished survival to lingering sadness that lately had claimed a chunk of his attention.

Why? Memories of her had been dormant for the past year but now were a constant companion. Maybe Gram was right. He should take the time to say a proper goodbye to Beth. The visit at the cemetery had seemed to help Ella move forward with her life.

He believed things happened at a particular time for a purpose. Perhaps this trip home was a jumping-off point for a visit to Nashville. He'd never thought about going while in San Francisco.

Jackson stood and placed the picture frame on the desk. Granddad's attack was the stimulus that had brought him home. It had provided him the opportunity for conversations with Dr. Williams and Valerie. Made him see the need to make a significant change to care for them.

And the time away from Ella made him realize how much he wanted her in his life. Would the choice to care for his grandparents someday turn him into a lonely, bitter man?

Chapter Sixteen

Ella settled into the first-class seat next to Alex. She activated the airplane mode on her smartphone. Conserving the battery life was a must since she wouldn't be able to charge her phone until later that night. "This was a wrong move on your part."

Alex buckled his seatbelt. "What's that?"

"Quick flight to San Diego versus an eight-hour road trip with me."

"It could be fun and revealing, but I need to be ready to roll when I show up for that first rehearsal. Traveling eight hours by car isn't conducive to that."

"I've booked enough flight hours to last a lifetime. It sounds like heaven to me."

"We'll plan to take one. Just decide where you want to go."

Shifting in her seat, Ella studied Alex's profile. "Why did you push so hard for me to agree to visit the Windom school?"

"Your proficiency at being subtle is incredible."

She punched playfully at his upper arm. "If there's something I want to know, I don't tip-toe around it. Why did you push?"

"I didn't know I was pushing."

"Yeah, you were. So you want me to take a position hours away from San Francisco?"

"The truth? I'd rather you stay, but Scott wants to claim you as his addition to the conservatory, and I owe him. Don't get me wrong; I think you'd be an excellent artist in residence. A way to bring out your talent from another angle. All I did was get him an introduction. It's up to Scott to reel you in."

"I do like the San Diego Chargers. But I'm not ready to jump into something so different from performing just because of a sports team. Or to be responsible for shaping new talent."

"Let's just see where the next few days takes us. No expectations. Just absorb the atmosphere."

"No pressure?"

"Promise, no pressure *from me.*"

"Are you excited about working with the state's best high school musicians?"

"Yeah, I like finding new talent and then following those students as they pursue their future."

The flight attendant interrupted the flow of conversation to give pre-flight passenger instructions.

They rode in silence while the plane taxied to the runway and then lifted effortlessly into the sky. Ella tilted her head against the seat and closed her eyes.

Preparations for the trip to San Diego had filled the last two days, a good distraction from thoughts of Jackson. Then she'd had the conversation with Lois. Now she sat on a plane with no distractions and no escape from the memory of last night.

After battling with her conscience about calling Jackson, she caved and tapped his number on her phone. She had been shocked when Lois answered.

"Hello, Ella. It's so nice to hear your voice."

"Hi, Mrs. Hart. How is Mr. Hart?"

"His recovery is going well. Thanks for asking. I'm sorry Jackson's not here. He was going to the park to run, and I guess he left his phone behind. If this is important, I can step outside and get him."

"I thought he went to the park."

"That was his intent, but I see he's ended up on our neighbor's porch. I guess he and Valerie are doing some catching up." At her words, Ella's stomach fell.

"Don't bother. I just called to check on everyone, and you all seem to be doing fine. I won't keep you. Goodnight."

Alex's voice pulled her into real time. "You're deep in thought about something or someone."

"Mmm," she replied.

"Have you heard from Jackson?"

Without making eye contact, she said, "No, but I heard that his grandfather's recovery is going well. I'm not sure when he'll be back."

"That's good news."

"His grandfather's recovery or the part about not knowing when he'll come back?"

"That's not fair, Ella. Jackson and I were at odds when we first met, but I have no ill will against him. I just haven't found much about him to like. Except that he's smart enough to know you're special."

"Stop, please. There were sparks between us, but that doesn't mean it's going to work into something deeper."

"That will make or break my opinion of him. If Jackson doesn't have the good sense to commit and make a go of it, then I don't think he has much intelligence after all."

THE DRIVE TO NASHVILLE had been quiet. Lonely. Jackson had wondered more than once if this was a wise move. It could backfire, and instead of figuratively putting Beth to rest, it might stir up feelings better left buried. Beth would always have a piece of his heart, but he needed to say goodbye to the one he'd loved fervently and lost too soon. At thirty-six, he had a long life ahead. He wanted a chance at love again. Wanted that love to be Ella. The idea of her coming to Atlanta had taken root, but how could he compete with her family ties? Wasn't he doing the same thing; moving to be with family?

Jackson turned onto the long driveway that led to the River View Bed and Breakfast. According to a letter he had received last year, his in-laws had taken account of their life after Beth's death and purchased the B&B. They intended to draw people into their lives. They didn't want to lock themselves away with memories of the past and become stagnant and bitter.

He hoped this impromptu visit was the right thing to do. He hadn't seen them since the day they took Beth back to Nashville. The walk from the car to the door was a slow one. Drawing in a deep breath, he followed the instructions on the door and stepped inside. He approached the foyer table and rang the bell.

"Be right there," a voice sang out.

Dread caused his legs to shake. Before he could retrace his steps and leave, Sharon Lambert came through the door wiping her hands on a kitchen towel. She stopped abruptly as their eyes met.

I shouldn't have come.

After a brief pause, she stepped forward and placed her arms around him as far as they would go. She pressed the side of her face to his chest. "Jackson. I've wondered if we'd ever see you again." She released her grip and stepped back. "Let's not stand out here. Come with me to the kitchen."

He followed her without uttering a word. Now that he was here, he didn't know how to start, what to say.

Sharon pointed to a chair, then moved to a cabinet and removed two cups. She poured coffee, then set the steaming cups on the table and took a seat.

He added some milk from the creamer then focused on her face. "I'm sure this visit is a shock. It's something I didn't plan."

"It's good to see you. How are you, Jackson?"

"I'm struggling with some things, and over the past few weeks, Beth has been prominent in my thoughts."

A screen door opened with a scrape. Sharon stood. "That's Keith." She reached the back door as he stepped inside. "Keith, Jackson's here."

Beth's father pulled his hat from his head and placed it on the table. He extended his hand as Jackson stood, then pulled him into a hug.

"It's good to see you both," said Jackson.

By the time they settled in chairs, Sharon had placed a third cup of coffee on the table.

"You know I don't mince words. What brings you to Nashville?"

That had always been something he'd liked about his father-in-law. Few words and he always knew where he stood. A short explanation of why he was here would be better than drawing things out. "I need to say goodbye to Beth."

An hour later Jackson hugged them again. He drove away with directions to the cemetery, ready for some heavy duty emotional lifting. Losing Beth hadn't been Keith and Sharon's choice, either. They had dealt with her death and reinvented their life.

They were happy, an example that it was possible to find happiness.

Maybe after relocating to Atlanta, he too could reinvent his life. But would it include Ella?

THE DAY AFTER ELLA RETURNED from San Diego, she stepped into the empty reception area. "It's lunchtime. Maybe Uncle's assistant is taking her break." She stepped to the door and stopped.

The events of the last eight weeks, a record for Ella to remain in one place, had shaken her picture of the future. She was struggling with emotions and desire. Not only about Jackson but how she should proceed with her career.

Ella ran her hand over the engraved nameplate. William McMillan, Chief of Surgical Services. "It must be nice to know where you belong professionally." Her knuckles made contact with the glass portion of the door.

"Come in."

She turned the doorknob and poked her head inside the door. "Do you have a few minutes?"

Bill stood and made his way around the desk. "For you, always."

She hugged her uncle tight as though she were trying to make up for the last few years of her self-imposed isolation. "I missed you while I was gone."

"I'm sorry I wasn't home when you returned last night. With Jackson in Atlanta, we're short staffed.

The emergency department treated multiple victims of a car crash. I stayed to help out."

"Maybe you should get a dog, so you'd have a reason to come home. You know, it would need to be fed and walked."

Bill led her to the seating area of his office. "You're reason enough to come home." He rubbed the back of his neck. "Do I need to get a dog? Is this your way of telling me you're moving to San Diego?"

Ella pulled her arms against her chest. "I don't know what I meant by the dog thing. I came by to share some news. I had my last appointment with my neurologist. He released me today."

"That's great." His eyebrow arched. "So why aren't you more excited? You've been waiting weeks for this."

"I'm happy about it. I also received a request from Mrs. Johnson to stop by her office. I've been relieved of my duties as the short-term children's entertainer. They found a volunteer to take my place."

"That was the objective from the start."

"I know. But all of a sudden, I'm at loose ends."

"You won't be for long. The rehearsal dinner is in four days and then the wedding. If I know Max, she'll keep you busy until after the wedding. Then she'll be with me on a cruise, so *you* get a break."

Ella laughed. "This is the stuff Aunt Maxine lives for. My job is to keep Claire from going crazy until she leaves for her honeymoon."

"Claire's happy you're here for everything. When we first thought you'd only have time to fly in for the wedding and back out again, it disappointed her. I guess when it's all said and done, things happen for a reason."

"I guess. Have you heard from Jackson? How is his grandfather?"

"Gene had his surgery and is doing well at home. Jackson should be returning in a few days. I told him to check in when he gets back."

"So you're not sure when that will be."

"I'm confused. I thought you and Jackson were back on track. You went out to dinner the night of Gene's heart attack. Why aren't you the one giving me the information about when Jackson will be back in town?"

Ella crossed her legs and set her gaze on the sofa arm as though fascinated with the fabric. "Our date did not end on a positive note. I told Jackson about my trip to San Diego, and things went downhill like a glissando on my keyboard. We haven't spoken since."

"Ella, if Jackson makes you happy, it's in your best interest to talk this out with him."

"I want it to be in person."

Bill took her hand and kissed it. "It's your happiness that matters to me."

"When I figure out what that entails, you'll be one of the first to know."

JACKSON KNOCKED ON THE OPEN OFFICE DOOR. Bill looked away from his computer screen. "Jackson, when did you get back?"

"Last night. I wasn't sure you'd even be here today. All set for the wedding tomorrow?"

"I needed to take care of a few details. Have a seat while I finish this email to Dr. Mann. He'll be in charge while I'm gone."

Bill tapped on the keyboard for a short time. "Done. The wedding? Maxine and the girls have handled all the work. My part is easy — just show up in my tux. Max did ask me to take today off, so I won't be late to the rehearsal dinner. I couldn't say no."

"Before you leave, I need to discuss something with you."

"What's going on?"

"I've made a decision, a big one. I need to do this, but it doesn't mean it won't be tough executing it."

"Does this have anything to do with Ella?"

"Indirectly, yes." Jackson stood and began pacing.

"Jackson, we're friends. Just talk."

He stopped and faced Bill. "I'm here to resign. I'm moving back to Atlanta."

Bill stood. "If the way I treated you a few weeks ago is the reason—"

Jackson held up his hand, stopping Bill's words.

"I have to be closer to my grandparents. I need to take care of them."

"Has something happened to Gene?"

"He's good. Look, they're getting older. They need me."

"What about Ella? What about you? I see the attraction."

Jackson pushed his hand through his hair. "I had to decide between family and Ella. My grandparents have to be my priority. I'm going to tell her after the wedding."

"Damn, your timing is terrible. Max and I are leaving on Sunday morning for a week-long cruise. I don't suppose you could wait until we return to have your talk with Ella."

"Sorry, I can't wait a week. She'll get through this."

"Ella *is* strong, and she'll be all right. But will you?"

"Eventually."

Though it doesn't feel that way now.

Chapter Seventeen

Ella returned to her room at the hotel, dubbed the bridal room for today. The bride-to-be stopped pacing, her forehead wrinkling as her fidgeting hands remained in motion. Her wide, brown eyes made it appear she might burst at any moment. "Well?"

Her heart filled with tenderness for Claire, usually confident about every facet of her life. Today had tested her composure. She was losing the battle, and it was Ella's job to restore her general positive mood. "He loved it."

Claire crumpled into a nearby chair. "Thank goodness."

"Why wouldn't he? You put a lot of thought into his gift."

"Ed had it easier than me. She held up her arm, showing off the new Mikimoto pearl bracelet. "What woman doesn't love jewelry? It took me forever to come up with his gift and since it's not tangible — I've been a nervous wreck. Are you sure he liked it?"

"Absolutely. Cindy got it on video so you can watch it later. The man loves tigers. His dream is going on a safari. You've started saving for his trip, and you adopted *a tiger* for him. Maybe one day he'll meet what's-his-name."

"His name is Jasper."

Ella pulled her lips together to suppress a giggle. It had a name. Were they actually talking tiger adoption on her cousin's wedding day?

A knock on the door brought a sigh of relief from Ella as she answered it.

Four women dressed in matching white silk bathrobes, gifts from the bride, entered the room.

"We're here," Cindy announced. She produced a bottle of champagne from behind her back. "It's time for the first toast of the day."

"Now?" asked Claire.

"A little champagne to get things rolling, but I'm only pouring half for you. Can't have the bride stumbling down the aisle. Everybody take a glass."

"Since Ella is giving a toast later tonight, I'll handle this one." Red-haired Bridget raised her glass, and the others followed. "Here's to a poignant ceremony and a high-voltage reception. Cheers."

Repeated "cheers" weaved amid the tinkle of glasses.

Pink cheeked, Claire fanned her face with her hand. "Thanks, everybody. My day wouldn't be complete if any one of you were missing."

Ella set her glass on the table. "All right, ladies, time for our bride to get dressed. Shoo, shoo. Go perform your magic on each other while I make her gorgeous."

Each woman took the time to hug Claire before departing. As they filed out the door, Ella called after them. "We meet the photographer downstairs in an hour. Don't be late."

Ella drew Claire into a hug. "I'm so happy for you and Ed. You're going to have a great life."

Claire pulled back, her hands remaining on Ella's shoulders. "You'll be in my shoes one day. Jackson will come back, and things will take off for the two of you. I just know it."

Did that possibility exist? Could they start over when he returned from Atlanta? "That's the last mention of Jackson. It's all about you today, Cousin."

Later, as Ella walked down the aisle in perfect step to the music, she held her shoulders straight. Happy that she was in San Francisco today. The group of bridal attendants in their medium-shade violet halter dresses made a beautiful picture as they faced the back of the ballroom holding their bouquets of white roses, lavender lilacs, and sweet pea.

As maid of honor, Ella's strapless dress set her apart. The deeper shade of violet complimented her skin tone and dark hair, arranged in an updo for the special occasion. Reaching the end of the aisle, Ella covered the small X taped on the floor with her shoe. She stopped smoothly and turned.

Claire appeared, and the guests rose. She floated down the aisle on Uncle Bill's arm, making Ella grateful for waterproof mascara when her eyes began to water. Tears of happiness for Claire. Tears of sorrow for herself. A moment she'd never experience since her dad was gone.

Today is about Claire.

She refocused. The silk dupioni and lace dress fit her cousin's petite frame to perfection. After reviewing the top three picks of wedding dresses, the scoop neck ball gown embellished with pearls and sequins, a dropped waistline, and chapel length train had been the only option for Ella's vote. It was as though this gown had been created especially for Claire.

Ella took that moment to glance at the groom. Ed's face filled with awe as he watched his bride come toward him. Would she ever have someone look at her that way?

"SORRY," ELLA SAID, as she bumped the arm of an elderly woman. The foyer of the ballroom overflowed with wedding guests waiting for the reception to start. After the last photograph, she had wanted a moment to herself, and she should have picked the door to the garden instead of heading into the foyer.

"There's my favorite cousin." Jeremy sidled up to Ella. "They're ready to open the doors for the reception, and the bridal party is gathering at the back entrance. Come with me."

"Sure, maybe I can corner you for a while since I haven't seen much of you."

"What can I say? I got the promotion, so now's not the time to be a slacker."

"Jeremy, you've never been a slacker. And I understand you want to do your best. It runs in the family."

They turned the corner. Ella followed him past the wedding party. Unable to resist the urge to peek, she partially opened the door. Once again, Aunt Maxine had created magic.

Candles and flowers were everywhere, a breathtaking scene. White china place settings rested atop purple lace overlays on white tablecloths. White napkins rolled up and tied with thin, purple ribbons were placed on each dinner plate. Purple tulips filled twelve-inch tall crystal vase centerpieces. Low lighting and candlelight created an ambiance of elegance. Claire would be pleased.

She closed the door and turned around just in time to watch as Ed touched Claire's cheek. The adoration for him was spelled out on her cousin's face for everyone to see. Ella's ribs squeezed tight at the thought she could be jealous.

No way!

She wanted only good things for Claire, but was it wrong to hope that one day she would be the bride? To have someone that adored her?

The volume of the music shot upward, signaling the guest had gathered in the ballroom. Time to celebrate. The DJ's golden voice welcomed the crowd and built their anticipation as he introduced each couple of the wedding party. When it was her turn, Ella danced into the room on the best man's arm.

The DJ dropped the volume of the music pulling off a dramatic effect. The roar of the crowd softened. "And now it's my pleasure to introduce Mr. and Mrs. Edward Richley." The crowd cheered, and the music resumed its earlier, vibrating level.

It didn't surprise Ella that the noise and general tension from the day had initiated a dull headache. She moved to the drink station at the south corner of the room and poured a glass of water. She'd only be gone long enough to take something before this headache became a raging pain.

Taking a sip, she turned to exit and stopped. Jackson stepped into the ballroom. Uncontrolled emotions whipped through her. Relief. Hope. Desire.

Relief from head to toe flooded through her. He was here. The two weeks they'd been apart had seemed a lifetime. Hope they could begin again caused fluttering in her chest. Time stopped. Ella perused the jaw-dropping gorgeous man in the gray Jones New York suit standing before her.

Their gazes connected. Jackson's eyes said, *"You're the only one I see,"* and her heart melted.

Desire that caught her unexpectedly was cut short by anger. She'd heard nothing from him while he had been away. Why hadn't he called?

Even so, her knees gave a little as she silently admitted she was hopelessly in love with him.

Jackson needed to pinch himself to prove he wasn't dreaming. Ella stood five feet away in a stunning strapless gown. Although her beauty was blindingly apparent, it was other attributes he would have to struggle to forget once he settled in Atlanta. Suddenly, the truth hit with the strength of a gale force wind.

I love her! I need her.

Fantasizing about how it would feel to touch her skin and to taste her, the fantasy went black as he remembered the verbal resignation he'd given Bill yesterday.

Ella spoke first. "Jackson, you're back. I didn't expect to see you here."

"A last minute decision. Beautiful ceremony."

My eyes were on you the whole time.

He cleared his throat. "I hope you'll share a dance with me tonight."

"I have responsibilities. I can't promise, but I'll try."

The DJ's voice filled the room. "Folks, if you'll find your seats we're going to get this party started."

"Claire has us seated at the same table."

"I'll follow you."

"It's to the left, at the front of the room. I'm going to take something for this headache. Save me a seat."

"I hope you're not taking aspirin or ibuprofen."

"Uncle Bill made it clear what's safe for me to take. I won't be long."

The DJ continued. "Put your hands together for the bride and groom as they enjoy their first dance as newlyweds."

He found his seat. While he waited for Ella, Jackson plucked the small menu card from its miniature easel resting on the table.

First Course
Roasted Red Pepper Bisque
Served with Cilantro Crème Fraîche

Second Course
Petite Hearts of Romaine with Shaved Parmigiano,
Toasted Focaccia Croutons, and Zesty Citrus
Dressing

Entrée
Filet Mignon with Zinfandel Reduction
Truffled Potatoes and California Baby Vegetables
OR
Grilled Pacific Halibut
Served Over Risotto Cake
Accompanied by Wilted Spinach and Tomato Coulis

Dessert
Wedding Cake

Bill and Maxine had gone all out. His and Beth's reception had been a scaled-back affair compared to the elegance that surrounded him. But it had suited them.

The bridal couple was still dancing when Ella took the chair next to him. When and how should he tell her about resigning? Her scent teased his nostrils, making him ache to hold her. As the song ended, Bill joined the newlyweds. Ed left to escort his mother to the dance floor. The music began again, and the couples performed the traditional father-daughter and mother-son dances.

The memory of his wedding day to Beth pushed its way to the surface. The therapist he'd seen in Atlanta had been spot-on about triggers of their memories. Jackson tried some deep breathing while allowing the image to play out. He acknowledged it had been one of the best days of his life. Then he turned his attention to Ella. Caring for Gram and Granddad would take away the chance to act on his newly discovered love for her. Would he survive the loss this time?

"THIS IS DELICIOUS," Ella said. "I haven't eaten since this morning, probably why I have a headache." She noticed Jackson consumed little of the offerings. He had something on his mind. Maybe her?

The evening progressed pleasantly. Ella danced with the other bridesmaids and took a few turns on the dance floor with Uncle Bill and Jeremy. Jackson stopped her as she and Claire headed out for a bathroom break.

"I'm trying to be patient. Is it my turn to dance with you?"

"The night's not over." It would feel wonderful to be in his arms as he twirled her around the other couples. "Maid-of-honor duty calls. I have to hold up Claire's gown so she can pee."

"Oh. I'll catch you later."

Entering Ella's room, Claire lectured. "You haven't danced with him yet? He's back, and you should make the most of it. Act on your feelings. How am I supposed to enjoy my honeymoon if I'm thinking about you and the mistake you're making?"

"Don't you dare give me a single thought while you and Ed are in Hawaii."

"I'll need some proof that you'll be okay if my thoughts are only with my husband."

Ella rolled her eyes. "All right. I *promise* I'll dance with him."

As they returned to the ballroom, Ed approached and took Claire's hand. "It's time for the toasts. Ella, are you ready?"

She smiled. "All set."

After the best man had given his toast, there was a pause as a spinet piano was uncovered and rolled to the center of the room. The best man handed Ella the microphone.

"I'd like to thank you all for spending your evening with us to celebrate the nuptials of Ed and Claire. It is my honor to stand here and wish them the best life has to offer."

She focused on the newlywed couple. "Claire, I love you like a sister. As I was thinking about this toast and what I would say, I took a stroll down memory lane. I thought of our teenage years when we would visit Grammy and Grandpa each summer, staying up late in our room and playing songs from their album collection. Enthralled by singers like Dusty Springfield, Aretha Franklin, and Barbara Streisand, we declared that when we got married, we would play these songs at our weddings. I've got you covered. DJ Michael has plenty of those 60's songs on the playlist tonight.

Ed, you've received a jewel of a woman from our family. We believe Claire has made a wise choice of the man we added to our family today as her husband. So it is with love that I sing this song for the two of you tonight." She held up her glass. "To Claire and Ed. And music and love." The guests agreed with a resounding murmur of "cheers" and a tapping of glasses.

Ella sat at the piano. After four bars of introduction, she began the lyrics to "At Last" by Etta James. Ella glanced up at one point and saw tears in Claire's eyes. She looked away quickly, or she wouldn't be able to finish without tears as well.

Ella stood at the song's end, and the piano was whisked away as DJ Michael made good on his promise and revved up the next dancing segment with "She Loves You."

Claire hugged Ella. "You can't get any more 60's than the Beatles. Thanks for making good on a silly agreement between two kids."

Ella smiled. "Not silly at all. We were serious back then about every plan we made. Hopefully, someday you'll have to return the favor."

"Don't hold your breath. You've always had a better singing voice than me."

As Ed and Claire began circulating the ballroom, Jackson approached Ella. "So, the lady sings the blues." He stepped close. "And sings to little children, too."

Ella raised an eyebrow. "How do you know about the children?"

"I listened outside the door during one of the sessions. You're extraordinary. You made them laugh and had them singing when otherwise they'd be isolated in their rooms. Some alone while their parents were working."

Choked with emotion, Ella managed a smile.

I think you're phenomenal. You fix broken children.

She needed to take their conversation in a different direction or risk falling to pieces in a sentimental heap. Her emotions had run the gamut today. "So, Dr. Hart" —she tugged on his tie— "Tell me about this. What made you pick lavender paisley?"

"It looks bad?"

"No. It compliments your suit well."

"I'm wearing it to appease Maxine. She gave it to me a few weeks ago and told me to wear it today. Something about the girls would be wearing lavender."

Jackson touched her shoulders. "I don't want to talk about ties. How's your headache? Can we have that dance now?"

"Between the medicine and dinner, it's gone. So, let's dance."

JACKSON LED HER into the crowd. People were everywhere, tuned into the "Good Vibrations" of the Beach Boys. Ella's eyes lit up as she laughed and danced. This was a side of her he'd like to see more often. Carefree and happy.

When the song ended, the energy in the room shifted as the tempo slowed and the volume softened. "Okay, men," instructed DJ Michael. "Find your lady and pull her close. Here's Michael Buble's rendition of "The Way You Look Tonight.""

Jackson had always been good at following directions and wasted no time in complying. He'd been waiting all night for this. Now he could hold Ella close, take in her scent and touch her soft skin. He leaned in and whispered, "You look beautiful, Ms. Maid of Honor."

As she rested her head against his chest, the enormity of what he had to tell her hit home. Jackson held her tight, committing the sensations to memory because their time together would end when he moved back to Atlanta. He dreaded telling her about his decision to take responsibility for his grandparents. The song ended long before he wanted to stop touching and smelling.

He didn't release her. Leaving Ella would be the hardest thing he'd ever done. He had no choice when he lost Beth, but this was his decision. A commitment to family over a possible future with Ella.

She looked up at his face. "You seem sad."

He tried to smile. "We'll talk later. You haven't finished your maid-of-honor duties." She didn't move. They were drawn together like two giant magnets. She'd have to break the bond because this was where he wanted to be.

Ella stepped back, separating their physical connection. "I'll see you later?"

"Count on it."

I'm not going to waste a second of the time we have left.

ELLA GRASPED THE ZIPPER of the wedding dress. "Let's get you out of your gown."

"I don't want to take it off because it will mean the end to the best day of my life."

"It's been marvelous."

Everything was perfect, wasn't it?" asked Claire, stepping out of her dress.

"It was, though I did see Aunt Maxine lurking a few times." Ella retrieved the garment bag and spread it on the bed.

"I know Mom was dying to tweak things. She held back and made it the best day ever."

Ella smiled at the phrase she and Claire had used as children. "Let's get moving. It's about time for you and Ed to leave for the airport. Why did you decide to fly out tonight instead of tomorrow morning?"

"I knew we'd be exhausted so we might as well sleep on the plane. By the time we make Hawaii, we'll have rested a few hours. Ready to start our honeymoon."

"You're such a planner. Being spontaneous has its merits. You should try it some time."

"What would you know about being spontaneous? You've had your life dictated to you for the last eight years. Ella now's the time for you to make decisions about what you want and why. I hope you're going to include Jackson in your plans."

"Why would I do that?"

"I see how you look at him."

"Maybe I've had thoughts about a future with him, but I can't ask him to pack up and move to San Diego."

"Oh — so you're taking the position at the conservatory? I didn't know."

"I haven't accepted yet, but I'm going to."

"I'd hoped you were staying here. I've missed having my cousin within driving distance."

"Come on. We can discuss this later. Right now, you've got a plane to catch. Don't want to keep your husband waiting."

"My husband. That sounds strange, but I like it."

"Hold on. You've got a smudge of mascara." Ella dipped a Q-tip into makeup remover and swiped under Claire's eye. "There, all gone. It's gonna get crazy in a few minutes, so I'll say goodbye now." She pulled Claire into a hug. "Love you, Cousin."

"Love you too," replied Claire. "I want you to be this happy one day. Don't throw away the chance to see if Jackson's the one."

Unable to speak, Ella nodded at her cousin and pushed her toward the door.

THE NEWLY MARRIED COUPLE left the reception in a shower of Ecofetti, and soon after, the last of the guests were gone. Ella took a final look into the ballroom for Jackson, but he wasn't there.

He's gone.

Ella's stomach clenched at the disappointment. As she contemplated going to her room, Uncle Bill and Aunt Maxine entered the ballroom.

Ella smiled. "All your hard work paid off. Claire loved her day."

"I'm glad, but I'm exhausted as well," admitted Aunt Maxine.

"A good night's sleep is what we all need. You ready to go up, Ella?"

"No, Uncle Bill. I'm going to take a walk in the garden for some air." She kissed their cheeks. "Goodnight. See you in the morning."

Ella turned and walked through the French doors on the back wall out into the cold night air. She strolled a bit then sat on a bench.

He said I could count on seeing him later.

His absence cut deeper than it should, especially if she was moving five hundred miles away. What chance could they have at that distance?

She closed her eyes. Dancing with Jackson had been wonderful. The sense of completeness had surrounded her as he held her in his arms. How could some position at a school compete with that?

"Ella."

She opened her eyes. Jackson stood before her. He had taken off his tie and unbuttoned the top of his shirt. Heat ignited in the pit of her stomach.

Gorgeous.

She rose. "I thought maybe you'd changed your mind and left." She couldn't take her eyes off him.

"I wouldn't have left without saying goodbye." The corners of his mouth turned upward. "Gram raised me better than that. I stepped out to call the hospital and check on a patient. I guess John and Maxine are gone?"

"You just missed them."

He took a step toward her. "So why are you here all alone?"

"Getting some night air before going to my room."

He touched her upper arms. "You're cold. Maybe it's time to call it a night."

The coolness of her arms had nothing on the electric pulses skimming through her body at his touch. "Probably not a bad idea. It's been a long day."

Talk me out of going to my room.

Moving to San Diego was not doable. She wanted to be near Jackson. Wanted Jackson.

He took off his jacket and placed it around her shoulders before they started walking. They exchanged no words before stepping into the ballroom.

The staff had changed from serving to cleaning mode. Some stacked chairs on dollies and others deposited dishes in rubber containers. One worker placed stray champagne glasses onto a tray. Ella changed directions to head back outside. "Where are you going?" asked Jackson.

I want to go with you.

"I left a packet of Ecofetti on the bench. I promised it to Natalie, a patient at the hospital."

"You stay, I'll get it."

"Thanks." Ella turned and collided with the worker holding a tray of glasses, some half-full. Caught off guard, the man released his grip on the platter, and it trailed to the floor. The sound of shattering glass caught everyone's attention. Ella attempted to dodge the onslaught of liquid but to no avail. She watched as the champagne from the glasses pelted her beautiful lavender dress.

"Sorry, miss. Are you okay?"

Ella stood amid the broken glass, a sad ending to an otherwise lovely day.

"Here's your confetti — what happened?"

"It's just me being clumsy."

The worker cut in. "Miss, the hotel will clean the dress for you, but I suggest you let them take care of it as soon as possible. I'll let the concierge know."

"Yes, you're probably right. Thank you."

Jackson took her arm. "Come on Ella. I'll walk you upstairs."

She gave her dress a shake and tiptoed around broken glass. The concierge met them as they walked past the desk to the elevator.

"Ms. Craig, I'm so sorry about your dress."

"It was my fault. I turned around so quickly the poor man didn't have a chance."

"I can have someone up to your room in ten minutes to pick it up if that will give you enough time to change. Our laundry service should be able to take care of it before it stains."

"We'll be waiting," said Jackson.

"Yes, thank you." Her heart raced as they stepped into the elevator. He was coming to her room.

THEY ENTERED THE SUITE. Jackson sat as he watched Ella disappear into the bedroom. He turned on the TV. Absorbed in the late night news, it wasn't long before the anticipated knock on the door sounded.

"I'll get it," said Jackson. He opened the door. "Just a minute, please."

He moved to the bedroom door and knocked. "Ella, can you hand me your dress?"

She peered around the door. "Will you please make them aware of the blood on the inside of the bottom here." She pointed to the stained fabric.

His eyebrow arched as he reached for the dress. "Sure, I'll take care of it."

A few minutes later, Ella emerged from the bedroom wearing a robe with a cloth in her hand. "I thought I did a good job of dodging all that glass, but apparently I didn't." She sat down on the sofa and drew her leg upward to place the cloth where the glass had made a clean cut above her ankle.

"Let me look at that."

"It's just a scratch. I don't have any bandages with me, and I don't want to stain anything."

He sat down beside her. "Well, I'm going to look anyway." He gently lifted her leg into his lap. Touching her sent a shockwave through his entire body. All evening he had wanted more than a dance and a kiss on her cheek.

"It's superficial, but a bandage and antibiotic ointment is probably a good idea. I'll call downstairs and see what they can send up."

Ella hadn't moved while he placed the call. His eyes traveled slowly up her body, finally resting on her face. Jackson shifted his body closer to hers. He caressed her face. She leaned in. He kissed her soft lips that tasted faintly of champagne. A knock on the door brought the kiss to an end.

"Efficient staff." Jackson stood. He crossed the suite and answered the door.

"You requested a first-aid kit. Is everything all right, sir?"

"Yes, just a shallow cut. We could use antibiotic ointment and bandages." Jackson opened the kit and surveyed the contents.

"Use what you need and leave it in the room when you check out. Is there any other way I can assist you, sir?"

"No thanks. This will do."

"Goodnight, sir."

"Night," answered Jackson as he pushed the door shut. He returned to the sofa. Ella sat in silence as he applied the ointment to her leg and covered the area with a bandage. His heart pounded in his chest. He wanted to hold her in his arms, but that wasn't the way to say goodbye before putting more than half a dozen states between them. "Not a bad job if I say so myself."

"Yes, it looks fine. Thank you."

Ella leaned toward Jackson, catching his shirt in her hands and pulling him close. Before he could react, her lips covered his. Another side of Ella, and he liked it. A confident woman, showing him what she wanted. Ella nipped at his bottom lip, and he took her mouth in a new direction filling him with desire.

She unbuttoned his shirt and pushed it off his shoulders. Her hands traveled slowly down his chest. A soft moan from her sent his hormones into hyperdrive.

"Ella," he whispered. "I missed you so much when I was away." He kissed the soft curve of her neck.

She pulled back. Her gaze settled on his eyes. "You're shaking up my plans for San Diego."

Jackson drew in a ragged breath and stood. They could keep going until they were in bed making love, but he wouldn't let that happen. Atlanta was his future. Allowing Ella to make a decision based on hormone surges and without full disclosure about his plans wasn't his style.

He picked up his shirt and put distance between them. "We can't do this."

After some silence, Ella rose from the sofa. "I see. You don't feel the same about me as I do about you." Her eyes glistened with tears. "Now, I'm just plain embarrassed."

Jackson stopped buttoning his shirt. "I have feelings for you. What you don't know is I've decided to move back to Atlanta. I gave Bill my notice yesterday. I'm sorry, Ella." He grabbed his jacket and walked away.

Chapter Eighteen

She closed her eyes to hold back the tears. When she opened them, Jackson was gone. A reeling sensation caused her to sink back onto the sofa.

What just happened?

Earlier in the evening, she had allowed herself to believe she was moving toward a future with him. His only intention was to move away. To Atlanta.

Exhaustion from the long day took a back seat to the searing pain burning into her heart. Her life was once again spinning out of control. It would take more than Dory's magic to settle things. This time it involved her heart, which had shattered at Jackson's rejection.

He said he had feelings for her. Maybe she hadn't been clear to him. Her decision about San Diego had changed enough times to cause whiplash of the brain. How was he supposed to know what she wanted if she didn't know herself?

She retrieved her cell phone, calling the one person she needed at this moment. Her voice wobbled. "Alex?"

"Ella, what's wrong?"

"I know it's late, but I need you."

"I'll be right there."

Her voice evened out. "Not at home. I'm at the Wilmont. Today was my cousin's wedding."

"Be there in no time."

"Okay, see you soon."

Ella tossed her phone beside her and picked up a decorative pillow. Her gut instinct on the outset of her second encounter had warned her to stay far from Jackson Hart. But she had pushed the impulse away, and now what did she have to show for it? A broken heart, compliments of the man with whom she'd wanted to spend the rest of her life. As she hugged the pillow, tears trickled down her cheek. A deep shudder ran through her body.

Ella returned to the bedroom and changed into jeans and a T-shirt. No matter how much cold water she splashed on her face, the red splotches remained. Next, she pulled the pins from her hair. Ella took a brush to the long curls covering her shoulders using more-than-necessary force.

As she entered the living area of the suite, a persistent, light knocking continued.

Tap, tap.

Ella opened the door. All it took was seeing her friend standing there to send her tears flowing again. Some, tears of relief that Alex was here. He stepped inside and held out his arms. She accepted his gesture and leaned against his chest. When he closed his arms around her, it was like being covered with a net of safety. The ugly cry took off. He pushed the door closed with his upper arm and guided her to the sofa.

She appreciated the fact he let her cry until there was nothing left but her shuddering and gulping for air. He handed her some tissues.

Ella straightened and dabbed at her eyes. She pushed back to the end of the sofa facing Alex. "I must look a mess."

"Talk to me, Ella."

She lowered her head. "He's leaving." A stray sob escaped from her chest.

"I assume you mean Jackson. Where's he going?"

"He's moving back to Atlanta."

"What's the draw — not the girl next door?"

Ella's head shot upward. "I don't know. There was no discussion."

"I'm sorry. Jackson's feelings must not be as powerful as yours are for him. How else could he leave?"

"This last part of the night has been surreal. Like I've fallen into a state of limbo, similar to what I felt after my parents died."

Alex reached for her hand. "Still, it's loss and you'll grieve."

"I can't go through that again. So, what should I do?"

"Wait a few days before trying to analyze your feelings. You need a distraction. Go back to your music. By the way, I spoke to Scott yesterday. He said you haven't committed to the position at the school. I'd hate it, but maybe San Diego is your future."

Alex pulled out his phone and clicked on a classical music app. The strains of Bach reached her ears. He motioned to Ella. She slid next to him. He encircled her with his arms, resting his chin on her head. "With time things will work out the way they should. You just need to be patient. And I'm here for you, Little Sister."

Ella sighed, grateful she had come home to San Francisco and found a friend-turned-sibling, who wanted to make her life happy and stable.

ELLA STOPPED TO CATCh her breath after a rigorous fifteen-minute warm-up session at her piano. It had been four days since Claire and Ed's wedding and three days since she had awakened to find herself alone in her hotel suite, swaddled in the plush comforter from the bed. After holding onto Alex, she had slipped into a much-needed sleep that brought her to the next morning with a much clearer take on the events of the night before.

If this were a stranger's predicament, it might be laughable. In the span of an evening, she had decided to stay in the same city with Jackson. It had felt right at the time. When she danced with him at the wedding reception, clarity had struck that her life would never be complete without him by her side. And she had believed he felt the same way.

The ringtone on her phone jerked her from her thoughts. She checked the caller ID. "Uncle Bill. How's the cruise? If you're calling to check on me, don't worry. I'm all right."

"Ella, we had some rough sailing early this morning. We were heading back to our cabin until the waters calmed. A freak accident happened. Max has suffered a bad break. She'll need surgery on her arm. We're waiting on a helicopter transporter to fly us to Bayside."

"Oh no! How's she doing?"

"The ship's doctor has sedated her, so she's okay for now."

"What can I do?"

"Nothing, baby. I wanted to give you a heads-up that we're coming home. I'm not calling Claire and Ed while they're on their honeymoon. I don't want to disturb Jeremy during his first out-of-town job in his new position. There's nothing they can do but worry. I'll let them know after the surgery."

"That's a good decision. If you think of anything I can help with, let me know."

"If this should become newsworthy and your cousins contact you, could you try to keep them from worrying too much?"

"I'll do my best. Tell Aunt Maxine I'm sending my love and prayers. For you too, Uncle Bill."

"Thanks, baby. Talk to you soon."

ELLA HURRIED FROM THE FLORIST SHOP to her car. She and her mother had never visited anyone at the hospital without an offering of colorful, fragrant flowers. Though worried about Aunt Maxine, a sense of comfort enveloped her at the thought of their flower ritual. Her latest communication from Uncle Bill had them arriving within the hour, and she planned to be there and stay until Aunt Maxine was resting in a post-surgical unit bed, ready for her flowers.

Ella turned the key in the ignition, but nothing happened. She tried again with the same results. She had to get to the hospital. Staying away was not an option. She fumbled in her purse, finally pulling out her cell phone. She clicked on Alex's name.

"You're going to change your mind about wanting a little sister if I keep calling you with my troubles."

"We'll see. What's going on?" Alex asked.

"My aunt suffered an injury on the cruise ship, and they're flying her and my uncle to the hospital. I stopped by the florist for flowers. I tried to start my car, nothing happens. My battery's dead."

"I did have a full afternoon planned, but how can I leave my little sister stranded? Where are you?"

"Oh, I didn't think...I'll call a taxi."

"Ella, I'm kidding. My afternoon schedule is fluid. I'll make a quick phone call, and I'll head your way. Where are you?"

On the corner of 6th Avenue and Broadway, about two miles from the hospital. I need to be there for Uncle Bill and Aunt Maxine."

"I understand. See you soon."

Forty-five minutes later, Ella walked into the emergency department carrying the floral arrangement with Alex by her side. She stepped up to the information window. "I'm Ella Craig. My uncle, Dr. McMillan asked me to meet him and his wife here."

"They're due any time now. Just have a seat in the waiting area. I'll keep you posted."

"Thank you."

Alex guided her by the shoulder to an empty corner of the room. He took the flowers and placed them on a table displaying the usual array of magazines found in a waiting room.

"It seems you're close to your aunt and uncle."

"They were my second parents when I was growing up. I guess that makes them my parents now that Mom and Dad are gone." Her jawline tightened.

"Your aunt will get top notch care, and it will be all right, Ella."

Her present emotions were reminiscent of those that had consumed her after those awful days following her parents' deaths. Aunt Maxine had to be all right. She wouldn't consider any other scenario. "In my head, I know you're right. But I can't help worrying. I'll need to see her before I can relax."

Just like Aunt Maxine.

Ella jumped from her seat as her uncle joined them. His face of worry prompted her to hug him tightly. "How is she?"

"They've given her pain medication while we wait on the specialist to evaluate her arm. Probably soon after that, she'll go to the operating room. Do you want to see her?"

"Please, take me to her."

She turned to Alex, who stood quietly by during the reunion. "Thanks for driving me."

"I'll be here when you're finished checking on your aunt."

Impulsively, Ella hugged him. She glanced up just as Jackson walked into the waiting area. A knot formed in her throat making her unable to speak. She pushed away from Alex.

Why did he have to show up? I don't need him.

Jackson approached Bill. "I heard about Maxine. How are you doing?"

"Fine, now that we're here. Max has a compound fracture."

"Ouch. Who's looking after her?"

"I called a favor. Wayne Preston's on his way to assess her condition. I'm taking Ella back to sit with her for a bit."

Ignoring Jackson, Ella took Uncle Bill's arm.

"Fair warning, baby. She's had narcotics, so she might not be herself."

"Tell her I'm here," said Jackson. He placed his hand on Bill's shoulder. "Tell her I'm not going anywhere."

"I will." Bill turned to Alex. "Thank you for being here with Ella."

"She can always count on me."

Without a word, she allowed Uncle Bill to remove her from the uncomfortable atmosphere.

JACKSON TURNED TO FACE ALEX without attempting to hide the scowl on his face. The jealousy at seeing him hug Ella pumped through him.

It didn't take him long to make a move.

"So, I hear you're leaving," Alex said.

"Going back to Atlanta, though I don't know how that's any business of yours."

"I'll tell you my concern. Watching my friend cry her eyes out over a man who I gave more credit for brains than I should have has been excruciating."

"So I guess you think she's lucky to have your shoulder to cry on."

"I prefer she has nothing to cry about. But you've given her reason for tears more than once."

"Like I said, this is none of your business."

"I can understand your pull to take care of your family, but you don't have to give up Ella to do it. Unless that's your plan."

"It's complicated, but I'm not going to discuss it with you."

"You're a smart guy. Figure it out. Tell Ella I'll be back. I'm going to find some coffee."

"Doctor 5423, call extension 7666. Doctor 5423, call extension 7666."

Jackson tuned into the overhead page. He tapped the numbers on his phone. "This is Dr. Hart."

The operator responded. "You have an emergency call from Jeremy McMillan."

"Thanks, you can transfer the call."

A few seconds delay and Jeremy said, "Jackson, I'm getting worked up. I can't get in touch with my dad. Ella's not answering her phone either. What's going on with my mom?"

"You're out of town. How'd you hear about it?"

"I used to date a nurse who works in the emergency department. She called to see how I'm doing. It's great. I have to hear about my mom from someone in my past."

"The staff is prepping Maxine for surgery. Ella and Bill are with her. Sorry that you couldn't get through to them. I'm not sure how long the surgery will last, and then she'll be in recovery for a while. I'll update you this evening. When will you be coming home?"

"I should have this wrapped up in about two days. Should I come back now?"

"And make me face the wrath of Maxine for taking you away from your first chance to shine in your new role? No thanks. You'll have to make that call yourself. She's stable. If things change, I'll let you know immediately."

"Thanks, man. I appreciate that. Hey, Dad gave me a heads up you might not be joining us for the annual quail hunting trip. He said you're moving back to Atlanta. That sucks."

"Sorry, Jeremy. I have to do this."

"What about Ella? You're close. I know you want to be with her. How can you just up and leave her?"

"I need to take care of my grandparents."

I want to take care of them.

"That's great. I admire you for that, but you need to find a way to make this work to include Ella. She doesn't need to have another guy walk out on her."

"What are you talking about?"

"She hasn't told you? About a year before my aunt and uncle's deaths, Ella was in what she thought was a serious relationship. The guy wanted her to give up her touring career, and when she refused, he broke it off with her. She had a rough time."

"I didn't know. Okay, I'll update you later." His stomach knotted.

What have I done to Ella?

Though he recognized her strength, he had just found a hole in her armor. The need to be the one to patch the hole was blurring his decision to care for the grandparents he loved. There had to be a way to do it all. He had taken the easy way out and picked one objective. With a little thought and a lot of repair to his relationship with Ella, could he make it work out for everyone involved?

ELLA CAME TO A HALT beside Uncle Bill just outside the pre-op cubicle.

"Try to distract her," he said. "Max has always hated hospitals. She's only been a patient twice in her life, and she took a baby home each time. I'm going to check on things while you're with her."

"I'll do my best." Ella plastered a smile on her face and pushed the privacy curtain to one side. Her resolve to be strong slipped as the image of her aunt took front and center. Her left arm, loosely wrapped with bandages rested against her body. Though her eyes were closed, she wore a grimace on her bruised face.

Ella's hands tightened into fists. She took the time to process the sight before moving forward. The first pro of the breakup with Jackson surfaced. She'd been so upset that the unsigned contract from the music conservatory remained in her music bag. Maybe that was an indication she should stay here, even if temporarily for her family. She blew out a breath and relaxed her fingers.

Focus on Aunt Maxine.

"Hey," she softly called as she moved forward.

Maxine's eyelids fluttered, finally remaining open.

"Uncle Bill said I could see you before they take you to the operating room. I'm sorry you're hurt. The cruise was supposed to be your time to relax after the wedding."

"Nobody's fault. Wrong place and time."

"Shouldn't the captain of the ship have known you were going into a storm? The technology we have today—"

Maxine touched Ella's lips. "Have to focus on getting back to normal. How about you?

"I want you back to normal too."

"Talking about you." Aunt Maxine rubbed her eyes. "Have you decided about San Diego?"

"I haven't signed yet, which is good. Maybe I should stay here now. You'll need me while you recuperate."

"Best thing you can do is move on with your life. Whatever you choose, be selfish and do it for you."

A nurse stepped into the small area. "Time to go, Mrs. McMillan."

A transporter moved to the head of the stretcher and pushed the pedal releasing the brake while the nurse slid a blue disposable bonnet over Maxine's hair.

Maxine turned to Ella and clasped her hand. "Do whatever it takes to be happy."

"I'll be here when you wake up. Love you." She released Aunt Maxine's hand as the staff pushed the stretcher through the door. Ella remained in the cubicle. Her mind hit replay, echoing Maxine's last words.

Lord, help me. I still want to be with Jackson.

She moved into the corridor. Before reaching the waiting area, Jackson stopped her.

"We need to talk. I can't leave things this way between us."

The toll of the past few days allowed a cloud of confusion to wrap around her brain. Seconds earlier, she admitted wanting him. Now she was plain angry with him. "Want to smooth things over so you can feel better about walking away? No thanks."

"There are things I want to say."

"You may want to talk, but I don't want to listen. Goodbye, Jackson." She proceeded through the doorway. The sight of Alex had a calming effect on her.

He stood as she approached. "How's your aunt?"

"She's coping. I know this because even in her present state, she gave me advice about my future."

"What did she tell you?"

"She said whatever I choose, do it for me."

"Smart lady. You're the one who's got to live with your decision."

Ella looked in the direction of the corridor. "But what if I can't have what I want?"

JACKSON PUSHED HIS HAND through his hair. Ella wasn't ready to listen. He needed her to understand how important the welfare of his grandparents was to him. They had taken him in, a lost, broken boy and had given him a tip-top life. The fact that he missed them had been undeniable when they had visited, the realization hitting hard when it was time for them to return to Georgia. He wished Ella would seek opportunities in Atlanta. His relocation to the South would be outstanding if it included her.

He needed to meet with her, convince her to stay in his vicinity long enough to have his say. The next hurdle, getting her to listen. The words uttered by Granddad more than once popped into his head.

Blood, sweat, and tears — the foundation to anything worth having.

Ella was that something and he'd gladly give any amount of blood, sweat, and tears to make her his future.

Chapter Nineteen

Ella paused at the now familiar townhouse door. Aunt Maxine's homecoming after four days in the hospital called for a family dinner. Trading in her nomadic, isolated life for closer proximity to family and new friends was also a good reason to celebrate. A weight had lifted from her shoulders when she passed on San Diego, opting for San Francisco. Her home. She would announce it at dinner tonight. Ella smiled and pressed the doorbell.

Claire opened the door and pulled her into a hug.

"You look relaxed and happy," Ella said. "Sweet tan."

"You can look this way, too."

"Doubtful. No plans to vacation in Hawaii anytime soon."

"Not the tan. I meant the comfortable, happy part."

"Oh... Well, I'm here with my family. That's a start."

Claire hugged her again.

"Who's at the door, Claire?" called Aunt Maxine from the sitting room.

"It's Ella. Be right there."

"How is she today?"

"Determined to cut out the pain medication. She intends to use it only at night, but I can tell she's hurting at times."

They stepped into the sitting room as Uncle Bill slid a pillow between Aunt Maxine's shoulder and the sofa.

"How's that?" he asked.

The vibe between them took Ella back in time. Their interactions, as well as memories of her parents' apparent love for each other, had prompted Ella at a young age to believe in happily ever after. Why was it passing her by?

Aunt Maxine smiled at him. "Perfect."

Uncle Bill could have hired a caregiver. Instead, he had moved into the townhouse to take on that role. Something in their relationship had shifted. For the better.

Aunt Maxine looked at her. "Ella, darling, I'm glad you're here."

Ella hugged Uncle Bill.

"Max, I'm going to make that phone call before dinner." He kissed Ella's temple, then left the room.

"How are you, Aunt Maxine?"

"Better than I was five days ago. Ask me again next week, and I'll be even better."

Ella laughed. "I do not doubt that. What can I do to help with dinner?"

"Not a thing. Lien pulled Jeremy into the kitchen as soon as he arrived. She's probably glad I have to stay out of her way with my broken arm." She patted the sofa with her good hand. "Come sit with me."

Ella obeyed.

"Come on, Ed." Claire waved. "Let's see if we can help make dinner happen sooner than later."

"As you wish." He pulled her from her chair.

"Good job," Ella said. "You've turned him into farm boy from "The Princess Bride.""

Claire wiggled her eyebrows before they disappeared from the room.

"You've made it through your surgery and a three-day stay at the hospital. What's next?"

"I'll find out at my next doctor appointment when I can start physical therapy."

"Whenever Uncle Bill decides to go back to work, just know I'm available to help out."

Jeremy walked into the sitting room. "I still blink when I see you to make sure you're not a fabrication of my mind."

Ella stood to accept a hug from him.

"Lien is ready to serve when you're ready, Mom. Can I help you up?"

"I'll wait for your father to finish his call."

"That gives Ella time to check out the table. Make sure I put the forks in the right place."

He winked at her, and she smiled.

Hooking Ella's arm through his, Jeremy led her to the dining room. Ella circled the table, checking each place setting.

"So, Jackson told me he's moving back to Atlanta. That must sting. I'm sorry."

Ella busied herself shifting flatware on the table. "His announcement came out of nowhere." She looked at him as tears pooled. "I'm working to accept it."

Jeremy handed her his handkerchief.

She blotted her eyes. "I thought we had something special." She shrugged and returned the handkerchief.

"You and Jackson need to talk."

Ella held up her hands defensively.

Before she could protest, Jeremy said, "Blindsided. You owe it to yourselves to smooth this out before he leaves. Give him a chance to talk."

"He wanted to talk at the hospital, the day of Aunt Maxine's surgery. I couldn't deal with him then. The agony of his walking away was too fresh."

"You both need to say what's on your mind and in your hearts. Just tell me you'll consider it."

"You've always been the man with the solid plan. I guess I shouldn't discount what you're saying." She gave a sideways glance. "I'll think about it."

ELLA SETTLED ON THE SOFA, passing on Lien's offer of after-dinner coffee. Her breaths were slow and easy as she contemplated the peacefulness surrounding her. She looked at her family, the love and support they represented. It couldn't replace the loss of Jackson in her life, but it meant not facing it alone. She just might survive.

"Hey, everyone. Could we focus for a minute?"

Surprised at the sudden silence, her breathing suspended for a split second. Her eyes shifted around the room to each person. The faces held similar expressions. If Ella had to put a tag on it, she'd say they all appeared hopeful.

"Don't keep us in suspense," said Claire. "Ed and I need to leave."

"I just wanted to let you know I officially passed on the San Diego contract today. I'm staying in San Francisco."

Like a giddy child, Claire clapped her hands. "Yay, I have my shopping buddy back."

"That's wonderful," Aunt Maxine said. "It took all the restraint I had to keep from telling you to choose home over the music school."

"Career-wise, what are you going to do?" Jeremy asked.

Ed and Claire stood to leave. "Please, save your answer for later. We need sleep. Badly." Claire said her goodbyes in the form of hugs.

Ed shook Bill's hand and placed a kiss on Maxine's cheek. "We'll check on you tomorrow."

The doorbell sounded. "I'll get that," offered Jeremy. He followed Ed and Claire as they left the room.

"Uncle Bill, I have plenty of time on my hands. I can take Aunt Maxine to her appointments, run errands. You name it."

"Thanks, baby, but I've got work covered for the next two weeks."

Jeremy returned. "Look who stopped by."

Jackson followed behind.

Oh, no.

Ella's chest squeezed tight and relaxed a degree as he moved immediately to Aunt Maxine.

"I see the hospital gossip is accurate. You look good. How are you feeling?"

"Most of the time I'm all right, but I do have my moments. I expect them to become less frequent day by day."

"Expectations are not controllable. Be patient with your body. It may not be able to perform the way you expect it to as quickly as you want."

"Great pep talk, Dr. Hart."

Uncle Bill stood. "Thanks for coming by to amend your resignation."

Butterflies took flight in Ella's belly. They crashed when she realized he'd said amend — not rescind.

JACKSON FOLLOWED BILL to the sunroom. "Thanks for the opportunity to see Ella."

"Let's settle your resignation first. I appreciate you extending your stay so I can take care of Max."

"It's not a problem. I don't have a solid start date for my position in Atlanta. You know Maxine would do okay with a personal care assistant during the day while you're at the hospital."

"Probably, but that's not how we're going to do it. Max spent the majority of our marriage carrying more than her share of — everything. Now it's my turn. I *want* to take care of her."

"Okay. I'll extend my leave date by two weeks."

For days, a chronic heaviness had settled in his chest, a likely side effect of his inability to control the direction of his future. Bill's admission of his love for Maxine hit home. He wanted the same deep-seated commitment for him and Ella. Would he be able to convince her to move to the Southeast United States?

"I'd better get out there before Ella decides to leave. Thanks again."

"I wouldn't lift a hand if I didn't believe you weren't right for each other. Good luck with getting Ella to believe it."

Jackson rolled his neck to push away aggravating tension before returning to the sitting room. "All finished with Bill, so I'm going to say goodnight." He leaned over and kissed Maxine's cheek.

"Goodnight, dear. Plan to stay longer next time."

"Will do." His eyes shifted to Ella. "Could I speak with you?"

"Be a darling and see Jackson to the door."

Ella chewed her bottom lip as she stood.

On the inside, he was dancing around like a boy who'd just experienced his first kiss.

Don't screw this up.

When she reached for the doorknob, he took her hand. The simple connection sent a rapid shock through his arm. "I know we've both had a lot going on since the wedding. I can't leave for Georgia without having a chance to talk with you. I have to tell you how I feel and why I'm going. Please, do this for me." He held his breath waiting for her reply.

"All right. Let me know when and where. I should get back to Aunt Maxine."

He allowed her to open the door and left quietly. He had two weeks to convince her they should be together. The stickler was to have a solid plan that could work. Not just a declaration of love for the woman he wanted by his side for the rest of his life.

THE CHOPIN NOCTURNE Ella played produced a melancholy air that reflected her mood. Though she had a bright future ahead, it dimmed without the possibility of a relationship with Jackson. And to top things off, she had agreed to meet for a final parting. Why had she consented to his request?

The doorbell brought an end to her time at the keyboard. She glanced at her watch. "Time for Alex already?"

She made a wholehearted attempt to boost her mood as she opened the door.

"Hi, you're right on time."

He stepped across the threshold. "Ready to work?"

"Sure, let's sit in the kitchen."

"Why don't we go on the patio? Something tells me you haven't seen the sun in a while."

"How about some tea? I had thought about making raspberry lemonade spritzers."

She sighed. "But it never progressed from my head into action."

"Tea is fine."

Once settled outside, Alex pulled paperwork from his satchel. "You don't seem as excited today about our project. Are you having second thoughts?"

She sipped her tea. "No, I love the idea of recording with the orchestra. It's just this unfinished business with Jackson is..." She searched for the right word. "Unsettling."

"What's happening with that?"

"I had dinner with my family three nights ago. He came by to iron out some business with Uncle

Bill. Before he left, he asked me to meet with him. Give him a chance to tell me why he's leaving."

"And you agreed?"

She nodded. "I had a weak moment. I want to know, but what will that accomplish except to make the pain of his rejection flair up again?"

"When's this meeting taking place?"

"He hasn't called. With Uncle Bill's absence, I know he's busy at the hospital."

The pity revealed in Alex's eyes was almost more than she could bear. "I'll meet with Jackson then get on with my life. I made a good decision, right? Everything I need is here. You and my family."

Alex took that moment to pull a yellow rose from his satchel. He offered it to her. "Do you know the meaning behind a yellow rose?"

She took the flower and breathed in its scent. "Tell me."

"It evokes warmth, caring, and pure joy. Things I equate with you. Linked to the yellow rose are friendship and platonic love."

She smiled. "Have I told you how grateful I am that Victor broke his arm and I became his substitute for the concert? That I met you and gained a friend that I never knew I needed."

He squeezed her hand. "You've had a profound effect on my life, so I'd say we're both lucky." He leaned toward her and spoke out of the side of his mouth. "Do you want me to lean on Jackson and tell him to go on his way and leave you alone?"

She laughed for the first time in days. "It's wonderful you want to fix this for me, but you can't. Maybe when Jackson's back east, things will get better for me."

"I hope so. But my offer still stands. Just give the word."

She preferred a smooth exit from Jackson's life. But having experienced rejection in the past, it was likely to be a turbulent ride. She didn't need Alex's offer, just his shoulder.

JACKSON WALKED INTO BILL'S OFFICE. "I thought you were taking some time off. What are you doing here?" he asked.

"Max is having a physical therapy session, so I thought I'd check on a few things. I'm in the dark about you and Ella. How did your talk go?"

"We haven't talked. I need to make some arrangements first."

"I guess I'm old fashioned. If I want to have a conversation, I just do it."

"Yeah... Presently, I'm not Ella's favorite person. I need a way to ensure she'll stay put until I've said everything on my mind. I've decided to take her up in a hot air balloon. That will eliminate the walking away factor. She told me once how she always wanted to try it."

"Looking for some brownie points?"

"If we have to say goodbye, I want it to be memorable. At least partly in a bang-up way."

"Oooh, don't say that when you're discussing hot air ballooning."

"Okay, but I don't see you as the superstitious type."

"Look, I know someone in the business. I'll set it up." Bill picked up the receiver. "Shelia, get me Gus Bishop on the phone."

Jackson shifted in his chair. He could always count on Bill for support. "Thanks. I'm going to miss you and Maxine."

"Are you one hundred percent sure about leaving?"

"Line one, Dr. McMillan."

"Thanks." He put the receiver to his ear. "Gus, how are you? Glad to hear it. I'm going to put you on speaker." He hit speaker and settled the receiver on its base. "My associate, Dr. Jackson Hart is here with me. He wants to do some hot air ballooning. Can you fix him up?"

"Sure thing, Bill. When do you want to go up, Dr. Hart?"

"Please, call me Jackson. I'm looking for a private flight for two. Can you accommodate me?"

"For Dr. McMillan, I'll work it out. What day, son?"

"Next Wednesday."

"You got it. Bill, give him my number. I can't talk now. Call me back in an hour."

"I'll do that. Thanks, Mr. Bishop."

Bill stood and clasped his shoulder. "Done. Now, go figure out how you're going to make a relationship with my niece work."

He had been through enough to know life offered no guarantees. He'd just pour out his heart and hope she might want to go with him.

Chapter Twenty

Nervous energy kept Ella pacing in the foyer. Jackson would be here soon. The only clue he had given was to wear comfortable clothes, preferably pants and sturdy shoes. A sense of adventure mixed with the nerves. If he didn't arrive soon, she might explode.

Ding. Dong.

Ella jumped at the accentuated sound in the quiet morning. She paused. An overwhelming sense that a profound change of life would occur when she faced Jackson made her shiver.

Help me accept whatever happens today.

She pulled the door open. Suddenly shy, her voice came out in a whisper. "Hi."

"Morning, Ella. I know it's early, but there's someplace special where I want us to talk. Thanks for indulging my request. Ready?"

She nodded and followed him outside into the morning dawn. A blanket of purple and blue hues covered the sky. Toward the east, a narrow ribbon of orange peeked beyond the treetops.

As they drove away, she asked, "Not even a hint of where you're taking me?"

"Okay, but just one. It's a short drive to the first part of our destination."

"There are parts? I thought we were just going to talk."

"How's Maxine doing?"

My nerves strung to the breaking point, and he picks now to be mysterious?

"Her physical therapy is going great. My determined aunt will come out of this a winner. Which means Uncle Bill will return to work soon, and you'll be free to go."

"Let's not touch on that now. Have you made any career decisions?"

Her muscles relaxed as her good news came to mind. "I just signed a contract with the San Francisco Philharmonic Orchestra and Sound Knowledge Studios to do some recordings. An appealing new arena for me. And it gives me a goal until I decide my next move."

Jackson pulled off the street to the valet area of a century-old hotel. He accepted a ticket stub and joined Ella at the front entrance. Jackson touched the small of her back to guide her forward.

How could such a slight gesture cause such great confusion? His touch soothed her frazzled nerves, but what was the point? Jackson would be out of her life in a matter of days.

She turned and faced him. "Why are we here?"

He took her hands. "Do you trust me, Ella?"

The purple sky had given way to light blue. The orange ribbon scattered wide into a rosy pink with edges of peach. She searched his eyes. Shaken to her innermost core at the realization she'd do anything for him, she stated with conviction, "I do."

"Let's get started."

They walked into the coffee shop off the lobby. After glancing around, Jackson pointed to the back. He led her to a large table with a full carafe of coffee, cups, plates, and an array of pastries. An older man with thinning gray hair and a mustache of the same shade, the only person at the table, rose when they approached.

"Good morning, Mr. Bishop. This is my friend, Ella Craig."

He nodded and held out his hand.

Ella responded. "Good morning."

A waitress appeared. "Would you like anything in addition to the coffee and pastries?"

A collective chorus of "no" and "thank you" had the waitress replying, "Let me know if you change your mind."

Mr. Bishop picked up the coffee pot. "Ella?"

"Usually I have just one cup in the morning, but this is probably a two-cup day."

Jackson snagged a pastry and dropped it on his plate. "I guess it's time to let Ella in on today's activity."

"I'm here to give you pre-flight information for your hot air balloon ride."

"Oh, Jackson. Really?" She reached over and hugged him, nearly spilling her coffee. The contact with his hard chest had her recalling the night that could have deepened their relationship but instead sent it into a downward spiral. She pulled back. "I've never done hot air ballooning."

Jackson nodded. "I know. The sooner we hear Mr. Bishop's instructions, the sooner we can head to the launch site."

To calm herself, Ella pulled in a deep breath. "Okay, I'm ready."

Her spirits lifted at the anticipated launch, pushing the overwhelming thoughts of Jackson's departure aside. At least for part of the day.

THE VAN CAME TO A STOP in a large field. Jackson stepped out first then extended his hand to Ella. The sixty-foot balloon lay upon the ground. An inflator fan sat at the neck of the envelope pushing air inside.

"Give us about twenty minutes, folks, and we'll be ready to take off," Gus said. "Got a couple of camping chairs in the van. Help yourself."

"Thanks." Jackson located the chairs and arranged them so they could observe the balloon-filling process. They watched in silence as the colorful fabric began to take shape.

"I'm grateful you agreed to come with me today, Ella. There are things I need to say."

She shifted in the chair, her eyes trained on his face.

"I'm going to be open and honest. It's the only way I'll be able to move on with my life when I return to Georgia. To know that I've told you how I feel."

She clasped her hands, fingers interwoven, but didn't speak.

"I love my grandparents. It was their idea to start fresh after losing Beth. So I came to the West Coast *temporarily* to figure out my life. How I wanted it to be. About four months ago, I starting receiving job offers, a few were quite tempting. My loyalty to Bayview and Bill kept me stalling any decision to leave. Meeting you cemented my choice to decline the offers and put down permanent roots in San Francisco. Then Granddad had his heart attack, and a new factor of consideration popped up."

Ella reached out and touched his arm. "Has something happened to your grandfather?"

Jackson covered her hand with his. Touching her made his determination for transparency about his feelings turn paramount. "He and Gram are fine. But that's the thing. They're okay now, but it's inevitable that at some point I'll need to be with them. Physically in the same place, taking care of them permanently."

He stood and began pacing. Rubbing the back of his neck, he halted in front of her. "It's tearing me apart that I'm leaving you, Ella. I need you to know that I didn't make this decision lightly."

"Have you discussed this with your grandparents?"

"When Granddad was in the hospital, I told Gram I was considering a return to Georgia."

"So no discussion, you just sprang it on them, as you did to me."

He took a step back. "Well...I guess."

Ella rose and poked a finger at his chest. "How dare you make decisions for me, Jackson Hart. Just like after the wedding, when you left my hotel room. I didn't want you to go, but I wasn't a part of *that* decision. Until now, I believed you left because of your lack of feelings for me."

"I left that night because of my feelings. I couldn't make love to you and then move away."

What a freaking mess.

A man approached. "Dr. Hart, Gus says it's time to load up. Follow me."

Jackson turned to Ella. She stood silent, hands planted on her hips.

"Are we still doing this?" he asked.

She leaned in, her voice low. "You bet your sweet derriere! I'm not giving up a chance at hot air ballooning because you need to learn to communicate." Frenzied, she strode away.

Overwhelmed by her outburst and a hardening desire for her, he stood rooted to the ground.

Never saw that coming.

He'd had no clue that a touch of spitfire was part of Ella's DNA. In the last few minutes, he'd seen more backbone from her than in all the weeks of their time together. Though convinced his chance to pitch a life in Atlanta to Ella probably wouldn't happen, and having no idea what to expect from her once they were air-bound, he joined her.

The balloon stood upright, the wicker basket attached with sturdy ropes. Gus was already inside. "Come aboard."

The rising sun cast a stream of sunlight through the trees a football field's length away. He paused a few feet from the oversized picnic basket. Caution stirred in his gut. "Are you sure, Ella?"

"Positive. I just need some help to make it inside." When Jackson moved toward her, she turned to a nearby crewmember and extended her hand.

I'm adventurous — I surf. But I don't do crazy stuff. Is this crazy?

Jackson had never flown until after his parents' deaths. The first time had been terrifying, and he'd struggled to hide the fear from his grandparents. He was okay with flying now. But to take off with no safety equipment slightly rattled his composure. It was a clear sign he wanted Ella in his life more than anything, especially if he was willing to risk his life to voice this to her. Jackson tugged on the rope for assurance it held firm before following Ella over the side.

The ground crew untied the basket.

"Get ready for the best ride of your life," Gus said. "But move to the other end. We want to keep the weight distributed as evenly as possible, and I've got a few pounds on the both of you. Hang on." Gus pulled down on the handle for ten seconds, engaging the burner, and the balloon lifted upward. The basket never swayed as they moved higher.

Ella clasped her hands as she moved slowly from corner to corner taking in the view. "A gentle ride, like we're weightless."

"This is wild," Jackson said. "It's like the earth is pulling away from us. The total opposite of flying, being pushed upward in an airplane."

Ella nodded. "It's beautiful and scary all at the same time. I guess Mother Nature is in control while we're in the air."

Jackson thought about giving up control. He had been easy going and up for adventure before Beth died. After losing her, Jackson had changed. Making a quick analysis of his life made him aware he worked to hold control over everything. From performing surgeries to how his grandparents should live out their remaining years.

The balloon floated up and down with the wind, gliding over the countryside below. This excursion had been one of his better ideas. The relaxing ride coupled with a mesmerizing quiet allowed his muscles to loosen. Giving Ella time to absorb nature's beauty, he viewed the 360 degrees of spectacular in silence with only an occasional sound of birds, barking dogs, or the periodic whoosh of the burner. He knew the rough edges between them were disappearing when Ella began commenting on the sights below.

"Jackson, look at the deer."

He took advantage of the moment and moved closer. "Fantastic view. Reach out, Ella and touch the air."

"And feel the warmth of the sun."

"If you think about it, we're part of the landscape."

Several minutes later, she pointed to his right. "I can hear those cows as if we were standing in the field instead of floating two thousand feet in the air."

"Great acoustics."

Ella turned and found Jackson's eyes. "Thanks for arranging this. It's breathtaking."

He watched as her gaze shifted to his mouth. She leaned in and rose up on tiptoes to capture his lips with a tender, sweet kiss. His arms encircled her waist, and she pressed into his chest.

"I feel complete when I'm with you, Jackson. That's my heart talking. My head understands your need to care for your grandparents. I just wish you didn't have to go."

The weight lifted from his chest. Ella didn't hate him. Maybe there was a chance they could be together.

"Boy, I've screwed up. It took more than one phone call to my grandparents to convince them I was doing the right thing moving back. I could hear the excitement in Gram's voice the last time we talked. I can't tell them I've changed my mind." Holding Ella in his arms provided comfort he didn't want to lose. He started to speak.

Whoosh.

The burner cut off all sound momentarily, and then Gus spoke. "The area below looks good for a landing. Time to vent the top of the envelope. Get ready. We're going down."

The basket dipped lower and lower then shifted to a forty-five-degree angle. The speed slowed, and the contact with the ground was smooth.

"That wasn't so bad," Jackson said.

The basket touched the ground a second time and tipped over. They bumped and dragged across the grass before stopping with a jolt. Jackson landed on top of Ella. The floral scent of her hair had him longing to grow old with her at his side. Like Granddad and Gram.

Old hat at landings, Gus had managed to land beside them. He slid out of the basket. Jackson rolled off Ella and turned her on her back.

Ella scooted into a sitting position. "Hands down, this ride goes on my top ten list. Don't move. There's something I want to say." Her hazel eyes sparkled with excitement.

"I'm listening."

"I'll go anywhere to be with you, Jackson."

His heart hammered as he pulled her close. There were things to work out. The knowledge of a future together sent blood charging through his veins.

Renewing his zest for life.

In the van, Ella leaned against Jackson's firm chest. The scent of soap and musk invaded her nostrils, making her want to burrow deeper into his embrace. She couldn't think of a better place to be. He loved her. And with that love came an unspoken promise of a lifetime together.

She didn't want to ask, but obtaining the facts was the first step in dealing with a difficult situation. "When are you leaving for Georgia?"

"I don't have a firm date. I've put things on hold while Bill is taking some time from work. After he returns, I'll be targeting to leave about two weeks later."

"So soon."

"Ella, the reality is we have some issues to resolve if we're going to be together. You've just signed a contract obligating you to the West Coast for...how long?"

"The timeline hasn't been finalized. The contract is specific for three concertos, possibly with a live performance as well as recorded ones. So it could be anywhere from one to three years depending on how far apart we would space them."

The van came to a stop. Looking out the window, Jackson announced, "We're back."

They exited the vehicle. Jackson held out his hand to Gus. "Thanks, Mr. Bishop. We had a fantastic time, might have to do it again."

Gus waved his hand away. "We're not finished. The traditional after-flight champagne toast is next."

"Oh," Jackson said. "It's a nice gesture, but we don't want to take any more of your time."

Ella touched Gus's arm. "Fabulous experience. I loved every minute."

"Folks, it's not an option. Follow me."

Jackson shrugged and intertwined his fingers around Ella's.

Ella couldn't hold her thoughts back as they walked through the posh hallway. "Our clothes. They're not appropriate for these beautiful surroundings."

"Don't worry; I have an arrangement with the hotel. Sometimes we offer a champagne brunch for a large party of clients. Other times, it's just a simple affair of champagne and hors d'oeuvres. But they're all dressed the same as you."

He stopped before a closed door and turned. "I enjoyed being a part of your first time going up in a balloon. And I hope you'll decide to do it again." Then he winked and pulled the door open.

Ella stepped into a small, but elegant room. A large table set for ten occupied the center of the space beneath a large crystal chandelier. A bank of windows allowed the bright sunlight to add pleasant warmth to the area. A full-length buffet set against the wall on the right. The delicious aroma swirling through the air caused Ella's empty stomach to gurgle. "Are we in the right room?"

Gus returned to the door and pushed it open. He stepped aside as Bill, Maxine, Jeremy, Claire, Ed, and Alex entered.

Ella turned to Gus. "I don't understand. Why is everyone here?"

"Good morning to you, too, Baby." Bill walked over to Ella and gave a kiss that landed on the top of her head. "We heard about the champagne toast and decided to join you."

"Okay," Jackson said. "This is weird."

"Even though small groups usually have their toast beside the balloon after landing, Gus helped me set this up."

A waiter appeared with glasses of champagne. When everyone had a flute of the bubbly wine in hand, Bill nodded to Gus.

After giving a short history of the post balloon ride toast, Gus recited *The Balloonist's Prayer*.

Bill raised his glass. "Hear, hear."

The group followed his lead.

"Okay, folks. Enjoy your brunch."

Before Ella could react and invite him to stay, Gus was gone.

Maxine tapped the side of her water glass. "Let's all have a seat, shall we?"

Ella found herself between Alex and Jackson. It felt right. Alex's unwavering support had allowed her to risk rejection and reveal her feelings for Jackson, who in turn, proclaimed his love. And now they were contemplating the future as a couple instead of two single adults.

Ella leaned toward Alex. "How'd you end up here?"

"Maxine. She insisted that as your adopted brother it seems I'm part of the family."

"Oh." Ella rolled her lips inward to withhold the laughter wanting to escape. "It's hard to say no to Aunt Maxine."

Claire pointed to the empty seats. "Mom, who's missing?"

Bill looked at Maxine but remained silent. He stood. "Jackson, Ella, there's a reason we decided to crash your champagne toast."

"Yeah, Dad. Why did you insist I take a two-hour window from work today?" Jeremy asked.

Maxine rose, and Bill took her hand. "Your mother and I have some news to share. We wanted to say this once with everyone present."

Maxine broke in. "Bill, honey, sometimes you can be long-winded. Everybody, we've decided to remarry."

Like a little girl, Claire scooted away from the table and ran to her parents. Hugging them both while crying, she finally managed, "I'm so happy for you."

Jackson heard the door open and assumed Gus had returned. When his grandparents appeared at his side, he was stunned.

Jackson leaped from his chair, nearly knocking it over. "Granddad, Gram! What are you doing here?"

"We received an invitation to brunch, so here we are," Gene stated.

Lois hugged Maxine gently as not to bump her injured arm. "Sorry, we missed your announcement. We hadn't counted on the delay to the gate."

"You're here now. That's what matters."

Jackson pushed his hand through his hair. "This doesn't make any sense. I'll be moving back soon..."

Gene patted Jackson's shoulder. "About that — Lo and I have decided to move. We found a really nice senior community."

"We never discussed that option. I insist I look it over first. You haven't signed anything, have you?"

"We're planning to do that today."

Jackson's confusion resonated with Ella. They had enough to figure out between the two of them without throwing Gene and Lois's move into the mix.

"Wait, wait. Gram, sit here beside me. Granddad, take that seat next to Gram."

As everyone settled around the table, the room became silent. Jackson rubbed his temples.

"Gene, let's get to the chase," Bill said.

He nodded. "Jackie, we're here to sign papers on a unit in San Francisco. We thought about your decision to move back to Atlanta and felt like we were the primary reason. Your past is there, but your future is here. So Lo and I decided to join you. We've seen about everything Georgia has to offer. So now we'll have new places to explore."

"But it takes time to hunt and find the best place possible."

"That's been done. Bill and Maxine scouted out some places, and we looked them up on the web. We've found the best place because it's near you."

Ella touched Jackson's arm. "Let's take a walk." She guided him to the hallway and glanced around. It was just the two of them. Her hands began massaging his shoulders until she felt his muscles relax.

Her hands moved to the back of his neck and continued pressing. Without warning, she pulled his head down. Their lips connected. Ella found the faint champagne aftertaste appealing. Jackson's enthusiastic response told her she had succeeded in soothing his acute distress over his grandparents.

She ended the kiss then guided him to a wooden bench with a cushioned seat. "Let's sit."

"I'm sorry about going off the deep end. It's a shock to see my grandparents in California and hear talk about leaving the home they've had for forty-plus years."

"It will probably have to happen at some point. It's a great plan." She counted on her fingers. "A senior community, lots of sightseeing, and we're all in San Francisco together. It's a win-win for everyone, especially us."

He pulled her close. "You're good at making me feel better when I'm stressed."

"You give as good as you get. You helped me take that first big step to say goodbye to my parents."

"I admire couples like my grandparents, Bill and Maxine, and probably your parents if I'd known them. Commitment like theirs is rare in today's world. Even when Maxine and Bill were apart, their souls remained connected. I hope one day we can have that, Ella."

"I'm convinced we will, Jackson. We'll just polish to perfection."

THE END

Note from the Author

Thank you for purchasing my book. Your support is appreciated! I started this creative journey in 2012 as a personal challenge. I had no idea that six years later I would be the proud author of three full-length novels and two short stories.

I am presently working on my first series: The Bennetts of Harmony Point, the story of four grown siblings; two men and two women. A Broadway performer, a composer, a conductor, and a music therapist, each submerged in their musical realm. One resides in the coastal town where they grew up, and the others find the need to return to Harmony Point to bring peace to the upheaval in their lives.

I will give updates to the progress of each book in my monthly newsletter. I invite each of you to subscribe by going to my website and filling in your information in the pop-up box.

http://rachelwjones.com

More by Rachel W. Jones

To Dance One More Day

Taking A Chance On Love

Love Around the Table

Christmas in Jubilee

About the Author

Her love of reading romance novels prompted award-winning author Rachel W. Jones to write her first contemporary romance manuscript at age fifty-seven. She enjoys composing stories about strong women and sweet romance. Her books reflect her passion of the performing arts and a twenty-nine-year career in healthcare has influenced the threads of medical drama woven into her storylines.

When she's not writing or working as a registered nurse, Rachel loves traveling, sewing and the music enthusiast in her still believes in practicing her clarinet and piano. She lives in metro Atlanta with her husband of forty years and one spoiled Labrador retriever who claims a full-size bed but sleeps wherever she desires.

You can follow Rachel at:

http://rachelwjones.com
http://www.facebook.com/RachelJonesAuthor
http://twitter.com/rjonesauthor

www.ingramcontent.com/pod-product-compliance
Lightning Source LLC
Chambersburg PA
CBHW051609100726
47898CB00001B/285